AFTERMATH

Copyright © 2015 by Casey Hill
All rights reserved.
No part of this book may be reproduced in any form or by any electronic or mechanical means, including information storage and retrieval systems, without written permission from the author, except for the use of brief quotations in a book review.

ISBN: 1517378494
ISBN-13: 9781517378493

AFTERMATH
CSI REILLY STEEL #6

CASEY HILL

ALSO BY CASEY HILL

TABOO
INFERNO
HIDDEN
THE WATCHED
CRIME SCENE
TRACE
AFTERMATH

1

"WHO ARE YOU WEARING? IT'S gorgeous."

"You're a dote, thank you! It's nothing really, I just picked it up at the sales."

"You have the most beautiful clothes, Annabel. Always."

"Ladies, ladies…okay, that's lovely, you both look *gorgeous* this morning. Can we move on though? Our viewers will want us to get on with the show."

"Oh Patrick, I'm sure *Good Morning Ireland* viewers will be just as distracted by Annabel as I am. You must admit, honey - you are distracting."

"Ah stop it, Tara. Patrick's right. We'd better get on with the headlines."

"Then hit us with it. What's going on in Ireland this beautiful summer morning?"

"Well, for starters it *is* beautiful for a change. No need for coats or jumpers - or so our favorite weatherman tells us. What's the high going to be today, Dave? Twenties maybe?"

"If we're lucky. But don't forget, a little rain forecast for later this weekend, so dig out those brollies just in case."

"Never leave home without one! So what else have we got on the show this morning, Annabel?"

"Well…do you remember the band N'Sync?"

"Course I do! I had such a crush on all of them. And Justin's made quite the name for himself since then, hasn't he?"

"Of course. But we can't forget JC either."

"Which one was he again?"

"Justin's sidekick, remember? He's been solo for a while, and this morning he's coming in to tell us all about his brand new single."

"Oh my god, I might just *die*."

"Please don't Tara, we need you to report the news."

"Haha, but you must admit, Annabel, you always get the best guests."

"I wish I could take credit. Oh, while I think of it, did you see Kate Middleton's amazing red dress at the races yesterday?"

"I know! Fabulous as always. When are we going to get *her* on the show?"

"I wish, and don't think we haven't been trying! I do think our purple sofa might be a bit beneath the Duchess, though."

"Ah Annabel - you could *be* the Duchess, the Irish version at least. You and Josh are Irish royalty anyway."

"Oh stop it."

"What happened with the rugby on Saturday, though? The boys in green could have certainly done with your husband out there."

"Oh I know, bad day at the office. But as Josh always says, one bad game doesn't make a bad season. Our boys will come back strong against Scotland, I'm sure of it."

"You know, I can only imagine the conversations in your house. Such a lovely couple, truly the nation's sweethearts! I'm sure our viewers would love to hear your own story sometime, get the scoop on the more intimate side of Josh and Annabel Morrison? We should have him on the show soon. Doesn't your lovely husband want to come on our show?"

"Haha, knowing Josh, I'm sure he's only *dying* to."

2

LATELY, SLEEP WAS NOT HAPPENING for Reilly Steel.

If it wasn't palpitations, then it was the pressure in her head. This night was no different, and no amount of looking at the numbers on her bedside alarm clock would change it. It now read 3:33.

Precisely three hours before she needed to be up and into the shower - and that was if she chose not to do the morning run.

There was an overwhelming sense of dread running through her bones recently—no doubt doctors would call it anxiety. And when they used that word, they would crinkle their noses just so—because doctors truly believed anxiety was something patients made up.

Still, Reilly's heart was racing. In episodes like this it felt like the damned thing was going to break out of her chest like some rabid weasel breaking through a shoebox.

She tried holding her breath. Then she tried a prana yana breathing routine she'd found in a yoga manual that was supposed to help with this kind of thing.

It didn't work; her heart was still in overdrive, and so was the ache behind her temple.

At last, Reilly got up and put on her robe. Dublin was still asleep outside. She observed the rainy dark streets of Ranelagh from the window of her ground floor flat, sipping chamomile tea. At least she thought it was chamomile.

Back home in California there were two types of tea: iced or hot.

The tea helped her palpitations though. She sat down on the bed, and collected her thoughts, the watery intoxication of insomnia swimming through her brain.

This was the third night in a row now. A week or more of this and she would be absolutely useless at work. Jack Gorman would soon be pulling her aside and telling her to get her act together.

Could she call him Jack now that she'd solved his daughter's murder? She guessed it was something that should put people on first name terms. Especially as she and Gorman had been GFU colleagues for almost over two years now.

The palpitations slowed a little.

Reilly got up, went to the bathroom and then settled back into bed. Her eyes closed, and it felt as if sleep would finally descend…until her phone buzzed.

Resisting consciousness, she slapped around until she felt the familiar digital appendage on the bedside table.

Flipping it on, she saw a row of texts from Detective Chris Delaney and a missed call. Then a voicemail. Then another text.

She thumbed sloppily on the screen and soon, Chris's familiar soothing voice answered.

"Wake up, Sleeping Beauty. Time to go to work."

"What time is it?" Reilly groaned, realizing that she had in fact fallen asleep.

"4:30," he said, "Sorry for the wake-up call. But we've got a big one on our hands this morning."

"Big one?" she repeated, running a hand through her hair as she struggled to wake up fully. "Is there any other kind?"

"Ha. I've just sent you the address, so I'll see you here. Oh, and Reilly," he added. "Don't tell anyone about this. And I mean no one."

Just like that, Chris was gone, and now her phone was lighting up like a christmas tree. Texts from her Garda Forensic Unit colleagues confirming they were en route to the scene, and even one from the department chief, Inspector O'Brien.

Chris must be right; whatever this thing was, it was a big deal.

Adrenaline kicked in and she was dressed in less than three minutes—wearing unpressed trousers and her only button-up shirt not at the cleaners.

She paused a little just as she was about to bite into a blackening banana, and apologized silently to the nine week old foetus growing inside her.

"Sorry Blob, I'll get us something tastier soon, I promise."

She was lucky that she didn't seem to be suffering from morning sickness. Yet.

But the hormones…man those were a killer. Though the worst of them seemed to have abated now, thank goodness. Or else she'd just managed to get a better handle on them.

Unlike the insomnia.

Her long blonde hair went up into a practical ponytail, and just before she stepped outside, she ran back in, almost forgetting to brush her teeth.

The cold early morning mist bit through, but Reilly knew once the sun came up the day was supposed to reach somewhere in the low sixties. The twenties, she reminded herself. Twenty degrees. To the Irish that was almost a sweltering heat wave.

Even after two years in this country, she still needed a sweater during summer. Or jumper, as they called them here.

Parked outside, a few steps away on the street outside the row of neighboring red-brick Victorian conversions, was her car.

Taking out her phone once again, she checked the address Chris had sent her and raised an eyebrow.

Killiney Hill. Aka Millionaire's Row and home to the most expensive real estate in South Dublin. Known as Dublin's Bay of Naples because of its stunning elevated coastal views, the area was located approximately ten miles south of the city in a well-to-do seaside suburb.

Hence the call from the chief, she thought, quickly putting the pieces together.

A serious crime in such a salubrious neighborhood would always be a Very Big Deal.

THE TRIP OUT TOOK ONLY about fifteen minutes at this time of the morning.

As she drove up along the steep hill from Dalkey Village, passing homes with exotic Neapolitan names, meandered along the high elevation, and lush Mediterranean gardens rolled out on either side behind castellated cut granite walls, and around stunning castles & mansions.

Upon reaching the crest of the hill, Reilly didn't even need to double-check the street address to find the crime scene location.

Clustered outside the high stone walls of a property called Villa Azelea, she counted six patrol cars and several support vehicles, including a fire engine, ambulance, and a couple of unmarked detective cars.

Who the hell owned this place? Was it Bono? She knew the rock star lived in the area, but figured that Chris would have mentioned that much at least…

Her curiosity growing by the second, Reilly jogged forward to the gated entrance, throwing up her badge to the uniforms securing the perimeter.

"Reilly Steel, GFU."

The young guy she reached first waved her past. "Welcome to the jungle."

She quickly understood what he meant. The long pebbled driveway alone was chaotic. There were easily a dozen uniforms rushing about, several paramedics, and a couple of civilians whose function she couldn't immediately identify. Neighbors perhaps?

As she approached the granite front steps of an imposing Georgian-style house the size of a small palace, she noticed police tape falling from across the door where it was poorly secured.

Reilly's mind reeled. If it was this chaotic outside, how messy was the inside? Though unaware of the nature of the crime, she still thought of the things every person here could have done to destroy or otherwise make irrelevant any evidence that might be in there.

As a crowd of whoever-they-all-were parted, Reilly's eyes fell on a rotund man in a bad suit with bushy eyebrows and sideburns.

Detective Pete Kennedy looked up and offered a friendly grin, a freshly-lit John Player cigarette hanging out of his mouth. He raised up two hands, both holding Starbucks cups.

Reilly immediately softened as her nose instinctively picked up the alluring scent of caffeinated vanilla.

"Bit of a madhouse here," he said handing her a cup.

"What in the hell is all this? Didn't you guys secure the scene?"

He gestured absently with the other cup, "This *is* secure, Blondie. You should've seen it half an hour ago."

"Is Chris inside?"

"Yeah, he's with Helen."

Her eyes widened. "Helen Marsh? What's going on here, Kennedy? Why is the prosecutor here? Who's house is this?"

"Didn't you check your messages? You really should check your messages, Reilly. And your emails. Or FaceGram and TwitterBook."

The problem with Kennedy was you could never really be sure if he was deliberately mispronouncing, or being dead serious.

"Do I need to ask Chris, or are you going to tell me what the deal is? What happened in there? And why so much fuss?"

"Rightio," he said and took a swill of Starbucks. "This humble abode happens to be Josh Morrison's residence. Poor divil's been stabbed."

Reilly waited for more, and when none came, she squinted at him.

Kennedy's eyes widened. "Josh Morrison? *The* Josh Morrison."

"Who the hell is Josh Morrison?"

"Who is…ah come on. I'm gobsmacked. No honestly, this time you have really smacked my gob."

She shifted her feet and then crossed her arms. Patience had never been one of her virtues.

"Josh…. Morrison…" he repeated with slow emphasis as if that would make it clearer. "The rugby player. Former Ireland International Team Captain? Played for Leinster?"

The additional information still meant nothing to her.

Not that it mattered anyway.

"Reckon that baby must be absorbing your grey matter, love," he muttered wickedly.

Reilly shook her head. He was lucky she was so fond of him; no one else would get away with daring to make such a joke.

Since he'd found out about her pregnancy, Kennedy could hardly go two sentences without ribbing her about it.

Now approaching the end of her first trimester, and thankfully over the worst of the hormone swings, Reilly barely noticed from day to day. Sometimes she was distracted enough on the job that she'd even forget all about it.

But when she was reminded, she was reminded. Over and over.

Wait until she started showing. Then the real jokes would begin.

She looked forward to that.

Reilly took a swig of whatever vanilla thing was in the Starbucks cup, reminding herself that she probably shouldn't be drinking it.

"A stabbing, you said?" She turned to go into the house, a huge monolith, set in magnificent grounds. It wasn't an original Georgian house, she realized, but very definitely 'inspired by'.

Obviously Irish rugby paid well.

"Yep," Kennedy inhaled hard on his cigarette. "I'm just finishing this and I'll follow you in."

At the front door, Reilly was surprised to be waylaid by a short, stressed-looking woman with hair tied back into a bun so tightly it stretched her pockmarked face. Thick glasses atop her raven's beak nose magnified her grey eyes and oversized pupils. The perfume radiating from her pristinely pressed navy suit was humbling.

Agent Provocateur, Reilly decided, cataloguing the scent instantly.

Figures…

"Hello, Ms Marsh," Reilly said, holding out a hand to greet Helen Marsh, police liaison to the Department of Public Prosecutions. The woman rarely appeared at a crime scene, or interfered this early on in the course of an investigation, unless…

"We have a situation here this morning, Ms Steel," the woman said, her voice barely above a whisper, "one with certain sensitivities that the GFU needs to be aware of…"

"All cases come with sensitivities," Reilly said. "Now, much as I'd love to chat, I really need to…"

"No rush, you have plenty of time."

"Has the ME been called? What about the victim…?"

"Josh Morrison is in critical condition at the hospital, no need to fret. And thankfully no need for Doctor Thompson either."

She furrowed her eyebrows. "So this isn't a homicide?"

"Not yet, at least. But a bit of a zoo in there as you can see, so I wanted to talk to everyone about certain… sensitivities."

That word again. Reilly's furrowed eyebrow was getting deeper by the second.

"The Morrisons solicitor is already inside. Now don't worry; I've already spoken with him and obtained consent for the GFU to examine the property."

"Consent? Of course we're going to examine the property. Isn't this a crime scene?"

"Perhaps but as I said, and especially given the victim's…profile, we also need to tread lightly."

Tread lightly…. Who the hell *was* this guy?

"And if anyone wishes to question Mrs Morrison at the hospital, the solicitor will of course need to be present."

"So the wife witnessed the knifing then?"

Helen shook her head. "You'll need to speak to the detectives about the nitty-gritty, I'm only here to mitigate the legalities."

"I thought the DPP's role was to put the bad guys in jail, Ms Marsh. Do we already have the attacker in custody then?"

"Not yet, no. But we're talking about *Josh Morrison*," Helen Marsh repeated with extra emphasis on the victim's name. "The man attacked here tonight is Josh Morrison." She blinked at Reilly several times before she finally added, "obviously you are not a rugby fan."

She shook her head. "No, I'm not and the victim's profession has no bearing on my job at this time."

Helen crossed her arms. "I'm pretty certain you will have heard of his wife though. Breakfast TV presenter Annabel Morrison?"

"The blond from *Good Morning Ireland*?" Bit by bit, Reilly started putting it together. This was the residence of not just a former Irish sports star, but a bona fide celebrity couple. The wife, Annabel Morrison, was one of the most beloved television personalities in the entire country.

Reilly's broad-stroke opinion of the woman was that she was insipid, annoying, and completely fake. Apparent behind the ditsy blonde TV persona was an obviously shrewd mind, and Reilly disliked intelligent women who liked to pass themselves off as bimbos to come across as likable.

Though apparently it worked, based upon the presenter's popularity and the breakfast show's viewership.

Reilly usually only caught snippets of *Good Morning Ireland* here and there if the TV happened to be on when she was getting ready for work, and as for Annabel, she'd come across the occasional clip on social media praising the presenter's wardrobe or hairstyle.

She'd been aware that the woman was one half of a celebrity couple of some kind, but having little interest in these things, had no clue she was married to a sportsman.

And a highly revered one by all accounts.

"I see," Reilly said at last.

"And sadly no, we don't have a perpetrator just yet. It seems Mr Morrison interrupted a robbery-in-progress, and his attacker fled just as Mrs Morrison returned home."

"Did the wife get a good look at the attacker?"

"The detectives haven't been able to take a full statement from her just yet. Obviously she's in great distress and has accompanied her husband in the ambulance to St Vincent's. His condition is critical, so it's unlikely she's in a clear state of mind at the moment. But again, the Morrison family solicitor is on hand if you have any questions."

Fat lot of a good a solicitor was going to do, Reilly thought, marveling at the unwavering ability of celebrities to get not only the authorities, but the justice system to bow to their whims. This wasn't even a homicide for goodness sake, and already the prosecutor's office was breathing down their necks?

She sighed and cast a cursory glance around the property. She wasn't even inside the house yet, and already it was clear it would be nigh on impossible to get this thing under control.

In more ways than one.

Going inside the Morrison house, she was confronted by an impressively huge limestone-tiled reception area, and kit-bag in hand, headed straight for an older uniform standing sentry beneath a grand staircase. On the left was a glass case full of trophies and medals and framed sports jerseys that very quickly left you in no doubt that you were in the home of a major achiever.

She just hoped the glass and limestone themed interior continued throughout this place; such glossy surfaces were optimal for picking up fingerprints and trace, and limestone's porous tendencies made it a nightmare for household spills, but a boon for crime scene investigators.

"Could you move everyone out now please?" she asked the cop. "We need the area completely cleared so we can begin."

The guy nodded and began ushering out first responders, other uniforms, random legal people and whoever else happened to be wandering around.

Fortunately, Reilly had yet to spy any press at or near the property. But given the house's occupants, it would be only a matter of time.…

Further into the hallway, the distinct piney-sweet scent of bourbon overwhelmed her senses. While Reilly's nose was famously sensitive to smell, the vapors were so intense just then, they actually made her stomach roil.

Sorry Blob, she muttered inwardly, trying to clear her head.

"You all right?" came a voice from beside her, and she shook her head, trying to regain her composure just as a surge of dizziness exploded in her brain. She put her head down, kneeling over.

"Reilly?" Chris Delaney asked again. She felt his warm hand on her back, inviting an automatic spark of emotional electricity that was quickly subdued by nausea.

"I'm fine," she managed.

But she wasn't just yet. The room reeled as the bourbon scent continued to assault her. Taking a few short breaths she recalled from those prana yana exercises, at last things settled down and she stood back upright.

"Morning sickness?" he offered. His deep brown eyes were wide with concern, unkempt brown hair framing his dark, almost Mediterranean looks. Unlike Kennedy, there was no hint of irony or jest behind the words.

"I don't have that - *yet*," she said a little more bluntly than she'd intended. "I just smell bourbon," she explained. "Enough to make me gag."

Finally, Reilly was able to take a proper look around. The colorful abstract paintings on the clinically white walls looked expensive and in keeping with the entryway's minimalist decor.

As she passed the doorway of a more plushly decorated living room, she caught a glimpse of the occupants in a large family portrait positioned above the marble fireplace.

Though she still didn't recognize him from the photo, she saw that Josh Morrison was - fitting for an ex rugby player - a big guy, with manly Harrison Ford-like good looks, and dark hair slightly gray at the temples.

Alongside him, his wife, the famous Annabel, was all perfect white teeth and bouncy blond hair. A dark-haired boy in a striped rugby shirt who looked to be in his late teens looked uncomfortable and solemn, while his cute-as-a-button little sister, a mini-version of her mother, grinned winningly at the camera.

The perfect family.

"So what happened here?" she asked Chris, as Kennedy shuffled up alongside them.

They led her through into a huge kitchen diner - about the size of Reilly's three-roomed flat, where three uniforms milled about a expansive stainless steel island unit with its own stove-top and sink, that put her immediately in the mind of a mortuary slab.

The comparison was fitting, as just then the island and surrounding area were spattered with ridiculous amounts of blood. All over the floor, the cabinets, and behind it to where an opaque glass dining table had shattered into countless shards on the floor.

This wasn't just a stabbing, she realized, it was a butchering. And there had been a struggle.

She tried her utmost not to, but unbidden, her mind immediately began playing out what had happened.

The victim, taken by surprise, (possibly slashed?) by his attacker while standing at the island had turned to defend himself; there was a struggle, and likely some defensive lacerations and a deeper sharp force wound inflicted before the victim collapsed backwards against the table, shattering it with the weight of his (and with luck the perp's) fall, before bleeding out amongst the splinter.

Mixed in with the broken glass was the source of the scent that had so overpowered her just then, a smashed bottle of Jack Daniels.

Associated secondary tissue lacerations from glass shards, mixed in with all that blood would muddy the waters, but the great thing about a stabbing attack from a forensic point of view, Reilly thought, was that it necessitated close contact between the victim and the attacker.

Lots of opportunity for transference of trace fibers, fluids, hair. And if the attacker sustained an injury during the struggle all the better.

Though of course, she realized then, her spirits falling a little, the victim in question was still alive, wasn't he? Good news of course, but with so many people along the chain - the wife, first responders, paramedics, hospital staff and theater nurses - contaminating and often even removing evidence from the body, living victims presented their own problems.

"Clear the room, please," she ordered the only other person besides the detectives in the kitchen, as she set down her kitbag and began putting on latex gloves.

The man, who looked a little like the actor Steve Buscemi, didn't budge. Reilly stared at him a moment and then gestured again to the door with her eyes.

"Ah the forensic unit I presume. Your name?" he asked, extending a hand.

Reilly didn't bother to look down at his hand and certainly didn't shake it—not only was she not in the mood for pleasantries, but it would contaminate her gloves.

"Reilly Steel, GFU," she replied just above monotone.

"Flanagan, Cormac Flanagan," he said in a blustering tone. "I represent Mr. and Mrs. Morrison."

"I see, Flanagan, Cormac Flanagan," she replied tersely. "If you'll excuse me, I have work to do."

"Actually…"

Flanagan was still saying something, but Reilly didn't hear what. Instead, she stood right in front of him as he blocked her way to the island.

"Detective, this man is in my way. And his presence is contaminating the crime scene."

"Come on, mate," Chris urged, typically placating.

Cormac Flanagan stuttered a moment. "Excuse me, but I have a responsibility to my clients to ensure that nothing…"

"Right," barked Kennedy suddenly, muscling forward. He grabbed the solicitor's arm and pushed him forcibly out the door. Then turning around with a satisfied grin, the big man wiped his hands dramatically and rested them on his hips. "That's how it's done," he said pointedly at Chris.

"Remind me of that when an official complaint arrives on O'Brien's desk," his partner muttered. "So, here's the run-down," he said to Reilly, straight back to business. "We're guessing the attack began here at the island, because the carnage proceeds from that point forward."

Chris went on to outline pretty much the same thought process as her own, while Reilly was mindful not to let such conjecture get in the way of her examination.

"Then," Kennedy continued, "the struggle ends over there at what was once the dining table. Wife comes home, maybe spooks the attacker, sees her husband bleeding out amongst broken glass, and panics. Calls 999 and reports the break-in. Medics come in, Morrison is half-dead—or mostly dead, likely. In shock and unconscious anyway. They stabilize him and take him to A&E. And here we are."

Reilly looked at Kennedy. "A break-in, you said?"

"Supposedly."

"The victim - Morrison - confirm that?"

"The man's unconscious and intubated at the moment," Chris pointed out. "Hardly in a state to corroborate anything."

Reilly nodded, and looked again around the room.

Incidents like these were always best examined through a process, and already the process was messed up. She began a preliminary examination of the crime scene, circling the perimeter as was her usual mode, but she'd already taken in the scene without paying closer attention to the entry points.

So she retraced her steps.

First back out the hallway to the front door. It was still open to the driveway, sloppily so.

But even on cursory inspection, Reilly could ascertain that there were no obvious forced entry points, and the front glass panels on either side were intact.

Door mat was also still in place, but slightly askew. Alarm panel active, no hint of tampering.

Carefully moving back through the reception area and through to the kitchen, she kept a close eye out for anything that suggested break-in.

The sliding glass patio door off to the side of the dining area looked somewhat askew, and on closer examination she soon realized that it was off its track a little, and looked to have been shoved open - leaving enough space for someone to slip through?

Enough for someone of her stature anyway she discovered, and having processed the door frame and surrounding areas, she slipped on a fresh pair of booties and stepped through the doorway and out onto the patio.

The morning sun still hadn't come up, but it was getting close. Night here seemed always coldest just before sunrise, and she wished she'd brought a jacket.

The Morrison backyard consisted of a wide granite patio area complete with easy chairs, another glass and rattan dining table and matching chairs.

Beyond this an expansive recently mowed lawn sat in the midst of an attractively landscaped border of lush tropical ferns, palms and bamboo, while a five foot granite wall bordered the property. All reassuringly expensive.

If anyone came in (and perhaps got out) the back way through the sliding door, it was not immediately apparent that they had done so.

There was no sign of disturbance on the patio, no shoe impressions on the lawn or amongst the planted borders along the perimeter wall.

"'Hey," Kennedy barked out at her through the patio door. "Crime scene's in here, you know."

Swapping out her booties for fresh ones, Reilly returned to the kitchen and muttered to herself as she prepared to walk the grid.

"Too early to say," she said, "but I'm not really seeing anything here that screams break-in."

"Fan-bloody-tastic," Kennedy drawled, wearily meeting Chris's gaze. "Here we go again."

A FEW MINUTES LATER, THE rest of the GFU team showed up.

Lucy Gorman arrived first, her demeanor these days a little more reserved than her usual bubbly self.

The fall-out of a recent case was still scarred on her young face. Following an age-old investigation, Reilly had helped her younger colleague uncover the truth about her missing sister Grace, and it was obvious she was still suffering in the aftermath.

Still, the girl worked on studiously, these days often more a soldier than a joker. She was careful with the evidence, light on her feet and typically insightful.

Though today, Reilly noted, she was more than a little distracted.

"I can't believe we're actually here. This is amazing," Lucy said when she first arrived at the house not long after Reilly had made the first sweep of the kitchen.

"A brutal stabbing that's left a man fighting for his life? Not sure I'd describe that as amazing."

"No. I mean…Annabel Morrison. We're actually in *Annabel Morrison's* house. And Josh…"

"Who's unconscious in ICU," Reilly reminded her.

"Oh God I know. I don't mean…"

"It's okay Lucy. Why don't you start upstairs; start dusting the staircase and the doors and keep an eye out for any signs of burglary in the bedrooms."

"Will do."

Rory and Gary arrived at the same time, so she sent the latter to comb the garden, and tech-maestro Rory to liaise with the Morrison's home security firm, and assess if the family used any related security technology to help identify a break-in.

While the team moved through the house, Reilly spent over an hour meticulously cataloguing the primary crime scene.

She took photos of the blood spray to allow for spatter analysis, shoe print impressions from beneath the island and surrounds (though the wife and paramedics had unfortunately tracked haphazard impressions all over the place) dusted kitchen appliances, utensils, surfaces, and combed for trace until every square centimeter of the Morrison kitchen had been examined in great detail.

Then she did it all again, but this time with her iSPI camera, so she could feed relevant data directly into the visualizer. Later, the software would be able to reconstruct the scene three-dimensionally, so the team could manipulate and assess according to their preference. The sun was long up by the time she was finished.

The detectives had since left for the hospital to check up on Josh Morrison's condition, and begin interviewing the man's wife about the attack.

Reilly was eager to hear about the victim's condition too.

If he was alive she would go on down to the hospital to examine his wounds and enter his bloodied clothes into evidence, but if he died she'd have to wait for the ME, Karen Thompson to do it.

She would also like to query the wife but while the detectives would be looking for suspects, Reilly would be looking for evidence, partly to eliminate Annabel and other family members from the investigation, but also to get a better sense of what exactly had happened last night.

Though she knew the wife would still be in shock, Reilly preferred talking to witnesses when they were still unawares, unable to craft answers to targeted questions except by simply telling the truth.

Her questions would be about specific details, the kind of thing that interviewees would never think about, so could only create an honest response.

'What shoes were you wearing?' 'Did you have your jacket on or off? 'Were you carrying a water bottle?'—those kinds of things. Questions that, by themselves, meant nothing, but when put together helped fill gaps, or more often than not created new ones.

She let the team finish off the messy business of dusting for partials, collecting environmental samples, and plucking fibers from couches, chairs and toilet seats, and in short - cataloging every nook and cranny of the entire Morrison property.

In any case, they seemed to be enjoying themselves in some weird macabre way, she thought, wondering again why so many people got off on being up close and personal to so-called 'celebrities'.

For her part, Reilly thought, looking again at the bloodbath that was the Morrisons' kitchen, she would not like to be in this family's shoes - Manolos or otherwise - for all the money in the world.

5

LATER THAT AFTERNOON, KENNEDY AND Chris returned, looking tired.

"You'd think the president had been stabbed," Chris sighed, confirming her suspicions about his mood.

"Is it bad out there now?" she asked, gratefully taking the sandwich he'd brought her.

"Unbelievable. Every journo, photographer and TV station in the country. With Morrison involved, we all knew this was going to be high-profile but…"

Undue media attention was never good for an investigation and despite all the high-profile cases they'd had in her time at the GFU, Reilly wasn't sure she'd ever been involved with anything involving someone so obviously beloved in Irish life.

"Whatcha reckon?" Kennedy asked, eyeing her. "Still not convinced?"

She shook her head. "About a break-in, no. There's no sign of disturbance anywhere else in the house, a wad of cash in one of the kitchen containers, expensive paintings in the living room, drawer of obviously pricey jewelry upstairs, not to mention a closet full of designer clothes and shoes and so on…Easy pickings for any thief worth his salt."

"You think Annabel Morrison is lying then? At the hospital she said she was certain her arrival interrupted a robbery," Chris told her.

"Did she happen to see the attacker?"

"She's still very distraught understandably, so we're holding off on a full interview for the moment. She did say she noticed someone rushing off, but didn't get a good look. Naturally she was more concerned about her husband."

"How is Morrison?"

"Stable but critical. He was still in theater when we left the hospital."

"Hopefully they'll let us examine the wounds soon. Then we can have a proper chat with the wife."

"Give Annabel some time, Reilly," Chris said shortly. "She's just spent all night frantic over her husband. Besides, we've already had a word."

But that was just an informal chat to establish the basics. Whereas Reilly wanted more. And what was with this 'Annabel' stuff - since when did Chris call material witnesses by their first name?

"What time are you bringing the style queen in tomorrow then?" Reilly asked somewhat petulantly, referring to the numerous media fashion awards and 'steal her style' articles that Annabel Morrison seemed to dominate.

They were both quiet. Sensing their hesitation, she stared. "What's going on here?"

"What?" Kennedy ventured, all innocence.

"You mean to tell me that the wife is not a suspect?"

"Not at present," Chris confirmed. "She's just seen her husband bleed out all over their kitchen floor. It's not like we want to treat her like a criminal after a trauma like that."

"I'm not suggesting that you do, but she at least needs to answer some basic questions pertinent to the investigation."

"Like what?"

"Like who was sleeping in the third upstairs bedroom?"

Chris looked at Kennedy, who shrugged.

"And why was the sliding patio door wedged open from the inside?"

She led them back through to the kitchen, and over to the door. "If a so-called intruder had forced it open, the bottom would be more likely to pop out on the outside."

"Well spotted Blondie," Kennedy said.

"And why didn't the alarm go off?" she continued. "Where was the couple's twelve-year old daughter? Who'd been drinking the bourbon? I'm assuming Mrs Morrison gave you the answers to those questions at least."

When they didn't reply, she paused dramatically and added, "And where's the cat?"

"How do you…?" said Kennedy.

"Litterbox, food…no kitty."

"Not sure why that's relevant," Chris put in. "All the ruckus probably just spooked it."

She shook her head. "That's not the point."

"Reilly, don't worry. We'll do our due diligence," Chris said irritably, evidently annoyed that she'd highlighted some shortcomings. "But you have to remember something. This is Josh and Annabel Morrison, we're talking about. They're very well known in Irish life, have been married for what seems like forever, and by all accounts are a hugely devoted couple.

Throwing suspicion at her right off the bat…well, we need to be judicious here. The chance that Annabel was actually involved in an attack so ferocious is remote anyway. Josh is five-foot-twelve and fourteen stone of solid muscle, whereas Annabel is barely a slip of a thing. Not to mention that when we saw her just now, she was traumatized and tearful yes, but barely had a hair out of place. Hardly consistent for someone who'd just been involved in a violent struggle. Sometimes a burglary is just a burglary."

"Not when the evidence is already strongly suggesting that it wasn't a burglary at all. Of course, it might be possible—if said burglar was also a sadistic killer," she added wryly.

"So now you're saying the attack was carried out by a sadistic killer? Someone who took great pleasure in inflicting multiple knife wounds on Morrison? And you're suggesting that this person is his wife of twenty-four years?"

"No," said Reilly a little too defensively. "I'm only suggesting we rule the wife out, and quickly."

"We will interview her, but only when it's appropriate," Chris argued, his tone firm. "These things are delicate and O'Brien will not only want - but expect - us to tread carefully. You already saw Helen Marsh here earlier."

"Hey, you two settle down," interjected Kennedy, breaking up the tension "We're all on the same team here."

Reilly sighed. "Well, I need Annabel Morrison's prints and blood type to eliminate her in any case - if that's allowed," she added, more annoyed than was strictly necessary. But just because these people were so-called celebrities didn't give them a pass. And she was surprised that the usually level-headed Chris seemed to have been taken in by such nonsense.

He nodded, taking a breath, "Let's just try not to piss her off, OK?"

"Mrs Morrison's emotional reaction to our investigation is not really a top priority for me," she countered automatically. "And since, as you continually point out, her husband was so brutally attacked, I'm sure she won't stand in the way of us finding the perpetrator. After all, they were high school sweethearts, right?"

She was very much trying to keep her snark level down, but something about Chris's mannerism today was really getting under her skin.

He was never condescending to her like this, nor was he flippant about potential suspects. Something was happening under the surface and Reilly worried that it had nothing at all to do with the case.

They'd had somewhat of a…breakthrough in their relationship recently, and while it looked that they might be heading for something more than a close working relationship, the discovery of her pregnancy (the result of a short tryst with someone else during a trip back to

States) had well and truly thrown a spanner in the works. While he'd insisted that he'd be there for her no matter what, she had been keeping her distance ever since, and it was likely Chris knew that—or at least felt it.

Reilly was no psychologist, but it seemed that he was acting out.

Or more specifically, acting like a wounded bird.

Poor Kennedy was stuck in the middle, likely having no idea why his colleagues had their claws out.

What really burned her up though, was that her snippiness and Chris's cutting reaction would likely be reduced to just hormones on her part.

She hated how every time a pregnant woman showed the least bit of emotion the entire world blamed it on the baby, and consequently invalidated the sentiment.

Beneath the surface, Reilly was certain that was the case. And she deeply regretted that her pregnancy had been exposed to the force so early, but there had been no choice.

She also resented the reaction- or *non*-reactive - equivalent of whispering to each other and thumbing back at her with rolled eyes.

After two and half years of working her ass off and doing her damnedest to prove herself to the Irish police force, Reilly Steel had once again been reduced to water cooler conversation.

6

"RTE HAS SOME BREAKING NEWS this lunchtime, tragic news in fact.

Beloved former Irish rugby hero Josh Morrison, was brutally attacked following a break-in at his home in Killiney in the early hours of this morning. We don't yet have a lot of specifics, but early reports are that he was stabbed a number of times, and remains in critical condition at St. Vincent's Hospital.

Morrison, best known as former Leinster and Irish International rugby captain, occasional RTE pundit, and now millionaire owner of Perk coffee, was brought to St. Vincent's following the attack, and is currently in intensive care.

We don't have word yet on his condition, except that it is critical, and he has been admitted into emergency surgery. On the scene in South Dublin now is Rebecca Murray. Rebecca, what more can you tell us, if anything?"

"Thank you, Declan. Well, it is indeed a dire scene at the Morrison residence today. Josh was stabbed while inside his Killiney home, Villa Azalea during the early morning hours.

Authorities have been very-closed mouthed about the incident, however we know that his wife, and much-loved presenter of *Good Morning Ireland*, Annabel Morrison allegedly interrupted the attack. Thankfully the perpetrator fled the scene and Annabel is believed to be unharmed. Detectives and crime scene investigators arrived at the house shortly before sunrise, looking for clues or traces on who might have committed this heinous crime."

"Rebecca, have the detectives imparted any additional details about the attack?"

"Declan, the authorities have been very quiet with the media so far understandably, as they are focused on the task at hand. Rumors have circulated that perhaps Josh Morrison stumbled upon a robbery in progress and was injured in the course of trying to apprehend the thief."

"Any further information about the family? Was anyone else in the house at the time?"

"Josh and Annabel Morrison have a twelve-year old daughter, Lottie who thankfully, was away at a friend's house, according to sources close to the family. As you may know, the Morrison's older son no longer resides here in Ireland; twenty-three year old Dylan Morrison now lives and works in the United States."

"Thank you, Rebecca, please keep us posted. Now over to Terry Ward, who is at St. Vincent's Hospital with a report on Josh Morrison's condition. Terry?"

"Declan, we've just received word from the hospital staff that mercifully, Josh is alive and now stable following the attack. While we don't have specifics, we believe that he was stabbed at least twice, suffered secondary related lacerations, and was rushed to the Emergency Room in critical condition. I have with me Roy McMahon, a paramedic who was on the scene. Roy, can you tell us any more about Josh Morrison's condition?"

"We arrived at the house just before two am this morning, following a 999 call placed by Mrs. Morrison who reported finding Mr. Morrison brutally attacked and unconscious. Upon arrival, we saw he'd suffered multiple lacerations and was in critical condition. We intubated him on scene and brought him here, where he has since been stabilized and admitted into surgery."

"I'm sure this was a shocking sight Roy. Can you tell us in your expert opinion how you think Mr. Morrison will do over the next few hours?"

"The surgeons have quite a task ahead of them, to be honest, Terry. They will need to immediately check for internal organ damage, and attend to all open lacerations. If a major artery was struck, Josh will need an immediate transfusion. The A&E did a stellar job of stabilizing his condition before too much blood was lost though, so we are optimistic he'll make it out of this okay."

"Thank you Roy. Hopefully when Josh does make it out, he can assist the detectives in finding the perpetrator of this horrific attack, which has brought Ireland's toughest rugby centre, down."

7

"WHERE'S THE GIRL?"

"Hm?" It was now early evening, and Chris was navigating through rush-hour traffic, spinning the car into quick turns and unpredictable lane-changes.

Josh Morrison was out of theater, and they'd been given the go-ahead to talk to the doctors about his condition, and examine his injuries.

Analysis of the lacerations and their characteristics would give them a better sense of both the perpetrator and the weapon. While Josh couldn't yet talk, his wounds would.

"The girl?" Reilly repeated. "They have a twelve-year-old daughter."

"The hospital," said Kennedy in between mouthfuls of coffee cake.

"Did she see it happen?"

"We haven't talked to her yet, but Annabel says she was at a friend's house," said Chris.

"Mrs. Morrison," Reilly corrected.

"What?"

"Mrs. Morrison, not Annabel. Unless I'm mistaken—is she a personal friend?"

"The face of *Good Morning Ireland*," Kennedy contributed. "A personal friend to each and every one of her viewers."

Reilly rolled her eyes and continued going through the brief incident file that Chris had compiled

The Morrisons had two kids, Lottie who was twelve, and twenty-three year Dylan who'd started work as a software engineer in Silicon Valley the previous year.

Forty-five year old Josh Morrison had lots of friends and business associates, it seemed.

She already knew he owned Perk Coffee—a major Irish cafe chain that he'd started not long after retiring from his rugby career. No business partners, but plenty of associates. One name popped out at her—Cormac Flanagan. Seemed Steve Buscemi represented the business side of things, as well as the Morrisons personally.

Chris's phone buzzed and so he tossed it over to Kennedy, who answered, following another heavy swallow of cake.

"Yeah? Yeah," he said. Then listened. "Yeah." More listening. "Yeah." Then he hung up, took another bite.

The car was silent for a moment.

"Well, who was it?" Chris asked finally.

"O'Brien," he said, full mouthed. "Wants us to talk to a producer."

"Hollywood finally take a look at my script?" Chris quipped.

That earned him another eye roll from Reilly.

"No, Annabel's bosses at the TV station. They're all in a frenzy apparently."

"What? They think they can get some kind of scoop on this whole thing?" she grunted. "Last I checked, you're not in public affairs."

Kennedy shrugged. "Be good at it, I reckon. Have a real face for TV."

Chris clicked his tongue. "It's not a priority though. Let's talk to Annabel…Mrs. Morrison first."

"And Lottie," Reilly said.

"Lottie?"

"Their daughter."

"Not sure that's necessary, Reilly. She's twelve years old, and she wasn't at the house when the attack happened."

"Maybe not, but it'd be nice to have a statement from each family member all the same. A little background in case we need to shore up any findings," she said as gently as she could.

"She's twelve and was at a friend's house," Chris repeated tersely. "What's there to shore up?"

"Are we sure about that?"

"We'll look after it," said Kennedy, rushing to avoid another confrontation. "Don't worry."

"Just looking at all of the angles here. What about the son?"

"We've already been in touch," said Kennedy. "Got him on Skype from the States at lunchtime - I'll show you the recording. Living in your neck of the woods apparently. He's getting a flight home tomorrow."

"Which part?" Reilly asked, feeling an automatic pang of homesickness. The mention of California reminded her that she really needed to call her father.

"Silicone Valley - wherever that is," Kennedy grinned, deliberately mispronouncing. "Sounds like my kinda place."

8

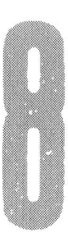

REILLY HAD BEEN AT ST Vincent's hospital a number of times, though mostly at the mortuary with the ME.

Her own GP was at a clinic in Ranelagh, and although the Irish constantly bemoaned their medical facilities, she figured they were miles better than the ones she grew up with back home in the States, where you had to plop down a fortune every time you got so much as an ear infection.

As Chris pulled the car up front, she quickly realized that the Morrison sensation-infection had spread.

The hospital entrance was inundated with media trying to get a story, and security staff trying to stop them.

Amidst this were hospital staff, nurses and patients trying to make their way through the doors to go about their everyday business. The security guys were doing their best to mitigate, but it was already out of control.

As they approached the entrance, a member of the press immediately recognized Chris and Kennedy as Serious Crimes Detectives.

"Detective, detectives!" a chorus of voices shouted all at once. Questions were lobbed unreturned, like a tennis practice session.

"What is Josh's condition? Was it a robbery? How malicious was the attack? Do you have any suspects?"

And a litany of other questions they would obviously not be inclined to answer. The three muscled their way through the crowd and finally made it through to reception where the scene was more contained.

This whole thing was going to very quickly spin out of control.

His wife's involvement in the media aside, Josh Morrison could only be described as a force unto himself. Former Irish rugby international, owner of a hugely successful domestic retail business, celebrity pundit and all-round media darling. His connections in the sports and business worlds would be wide and far-reaching.

If the attack on him was not an unfortunate case of robbery gone wrong, then there really was no shortage of other equally plausible scenarios, and an immense pool of suspects even in his immediate sphere of influence; anyone he could have crossed or done wrong in the sports, media or business sector.

Maybe someone who was resentful of his wealth and status? Rival businessmen, scorned colleagues, ex-lovers, who knew? Josh Morrison was one of those men who invited trouble just by existing. Such personally motivated attacks were random—and most of the time, without reliable witnesses, largely unsolvable.

After the first forty-eight hours the chances of cracking a case like that were practically nil. Add another day and you may as well close up shop on the investigation. All of the crime shows and detective books liked to glamorize this process, but really it was generally boring and fruitless.

But this case was different in a few ways. For one thing, it was extremely high profile.

Reminded her actually, of the fervor around OJ Simpson in LA at the time. Similar in scale for a small country like this—though she hoped not as messy and sensationalist.

Reilly's only hope was that this whole thing would be easily resolved and quickly, so they could move on to more serious crimes - homicides and suchlike - which were ultimately their bread and butter, and *should* be their priority.

The longer this took, the more pressure would be applied from both outside the department and in, and the more likely the investigative team were to jump to conclusions or make mistakes.

The entire thing was under a huge spotlight. The perp would feel unnerved and flee. The top brass already felt enormous pressure to wrap it up - hence the DPP liaison at the house earlier.

No matter how this was diced, it would be at best frustrating, and at worst very messy.

9

TWO UNIFORMS WERE THERE TO meet them, and hurriedly escorted them upstairs to where Josh Morrison was being treated.

Reilly recognized one from a previous case, Fitzgerald, she recalled. He had good hair, thick and lustrous. A cop-face—but the good kind. And blue eyes.

"You're just in time, Mr. Morrison is stabilized, and not long back from theater," Fitzgerald said.

"Is he talking?" Chris asked.

"Still intubated. And they induced a coma."

"Why?" Reilly asked. "Did he suffer head trauma?"

"Missed that bit," Fitzgerald shrugged. "Something about his liver?"

"Was he ever conscious?"

"No. Been under since he was found."

They arrived outside the ICU to find Josh Morrison in isolation behind a window, and hooked up on various monitors, breathing with a tube and completely covered in bandages.

There were several doctors and nurses in there checking charts, looking at equipment and clearing out other equipment.

The ICU head nurse, pretty and in her mid-forties, had a calm and gentle face as she came outside to talk to the detectives.

"Desperate day," she said with a thick Cork accent. "Poor divil had a terrible time of it. Nearly lost a couple of fingers defending himself."

"How many wounds altogether could you make out?" Kennedy asked.

"Some lacerations on his palms where he grabbed the weapon, incised wound along the shoulder blades, and a puncture wound just below the ribs. You'll have a better idea obviously, but to my mind, looks like it was a chef's knife."

The word struck Reilly cold, and for a moment she felt dizzy, but she regained composure.

It's been over a month. Get Over It.

Her recent run in with a psychopath known as "the chef" during a previous case, was all too fresh. Chris seemed to feel it too and gave her an unblinking, sympathetic look. Fortunately, he was the only one to notice her falter.

The woman continued. "Surgeon came down and admitted him once we had him stabilized. He was up in theatre for nearly three hours straight. The knife punctured part of his liver, now he's got nothing left in there to stop the blood toxins. We induced a coma until we can get that liver working again. Have a cocktail in his IV that should do the job in a couple of days. Higher brain functions bound to fail if we don't."

Kennedy let out a low whistle. They were all feeling that whistle.

"Blood alcohol level?" Reilly asked, thinking of the bourbon bottle.

"Not a dickie bird," the woman told them, which Reilly readily translated as 'nothing.' Interesting, so who was drinking from the Jack Daniels bottle on the dining room table? Assuming that was where it had been before the struggle.

"Thanks, nurse," said Chris. "GFU will need to examine the wounds soon if we can."

"Of course; I've already let the attending nurses know you were coming," she said. "One will need to stay to observe, or assist if needs be."

"Not a problem, thank you - and we'd appreciate the help. We'll also need the clothes Mr Morrison was wearing when he was brought in."

"Better talk to A&E about that. I'll buzz them now and ask them to get everything ready for you."

Reilly knew that any forensic trace found on the victim's clothing would have already been badly contaminated by the wife, paramedics and the hospital staff, who would likely have cut them off his body, but you never knew.

In any case the torn and bloody garments would help in assessing the nature of the damage inflicted, and if they were lucky, identifying the weapon used.

In the ICU unit, Josh Morrison was intubated, attached to a respirator and EKG. They'd turned off the audio, but she could see the regular slow heart beat on the monitor. He had bandages all over his body.

"OK to get a quick look at the sutured wounds?" she asked the nurse. "I need photos and measurements of the lacerations."

"No problem, I can change out the bandages now, while I'm at it."

Taking her time to gently remove bandages, Reilly snapped photos, and took measurements as the nurse went about her business.

From a forensic point of view, it was important that sharp force injuries (stab wounds) were distinguished from lacerations (tearing apart of tissues), which were a type of blunt force injury.

The presence of tissue bridging within the depths of the wound, below the level of the skin surface - represented by nerves, vessels, and other soft tissues that extended across the gap from one side to the opposite side - were indicative of a laceration, which was what she was seeing now.

The injury to Morrison's shoulder was an incised wound, where a cut or "slash," had resulted when an object with a sharp tip or sharp edge, made contact with the skin, with the direction of the force occurring in a more-or-less tangential fashion. Incised wounds were typically longer than they were deep.

As the bleeding from the incised wound had been stopped and the gash cleaned, that one was straightforward enough for Reilly to assess.

Examination of the stab wound - present under the victim's ribs - would be a lot more difficult, and would yield considerably less information, by nature of the fact that it had been sutured, and so some of the detail often so easily gathered from a corpse would be impossible.

These were caused by a pointed object typically having a sharp tip when the object is forced into the skin and underlying tissues, with the direction of the force in a more-or-less perpendicular angle with the skin.

Reilly carefully measured all the wounds' margins and angles and took note of the defensive injuries on Josh Morrison's fingers.

Such information, along with blood spill and drip patterns, foot impressions, handprints, and fingerprints taken from the crime scene, were all hugely important in helping the team determine what had happened during the attack, and she hoped, ultimately identify the perpetrator.

She tried to remain unaffected as she measured and recorded, keeping in step with the science, not the emotion, but it was difficult in the face of such a fresh attack, and while the man was still lying unconscious on the bed.

And she couldn't help but wonder if Tony Ellis would have done something similar to her if Chris hadn't shown up…

She shook her head. This was a brand new investigation and the attack bore no relation whatsoever to what had happened to her a few weeks' back. She needed to focus.

When it was all done, she thanked the ICU nurse and stepped back out to join the detectives.

But they were paying Reilly no attention, and she soon discovered why.

The TV Queen herself, Annabel Morrison was walking down the corridor. Even with tear-stained puffy eyes, an expression carved from sustained trauma, lack of make-up and whatever workout clothes she'd changed into in the meantime, she looked stunning.

Though as with most TV people, much smaller and thinner in person, the television presenter had lustrous blonde hair that hung in waves over her shoulders—quite the contrast to Reilly's own wiry locks that were often bunched up in an untamed ponytail.

With her brilliant green eyes, toned body, and sex appeal to match her stardom, importance seemed to emanate off her in waves.

As she approached, all the men standing nearby fell silent and stopped moving. Except for Kennedy, who kept shifting between his feet.

Annabel arrived at the door of ICU, and without saying a word, flashed everyone with a dismissive "who-the-hell-are-you and what-are-you-doing-here" expression, shot through with a deep sense of superiority.

Chris stood up straight, and came to life.

"Mrs. Morrison, hello again." he said, with the smooth tones and affable expression he used to put people at ease.

The woman's eyes widened. "You're still here since this morning? Why aren't you out looking for that *monster*?" she gasped, her voice barely above a whisper.

"We've just arrived with the GFU to assess your husband's injuries," Chris soothed. "Good to hear that he's doing better."

"Don't worry Annabel, rest assured that we are doing all we can to find this guy," Kennedy sputtered with such lack of eloquence Reilly physically turned to look at him.

"Surely the man who stabbed my husband is not at this hospital," the woman replied pointedly, eyes narrowing.

The man...

Unlike the others, Reilly wasn't about to tip-toe.

"So you believe the attacker was male?" she began, "that's helpful information. In any case, now that your husband's condition is stable, my colleagues and I would like to have a private word. The detectives need a full statement from you now, and the GFU also has some questions that will help us with our investigation. Also, we will need your prints and blood type, so as to differentiate you from the perpetrator."

"And you are?" the woman asked coldly.

"Reilly Steel, Garda Forensic Unit."

"Oh, of course, anything you need," Annabel said, softening a bit.

Chris waylaid a passing nurse. "Is there somewhere private we can speak?"

"Sure, this way."

They were led to a small six-person conference room with a white board, presumably for staff meetings.

Reilly closed the door and let Mrs. Morrison get settled for a moment.

"I take it you've changed your clothes from this morning," she said, and the other woman nodded.

"Yes...there was just so much blood."

"Where are those clothes now?"

"My co-presenter…Tara…she picked these up from wardrobe at the studio, wanted me to have something more comfortable. I'm not sure what she did with my dress - dry cleaning I suppose? My jacket…I don't know where that is…maybe downstairs somewhere. I used it try and stop the bleeding. It was Gucci."

Of course it was.

Reilly eyed Kennedy who automatically picked up the phone. "I'm on it."

"I'm so sorry, I didn't realize it was important…." the woman sniffed, looking close to tears.

"It's fine, and we appreciate what you are going through, Mrs. Morrison," Reilly began, softening a little in the face of the woman's obvious distress. "Thank you for co-operating."

Then she opened her kitbag and pulled out a fingerprinting kit along with a sterile needle, vial, alcohol and cotton balls.

"We'll do everything we can to find the person who did this to your husband," Kennedy told her, while trying to track down her clothes.

Chris remained stoic, but Reilly noticed he kept swallowing and clearing his throat as she took Annabel Morrison's fingerprints.

She'd wait until the interview was finished before taking blood, for fear that the witness might pass out.

Annabel barely looked up, and appeared to be holding back a fresh wave of tears.

Reilly waited for Chris to do his job, but after the third time he cleared his throat, she decided to jump in. He was nervous, she realized.

"Mrs Morrison, can you tell us exactly what happened last night? Step by step, please?"

The woman shook her head, her perfect hair hardly moving. "Call me Annabel, please," she replied as if by rote. "Oh, it's all such a blur," she continued, her voice a low whisper. "I came home and…and…Josh…he…"

The flood she was holding back escaped, and her beautiful face wrenched into a painful grimace, her mouth open in a silent and clenched sob.

Chris jumped up and pulled up a chair right next to her, and without missing a beat, Annabel buried her face on his chest, shoulders rolling with uncontrollable sobs.

Oh for crying out loud….

Then Kennedy got into it. He sauntered over and put his meaty hand on Annabel's back and patted it gently.

"It's okay, love," he said gently. "We'll get him. It's okay."

Reilly reached into her bag, found some tissues then passed them across the table.

"Please continue," she said, trying to get her back on track. "You were saying that you came home and saw your husband…can you describe the scene in as much detail as you can remember please."

Recovering quickly, Annabel took them and composed herself, wiping her face and nose.

Chris remained alongside her, concerned and sympathetic, gently tapping her arm as she recovered.

Suddenly, before she realized it, Reilly kicked him in the shin beneath the table. He jumped back, startled and then glared at her with a mystified expression. Fortunately, Morrison didn't seem to notice.

"I…saw him lying on the ground on top of broken glass, the dining table all smashed up. He wasn't saying anything…. there was so much blood. It seemed like there was blood all over the kitchen. So I checked on him, used my jacket to try and stop the bleeding, and then took out my phone and called 999…" she trailed off again, apparently reliving the scene.

"Did you get a look at his attacker at all?"

"I'm not sure…it's all such a blur…I thought I saw someone slip off out of the corner of my eye - "

"Slip off where - through the hallway and out the front door, or out the back way?" Reilly pressed. "And can you give us a description of this person?"

"I don't know, I really can't remember. I was just so… shocked. It was like everything just…froze."

"Anything at all would be really helpful, Mrs Morrison."

"He was wearing black I think, and his head was covered - a hoodie I think. Like I said - "

"Approximate height, weight?"

"I'm sorry, I really have no idea. It all happened so fast…"

"What time was this?" Kennedy asked, taking over.

She shook her head, "I don't know. It was late. I think maybe 1.30?"

"Where were you till then? Sounds like a late night."

"I sometimes go out with the production team on Friday nights. We celebrate wrapping up the week, and the fact that we can all sleep in at weekends."

Finally Chris started contributing. "You went out for drinks with people from *Good Morning Ireland?*"

"Yes. Sometimes we head to Roly's for dinner, and then onwards to the Gate House for drinks. Just down the road from the studio."

And also just a stone's throw from this hospital, Reilly noted.

"Great pub grub in the Gate House," Kennedy commented unnecessarily.

Reilly continued. "So who exactly was with you last night - at the restaurant and the pub?"

Annabel suddenly recoiled. "Wait a second…. why does that matter, and why are you questioning me like *I'm* some kind of criminal?"

Chris jumped in quickly. "Don't worry, this is just a standard line of questioning."

"The entire production crew was there," she barked, clearly incensed. "Call them if you like. I think I've had about enough of this."

"Please, Mrs. Morrison," Chris implored "we still have a few questions…"

"Bullshit!" she retorted standing. "Somewhere in this city the man who broke into my house and stabbed my husband is running from you. Hiding from you. And you are here in the hospital—instead of out there looking for him. For god's sake my daughter could have been in the house…I suggest strongly that you people put your energies where they belong. On finding the bastard that tried to murder my husband."

Annabel stood up and stormed out of the room—but before closing the door added, "I'm not saying another word without my solicitor. Are we understood, detectives?"

And she was gone. The three remained quiet for a couple breaths before Kennedy muttered. "Well that went well."

"What in the hell is wrong with you two?" Reilly asked, frustrated.

"What?"

"You especially. Oh let me give you my shoulder Annabel, you poor, sweet little angel."

"The woman was upset for goodness sake."

"And suddenly you're Sir Lancelot? You are a detective, Chris. Or has star power suddenly blinded you of that."

"Now hold on just a goddamn second…" he said standing up. "What's this about? Are you jealous or just hormonal?"

"Hormonal?" Now Reilly was standing.

"Settle down," said Kennedy. "Look, we need to focus here. We didn't get a blood sample."

Reilly took a deep breath, irritated that Chris's behavior had gotten under her skin like that, and worse that she'd shown it.

She began packing up her kit bag. "I'll take care of it," she said with a sigh and left to catch up with Annabel. "You two go and check out the pub."

"Gee thanks, boss," Chris retorted, "what would we do without you telling us how to run an investigation?"

Conceding that the comment had in fact come across patronizing and bossy, Reilly smiled and gave him a truce-making pat on the shoulder.

"Sorry, it's been a long day. If the food is good like Kennedy says, maybe you two should try pick up dinner while you're there."

But Chris's body language remained terse and cold. "Whatever you say."

10

ANNABEL MORRISON WAS WHERE REILLY expected. Standing outside the ICU, gnawing at her fingers and watching through the window in desperation as her husband lay in a coma.

Reilly felt a little pang of guilt watching the woman. Morrison was motionless, clearly lost in a vortex of trauma and worry.

She approached quietly and stood next to her. "The doctors said they are trying to get his liver failure under control."

Morrison didn't respond.

"It's a good sign, I think," she added gently. "If they can catch it in time, then they can work the toxins out."

"You're out for my blood, aren't you?" Morrison said, not changing her gaze or expression. "I know how these things work. Just be sure to pin it on the spouse and then wrap it all up in a nice big bow. Not happening."

"Don't you want to help us find the person who attacked your husband, Mrs Morrison?"

"Of course, but not if it means I'm automatically implicated," she retorted, casting a dismissive gaze at Reilly's kitbag.

"I just need to ascertain your blood type to eliminate you from the scene…"

"Well, you could have just asked me then. It's B plus. I hold a donor card," she added, when Reilly looked surprised.

"Your daughter," she asked, deciding to press while the woman seemed a little calmer. "She wasn't home last night?"

Annabel shook her head. "Lottie usually stays over with her friend Gemma on Friday nights."

"Because you're usually out late," Reilly guessed, wondering why the woman wouldn't be more eager to go home and spend time with her family after a hard working week, instead of partying with her colleagues.

But what did she know?

Morrison nodded. "She's with my mother now in the waiting room. Please don't bother her."

"I won't," Reilly told her. "What about your husband? He usually home on Friday nights?" It would be useful to know the habitual family comings and goings, as if this was a robbery, chances were the burglar might have had that information too.

"Sometimes. It depends on how busy things are. With the company."

"Were you in touch with Josh at all before you arrived home? Sent a text letting him know you were on the way maybe?"

"Josh and I are a little old school that way. Still remember what it was like in the days before mobile phones. No, I just took a taxi home, came inside and…"

Reilly didn't run the risk of her clamming up again, by asking the name of the taxi company. Instead, she made a mental note to get Rory to check with the taxi firm the TV station normally used, as she guessed a famous face like Morrison wouldn't just take random city cabs home.

"Thanks for your co-operation, Mrs. Morrison."

"Call me Annabel," she insisted again, but Reilly felt the response was by rote, the result of so many years playing the affable TV host. "You'll find him won't you?" she said then, with ferocity in her eyes. "You find him and make my house safe again for me. For Lottie?"

Reilly nodded, and then left the woman alone to watch over her comatose husband, her arms hugged close to her chest as tears streamed down her face.

So dramatic, and of course Annabel Morrison had every reason to be, but still she couldn't help but wonder if this too was all part of a performance.

She shook her head. She really needed to work on being more sympathetic, but something about Annabel Morrison rubbed her up the wrong way.

As she headed down the hallway, her phone buzzed with a diary alert. Checking the screen she realized she was about to miss an appointment.

One she'd been dreading for quite some time.

Fortunately for her, this Morrison thing was a hot case, so she could blow off the force's attempt to provide her with obligatory PTSD counseling, following the incident with Tony Ellis last month.

The first session was today, and Reilly was grateful for the opportunity to give it a miss. It was a dumb idea and a complete waste of her time. In her line of work she ran into crazies all the time, had done throughout all her time in law enforcement both here and in the US.

How was she supposed to find time to do her job if she had to get therapy every single time that happened?

11

WHILE THE DETECTIVES WERE OFF hunting down potential suspects and interviewing witnesses, Reilly once again turned her focus to the crime scene.

One thing that had bugged her from earlier was still bugging her, so as she found her way to the hospital cafeteria to grab a bite, she looked at the Morrison background file information-hound Rory had compiled, and dialed the number to PhoneWatch Security.

"Reilly Steel, GFU," she said to the woman who answered. "I need some data from one of your customers for an open investigation. I have the necessary codes."

While Reilly listened to the hold music—Peter Gabriel she guessed—she sought out a sandwich and a soda. And some sort of processed cookie.

The baby made her want sweets. Or at least, that's how she justified it.

Sitting alone at a formica table she got through both her sandwich and the cookie before another person picked up.

"Investigation Liaison, this is Brian."

"Hello, Reilly Steel here from GFU. I'm on the Morrison case."

"Of course you are," Brian drawled. "And no I don't have a comment."

"I'm not a reporter. My office should have faxed over an incident request?"

"Oh," he said apologetically. "Let me look. Yes, I see it now, sorry. Can you confirm the incident number?"

"Yep, hold on," she thumbed through Rory's carefully compiled info and found it. "X7 stroke 4989."

"Okay got it, so what can I help you with?"

"I know you guys usually send on a form report, but in the meantime, can you check the records for me? Was there an alarm or trigger event anytime last night at the Morrison residence?"

"We're already checked it, believe me," Brian said, in a tone that suggested he was (yet another) Josh Morrison fan. "Quiet as a church. Not a peep."

"You don't need to get too detailed, but what's the trip configuration exactly? Someone hops over the wall into their garden for instance?"

"That would trip the system, yes. The whole perimeter is motion-sensitive, plus there's a trigger on all the windows and doors. As a matter of fact, we get at least a dozen false alarms from there a month."

"False alarms from what?"

"The usual story. They have a cat. Sometimes it gets out."

"CCTV?"

"Nah, they didn't want it. Not many people do with a monitored system."

Made sense, Reilly thought, that a high-profile couple like the Morrisons wouldn't want live CCTV cameras directed onto living areas that random PhoneWatch staff members could access at any time. It would be like living in the *Big Brother* house.

Pity though.

"Okay, got it. Thanks for your time Brian, and just fax the report to us as soon as you can."

12

SATISFIED SHE HAD WHAT SHE needed - for now - from both Josh and Annabel Morrison, Reilly left the hospital and returned to Killiney Hill.

The media circus had since turned into an all-out mob. Television crews swarmed the neighborhood. Cops had to close down the main thoroughfare around the coast, and escort locals to their houses.

City TV stations, newspaper and radio journalists crawled around en masse. It put Reilly in mind of trips to Palos Verdes as a kid, when hundreds of crabs would scuttle around rocks in between wave crashes.

Several TV trucks were scattered around as she passed, masts raised all the way. There were even two or three from UK stations. Several reporters were speaking into cameras. Producers crawling around. Photographers snapping each moment.

It reminded Reilly of an average day in Los Angeles.

Walking into the house, she was confronted with the unsettling smell of bourbon again, though thankfully its intensity had since subsided.

The rest of the GFU team were still there, carefully combing the property in full. The interior was now completely photographed and dusted. Samples were taken and crime scene markers were laid out at locations of significance or potential interest.

Going upstairs, she found Lucy finishing up in the master bedroom.

"Anything interesting?" Reilly asked.

"Everything…" she replied, eyes beaming. "Such an amazing wardrobe."

Reilly looked at her. "What I meant was—did you find anything specifically of interest concerning the crime?"

"Oh sorry. No sign of disturbance, or anything out of the ordinary in here. Except for her *incredible* Blahnik collection…"

"Lucy, please. Focus." This was getting out of hand. First Chris and now Lucy, who Reilly considered her trusty number two.

How this couple (just a jock and a clothes hanger as far as she was concerned) had such a hold over supposedly intelligent people, she didn't know.

Reilly could never for the life of her understand celebrity culture - why people were so revered by the masses, solely because they happened to be in movies or on TV.

Maybe it was because she grew up in California. She'd seen countless so called 'celebs' over the years in San

Francisco. They were always shorter than you thought (and much, much thinner) and usually had smaller heads. Except for news anchors and reporters who oddly all seemed to have giant heads.

In fact, the only time she was remotely interested was when she happened across Michael Jackson and his entourage sneaking out the back of the Fairmont Hotel one time. Though she'd barely batted an eyelid at Orlando Bloom waiting in line at Panda Express after a late shift one night.

Celebrities were fewer and far between in Dublin, of course. But there were a few—and many in this particular neighborhood. Everyone knew Bono lived just down the block, and this part of town was full of actors and media personalities. Hadn't she heard that Meg Ryan had lived in these parts onetime too? Or maybe there was a romantic comedy in which Meg Ryan lived here. She couldn't be sure.

Maybe it was both.

The GFU's tech-maestro Rory was wrapping up in the study downstairs. Clicking at the computer he barely noticed Reilly and Lucy enter.

"You almost done?"

He nodded. "I've dumped the hard drive, emails, and browser history. I'll trawl through it all at the lab."

"Just one home computer here?"

"Josh's, I think. He has an obsession with MineCraft by the looks of it. Or maybe the daughter has. If Annabel used it, I can't tell."

"Maybe she has a laptop somewhere? Or an iPad."

"Well, it's not here if she does," Lucy said. "I've gone through everything."

"Mini-tablet? She must have some kind of personal organizer."

Rory shrugged. "She'll be carrying it around with her, so unless she hands it over…"

"That might be not be necessary just yet. Okay, thanks, Rory."

Next, Reilly went back to the kitchen and examined the incident markers the team had put up. Initial point of contact, position of struggle, and of course, where it ended with the smashed table.

Gary walked her through it again, giving her his initial impressions.

"Attacker came from behind the island, and made the initial slash here," he pointed to the blood spatter on the floor.

He had marked the knife block already, the assault weapon hadn't yet been found—and the chef's knife from the knife block was missing.

Premature to assume anything just yet though. They'd have to analyze the wound characteristics in more detail to be sure.

"That would suggest that the perp walked up to Morrison from behind?"

Gary nodded, and then pointed to a kettle sitting on the island's gas hob.

It had stood out to Reilly earlier because it wasn't a plug-in electrical type but one that whistled when boiled - the kind that Americans used.

She hadn't seen one of these in Ireland before, everyone seemed to prefer boiling water electrically rather than wait for it to heat up on the hob.

Looking at it more closely now, she realized that this was likely a choice of style over convenience, as the kettle was an expensive designer Alessi brand, with its signature whistling bird on the spout.

Known for it's artistic, rather than functional appeal, and glancing around the worktop area, she saw that the Morrisons favored this kitchenware brand quite a bit.

Figured.

"Recorded the water level. It was almost full, and at room temperature. And the hob wasn't on."

Reilly noticed the mug and a tea filter with dry-leaf in it, waiting.

"He didn't get the chance to start the kettle," she observed.

"Or someone turned it off," Lucy reasoned. "We've dusted it for prints, obviously."

Pacing around the kitchen, she decided to check the fridge. There was leftover curry inside, plus an assortment of typical groceries. She took a mental note, wondering if Josh Morrison had ordered in for dinner last night.

Her phone rang; it was Chris.

"Just wanted to let you know, her alibi checks out." His voice was terse.

"What?"

"We spoke to the barman on shift at the Gate House last night. Annabel Morrison was with her colleagues in the pub until the party broke up at about 1 am."

"Which taken with the time of the 999 call, suggests the attack happened while she was on her way home," Reilly observed, almost to herself.

"Sounds like it. Happy now?"

"Maybe."

Hanging up, she turned to back to the team. "OK then. Anything else?"

Lucy nodded. "Got a couple of decent tread impressions behind the island, despite the mess. Might be something once we eliminate the paramedics and first responders?"

"Great, double check the walls and countertop again for anything I may have missed first time round, fridge too. Use black light on the broken glass—maybe the perp drooled or something. And you printed the internal doors and the slider?"

"Of course," Lucy nodded, as she continued dusting.

Gary had gone back outside placing markers near the perimeter wall.

"Bit surreal isn't it?" he said when Reilly approached. "To be standing in Josh Morrison's garden." Again he had that dreamy look on his face. "I mean, I grew up watching this guy scoring unbelievable tries week after week, and now I'm standing in his garden, where he might have even practiced…"

"And now the guy is fighting for his life in the hospital," she reminded him, exasperated. "I'll want you to look over the medical charts with Julius. St Vincent's should be faxing them to the lab soon."

"On it," he said, recovering a little. "I'm almost finished here anyway. Take a look at this." He hoisted himself up on the wall, and pointed to a lane-way in the back that seemed to go nowhere.

Then she saw it.

Footprints in the dirt. On first impression they looked like they belonged to a heavy work boot of some sort, and were facing away from the wall. There was much more pressure on the first than the next, so easy enough to deduce that someone had jumped the wall and landed there.

"Impressions?" she said to Gary.

"Already done. Decent ones too. Look to be male - big feet, size eleven or twelve, even. Hopefully we can isolate something similar from the mess inside."

"Nice work, Gary." She was inwardly cursing herself for failing to check outside the perimeter during her inspection of the grounds earlier, but the wall was high and she remembered feeling instinctively reluctant to scale it.

Blame the blob.

Luckily Gary had no such issues.

"What are you marking there?" she asked him then.

"Cigarette butt."

She leaned in close and saw the butt half-hidden beneath a piece of bark mulch in the plant bed.

"Brand?"

Gary was studying it. "Looks like Marlboro. You'd know - give it a whiff."

Reilly didn't even need to bring it as far as her nostrils to confirm that he was correct.

"Great. Might be good for some kind of partial even if it's not our perp. I doubt that he took the time for a quick cigarette before hopping the wall."

"I agree, but you'd never know."

"Okay, let's try and wrap things up then - I want to be back in the lab before the day's out."

13

RETURNING TO THE HOUSE, SHE then caught up with Lucy to go through a step by step run through of the team's initial findings before everything was packed up and returned to the lab.

"How's your mum doing?" she asked, as they worked.

Lucy shrugged. "I think mostly okay. Dad and I are both throwing ourselves into work as usual. Good distraction, I suppose."

Reilly nodded. "I can relate to that."

"I'm not sure if Dad ever really thanked you for…you know," she said.

She smiled. "In his own way. And no thanks needed."

The psychological mechanics of losing a daughter had to be the hardest to understand. Humans were not engineered to see offspring die. It was the sons and daughters that were supposed to take care of the parents and see them pass, with full knowledge their legacy will live on.

Losing a child—no matter the age, but especially a young child—did something to a person. Reilly had seen it a few times on the job, but most noticeably with Jack Gorman. The truth was perhaps, not worse than the assumptions, but horrifying all the same. To confront that, to be forced to confront that, could take a toll on a person.

Reilly was surprised that Gorman didn't lash out more than he did.

In the end, though, he wanted to know the truth about Grace. And now that he did, he was forever transformed. It was a subtle transformation, but one none-the-less.

He seemed calmer these days. Or if not calm, more patient, and less spiky. He also seemed immensely sad. Like a fire was squelched deep within.

Lucy was that way too. The young had woman aged twenty years over the last month. The realities and ruthlessness of the world in which she lived and worked could now not be more evident.

Reilly knew from personal experience that incidents like these did more than just change a person. Senseless violence, death and murder had a tendency to dismantle people altogether. Not terribly different from say, soldiers in a war zone—all perceptions of reality get pulled apart, set aside and rebuilt more accurately and realistically.

It was beyond a new pessimism about reality, more a new sense of the randomness of it. And moreover, a true understanding of how powerless one is to change the course of their fate.

Or protect the fate of the people they love.

It could be said that tragedy anesthetizes people—makes them numb to the potential for atrocity. But it was more than that.

Although Reilly was still quite young when she lost her mother, she went through this dismantling as well. Certainly pessimistic (although she would argue "realistic"), certainly numb to atrocities other people reacted to, she was wiser. Not wise in the sense that she knew things other people did, but that she had a more thorough understanding of things without being told what/why/how.

She could put together pieces of a puzzle quicker and had fewer second-guesses, self-doubt or hesitation. She had a good sense of what needed to happen, without knowing the reason why. It was almost like the debris of everyday living that so clouded everyone else's judgment was no longer blocking her path, and so she could see forward easier than most.

She could see the bigger picture.

Lucy was like that now too. Something had changed in her since her return to the GFU after a brief spell of bereavement leave. She was more intuitive, focused, determined. She made fewer errors and was making better judgment-calls.

It was moments like these, when they were working closely that Reilly noticed the transformation the most. She seemed to be on auto-pilot, each gesture pre-programmed without error and with no hesitation.

She was so in touch with the flow of work that Reilly often just let her off. Even earlier she was in charge of the Morrison crime scene while Reilly was at the hospital.

As these thoughts surfaced, she decided to step back and let Lucy do her thing. She was already inputting data for iSPI, adding the shoe impressions Gary had found.

The data was sent securely to the lab, Reilly even noted that Lucy used encryption without having to be reminded. She followed up by phone to the GFU to make sure Julius had received it.

After that, the team broke up and agreed to stop off for a brief food break before reconvening later back at the GFU lab.

14

"WELL, WE ALL KNOW RUGBY legend Josh and we certainly know Perk. Clearly he has the Midas touch as the prosperous coffee chain pulled in over six million euro last year, and now rivals even the ubiquitous Starbucks. But we might not know about the money behind Annabel, or the couple's lucrative financial portfolio."

"That's right, Lee. Ireland's sweetheart Annabel Morrison is worth a couple of million in her own right."

"Surely that's not from her *Good Morning Ireland* gig? I didn't think TV paid that well."

"Well, that certainly doesn't hurt. Top Irish presenters typically clock in at around a couple of hundred grand. Not bad. Still, much of Annabel's wealth comes of course from her fashion endorsements. Irish and occasionally international brands pay the lady a small fortune to wear clothing, appear in commercials, or in the case of Steps Trainers, simply to walk down the street."

"Any guesses on the combined Morrison wealth?"

"Total? I'd say they pull in five or six million a year, or somewhere in that ballpark."

"They didn't start out that way though, did they?"

"No. It might have been Josh's early sports fame that brought the couple to prominence, but Annabel never missed a step as her husband jumped ahead. The Morrisons are every bit shrewd business partners, as they are a loving married couple."

"Ireland's own power couple."

"Well, I wouldn't call them Brad and Angelina, but basically they're Ireland's Brad and Angelina."

"And childhood sweethearts, too."

"That's what's so amazing, really. That they could have such aligned interests from so young. It really takes tremendous commitment to one another to amass this sort of family empire in a small country like this. And still relatively young too, both only in their mid-forties."

"Obviously beloved by the entire country and with good reason. But they've kept their noses clean too."

"True. Considering they're a couple with this kind of influence—not only in the Irish sports world, but in broadcast news, fashion and entertainment—they've really been stalwarts of their community. *Perk* repeatedly gets voted best place to work, Annabel is of course Ireland's sweetheart, and her TV colleagues and producers adore her, as do the media...really these two can do no wrong. Life is squeaky clean and they also find the time to contribute to so many charity events too."

"Such a shame what's happening to them now."

"Well, I suppose if you think about it, they were a prime target for such an invasion. They have not only money, but influence too. You get to them, maybe you can get to the keys of the city."

"True, true. Well thanks for joining us on *Live at Five* today. Gary Flynn is finance analyst for *The Irish Independent*. Thanks again, Gary."

"Pleasure."

15

ON THE WAY BACK TO the GFU, Reilly took a detour to Store Street to check in with the detectives and update them on the team's findings, while they shared information they'd since garnered from friends and family members.

Dylan Morrison was a handsome kid, and about five years older than he'd been in the family portrait, Reilly realized. He was now in his early twenties and of the "goth" persuasion, as he would have been labeled in Southern California.

His skin was deathly pale, hair dyed black and he wore a large ironic silver cross around a black button-down shirt.

Not your typical Silicon Valley tech.

Chris started the Skype recording, and flipped the laptop around so Reilly could watch the interview they'd taken from him earlier that day.

Dylan seemed to be answering the video call from a train—probably on an iPad by the look of it. The picture was washed out from the glare of the train window, and the angle of the shot came up at his nose, his head barely in the frame.

"Thanks for taking the call," Chris began. "I'm sure you're wondering…"

"Mom already called me. I know what happened."

"We're very sorry about what happened to your father, and are doing all we can to find the perpetrator," he assured him smoothly. "As part of this process we need to interview all family members. I'm sure you understand."

"No problem. I'm just on my way to a work conference in San Francisco. As soon as I'm done with that I'll get a flight home."

"Okay, thank you for that, but it's not necessary for our investigation. I'm sure your mother would appreciate it, though."

Dylan nodded, but his face remained impassive.

"A real bucket of emotions," Kennedy commented wryly.

"As you see, we didn't get much from him," Chris said when the video finished. "No grudges or arguments with associates of his father that he knew of, or was concerned about. Or if the business was having any problems. Nothing out of the ordinary."

"Yeah, except that he lives on the opposite side of the planet," Kennedy pointed out.

"Software engineer at Oracle?" Reilly shrugged. "It's a good job. Many college grads would leave home for a gig like that. So have you spoken to anyone at the station yet?" she asked, musing.

"The TV station?" Chris asked, somewhat incredulously.

She felt her hackles raise again. "Yes, the *Good Morning Ireland* production team to be specific." He was a good cop. Why was he so resistant to any angle involving Annabel Morrison?

"What is wrong with you?" Chris persisted. "I already told you - we talked to the barman at the GateHouse and the details she gave about her whereabouts last night checked out. More to the point, I sincerely doubt a slip of thing like Annabel Morrison came home and overpowered her fourteen-stone mountain of a husband."

"How would you know?" she barked back. "You couldn't ask her any questions earlier because she was too busy weeping on your chest."

"Woah," Kennedy laughed nervously.

"That's unacceptable, Reilly." Chris said, standing up.

"Is it? Because it seems like I'm the only one taking this investigation seriously. If it's not you consoling the poor princess in despair, then it's everyone at that house mooning over shoes and trophies and putting selfies on Instagram."

"Calm down…" Chris attempted.

"No, you know what? It's fine. And for the record, no I don't think Annabel Morrison could inflict such an attack on her husband without injuring herself in the process, but I definitely think a couple of holes in the story warrant some further investigation. So can we stop with the defensiveness?"

The table was quiet for a time before Kennedy attempted, "So…the TV station…"

"We need to know exactly who Annabel was with last night. And if anyone there has any indication on what or how much she drank. Also, I'm pretty sure there's more to this family than the PR spin, and if anyone could shed some more light on that, it would be Annabel's boss or colleagues."

"I'll set something up if we can," he said. "Anything else?"

"This wasn't a simple robbery gone wrong, I'm sure of it. That level of injury…the overt fury of the attack, it was personal. Somebody had a grudge against Josh Morrison."

"We've compiled a list of business associates, past teammates, old Blackrock College student buddies, the works."

"And the wife's?"

Chris rubbed the bridge of his nose. "Reilly, your job is to focus on the evidence. Ours is to focus on motive. Until the evidence suggests Annabel Morrison had anything to do with this, I'm going to ask you to stop."

"Look, I don't know what's going on between you two lately…" Kennedy tried to say.

"Nothing," both snapped at the same time.

Reilly stood up, "Nothing is right. Nothing at all."

That cut him, she could tell. And was a lie. There was indeed something going on between them, had always been.

But it was complicated.

16

SHE FELT DISCOMBOBULATED ALL THE way to the car, and the entire drive to the GFU. Her team was already busying themselves in the lab when she arrived.

Lucy had submitted trace samples for analysis, and Rory was busy going through the Morrison's computer records.

Julius was analyzing blood pattern photographs taken from the scene, and Gary was sorting through the physical evidence bags.

It would be a while before any kind of coherent picture began to emerge, so Reilly hunkered down at her desk and started absently going through the file, still thinking about her behavior just now.

The truth was, she wasn't sure what it was about Annabel Morrison, but she just didn't trust the woman.

She knew she would need a clearer sense of the attack and how and when it happened in order to take her out of the focus.

In this line of work she inherently latched onto something early, and eventually the evidence would either substantiate or negate her assumptions - her gut.

In this case, she had to admit that she also didn't like the way everyone seemed to be transfixed by Annabel, and held her up as this paragon of virtue, someone to be admired and adored. The woman was a trumped-up talk show host. So what?

She knew this cynicism was partly due to time spent working in and around Los Angeles.

Too many of these superficial nobodies took over the town there and tried their utmost to draw in every ounce of attention the world could bestow upon them. In Hollywood, fame came with a lot of perks, certainly.

But in a big city filled with rich and famous, it was all too easy to identify those with substance and those without. Those without - the wannabes - were always trying harder, working harder, putting up appearances. If you're Jack Nicholson, you don't need appearances. You are your own walking brand and the city will part ways for you. Whereas if you're just some guy with one movie under your belt, you want everyone to *think* you're Jack Nicholson.

Annabel Morrison was like that, Reilly thought. She was trying too hard. In a small place like Ireland, where celebrity isn't the currency that it is in LA, people can't really see through it. She could get away with the facade as long as she wanted, and so earned social currency through this manufactured persona.

Worse than being "fake," it was building an entire livelihood on a caricature. How could someone like that make an honest statement about anything?

And was her husband's stabbing truly a horrible moment in Annabel's life, or just an opportunity to further bolster her profile?

Perhaps it was unfair, but the thought was there nonetheless, and while Reilly couldn't articulate it, the concept was wedged beneath her thinking, making the investigative process uncomfortable.

Worse, she couldn't seem to discuss it openly with Chris, so there was no way to know if her suspicions were truly unfounded or not. He, like everyone else seemed smitten by the Morrisons' celebrity.

Of course the wife had to be a suspect, and if not the person—the caricature. Maybe Annabel Morrison wasn't the murdering type, but perhaps her caricature was?

Chris's assertion was correct though—there was no way a woman of Annabel's stature could have overpowered her husband that easily without displaying signs of a struggle. The guy was a rugby player for goodness sake, nearly two hundred pounds of raw muscle and bone, whereas Annabel looked like she hadn't eaten a good meal in a decade.

She needed to remember her training. Forensics investigators were trained to avoid criminal deduction, to ignore traditional motive and opportunity and focus only on what the evidence was saying.

But her gut rarely lied, and she was mindful that the evidence might well lead to places that would make, not only Chris, but a lot of people uncomfortable.

Her iPhone rang then and she picked up. "Steel."

"Hello Ms Steel. This is Dr Corcoran. We had an appointment earlier this afternoon."

She cursed under her breath. "Yes, I'm very sorry. I've been pulled onto a case.…"

"I understand and have been briefed. I do think it is important, however that we meet - soon." As he spoke, Reilly was distracted by the ding of an incoming message in her earpiece, and the chime indicating new emails.

"Clearly now is not a good time…"

"I'm not sure you quite understand, Ms Steel. HR and Detective O'Brien - your superior - has insisted. I'm available now if you are."

A headache began forming behind her right eye, as once again incoming information began pouring into the device she held to her ear.

This whole PSTD thing - was it about competency after the whole Tony Ellis thing? If she couldn't handle herself under pressure, what sort of investigator was she? If she couldn't keep it together through the thick and thin, how could the department rely on her? By pushing for counseling, was O'Brien implying she was inept? Not capable? Or was this some sort of sympathy card because of her gender?

Sure, she'd a nasty run in with a murderer yes, and had put, not only her own, but her baby's life in danger. Yes, the incident had put her on edge. Who wouldn't be on edge?

"Give me a couple of days until things calm down," she told the psychologist, putting him off.

But would things ever calm down? That was what she'd signed up for though, wasn't it?

No, Reilly didn't need some shrink pouring over her life, and talking about her shortcomings, or worse her 'feelings' about the pregnancy.

Instead, she'd do what she always did to cut through her demons; concentrate on doing what she did best.

17

HANGING UP ON THE PSYCHOLOGIST, she checked the phone's home screen and saw that she had a ton of messages and missed calls while she'd been on the line. Though a quick glance through the subject matter of most of them would be enough to make anyone think she did need therapy.

It was amazing the kind of impression - erroneous or otherwise - you could build up from someone's....

A thought struck her. Putting down the handset, she picked up the internal phone and quickly buzzed the lab.

"Where's the victim's phone?" she asked Lucy, who'd answered.

"Josh's? Not at the scene I don't think. I don't remember seeing it. I'll ask Rory."

But no, there had been no mention of the phone when they were itemizing the evidence, and discussing the Morrisons' tech hardware. A PC, iPad perhaps, but nothing at all about a phone. It must have been on Josh's person during the attack and stored at the hospital with his personal effects.

She texted Chris. *You and Kennedy pick up Morrison's phone at the hospital earlier?*

A minute or two passed before dancing ellipsis appeared on the screen, signifying Chris was replying.

Sorry forget to mention earlier but yes. Nothing there though, looks as though messages have been wiped. Will get into evidence asap. Maybe Rory can revive.

Reilly frowned. Who would delete the message data on Morrison's phone? His wife might, she thought automatically. If there was something to hide, that was.

In any case, she was sure Rory could get something from it. The guy could pull data from a dead turnip.

Reilly went down the hall into the computer lab, where Rory was dissecting the Morrison family computer, and was working meticulously on hooking up the motherboard to another unit.

"Victim's personal phone is on the way," she told him. "Seems the message data has been wiped, though."

"Let's hope it's not an iPhone, then," he muttered and circled the table, working on the connections.

"Find anything?"

He shrugged. "Emails, browsing data and docs are on that flash drive there, if you want to take a look. I'm only getting into the good stuff now. Or let's hope there's good stuff," he added wryly.

"Great," Reilly took the flash drive and began the arduous task of going through the information, email by email, in the hope of figuring out if golden boy Josh Morrison had any enemies.

She was about an hour into it when she was interrupted by a soft knock on the door.

It was Chris.

"Just dropped off the phone to Rory."

"Thanks," she said, without looking up.

"Reilly?"

"Hmm...?"

"Are you okay?"

"Why do you ask?" she said, still not looking up.

Chris stuttered a bit, trying to find the words. "You've been acting...odd today."

She sat back in her chair. "I've been acting odd? You're the detective with years of experience thrown off his game by the sight of a famous face."

He sat down in frustration. "I was keeping Annabel calm. Besides, jealousy doesn't suit you."

Reilly snorted. "Don't flatter yourself..."

He leaned in, urging her to face him instead of the screen.

"Look, I know things are still a bit...up in the air for you at the moment. I just wanted to remind you that I'm a friend. I'm on your side, remember?"

The gentleness of his words hit her harder than expected, and she felt an unwelcome surge of emotion rise up, then very quickly suppressed it.

"You're right - I do have a lot on my mind," she replied sharply. "Namely trying to get a grip on this investigation, while - thanks to celeb star-power - a million other *actual life and death* case files lie unattended in the meantime."

Chris leaned back, shaking his head with frustration.

Then he stood up and left without another word. She only turned to look after he was gone, watching the open doorway.

It felt cold in his absence and she knew she was wrong for treating him like this.

Yet she couldn't help it. She needed to push him away, once and for all.

It could never work between them. The prospect would have been hard enough before, but now with the baby…She needed to keep him at a healthy distance. Professional only.

It would hurt, but it was necessary.

Finally she decided to stop scanning email. She had made a thorough list of the people Josh Morrison seemed to correspond with the most. Generally associates involved in his coffee empire. There were some college friends and old rugby buddies on his Facebook page that she was able to match up through his email contacts.

It was a burgeoning list with lots of phone numbers.

She would begin the calls in the morning. But for now, Reilly was ready for some much needed insomnia.

18

"AND MEANWHILE AS WE ENTER the next twenty-four hours of the Morrison investigation, what's going on with Store Street's finest?

So far we only know two things: Josh got stabbed during a break-in at his house in Killiney on Friday night, and is still fighting for his life the ICU.

What's wrong with our police force? Still no suspects? No leads? And, perhaps most unforgivably, not a single statement to the press. With me on Dublin FM this morning to discuss the force's inability to zero in on a culprit in this captivating crime story, we have on the line forensic scientist Phil Palette from New York City's CSI. Hello there Phil. How's Gary Sinise?"

"Thanks for having me on the show, Martin."

"Well, you know the background on this one, I'm sure. Our former rugby captain brought to his knees by some vicious thug, and twenty-four hours later, still not a suspect to be found. Sounds like our lads could use your help!"

"Well, Martin, as you know, this is a critical period in any investigation…"

"That's right; all bets are off once the first forty-eight hours are up, isn't it? See listeners, I've watched the shows, I know my stuff!"

"In truth, that's a bit of a myth, Martin, but yes, the sooner the investigators get to grips with the physical evidence, the better. Especially when there's a perpetrator out there on the loose."

"So why don't they have anyone yet?"

"My understanding of the situation is that the investigative team will want to play their cards close to their chest. Especially as this is such a high-profile case which, given the parties involved, has an unprecedented amount of public interest. They may well have sensitive information that they don't want made public - or anything that could spook the suspect or tarnish their investigation."

"So tell us what usually happens in a situation like this, from a CSI point of view. Actually, Phil did you know our GFU here is fronted by glamor-puss Reilly Steel, actually one of your own?"

"I did know that, and you're in good hands, though I'm not sure she'd appreciate that description, Martin. Well, as per protocol the team would by now have collected forensic evidence from the Morrison house, and started to process it in the lab. In the case of a robbery gone wrong like this there will be any number of items to analyze, footprints, finger prints, blood spatter patterns as well as a multitude of trace evidence. The forensics team will be reviewing information about Mr Morrison's injuries from the hospital, all the while working alongside the homicide detectives, throwing out possibilities and directing interviews with potential suspects based on the evidence found."

"So when Gary Sinise goes to these crime scenes he's always pulling out his fancy equipment, looking at things under fluorescent light? Does Reilly Steel do that too?"

"I imagine your GFU is equipped with all of the standard investigating equipment, Martin. And I'm sure the team are working round the clock to assist the detectives in finding the weapon and the perpetrator."

"With your trained eye, Phil, can you tell us who you think might have dunnit?"

"Impossible for me to say without direct involvement in the investigation though, initial reports suggest that the attack was prompted by the interruption of a burglary in progress. But if Mr. Morrison was stabbed in the way the press report…well, I must admit it sounds personal to me. Stabbings are a very personal crime, and to my mind, a spooked burglar is more likely to make a few quick slashes and then run off, than remain at the scene to inflict a sharp force wound in such a location. A miracle the victim survived, actually."

"Well, in this country we all know what a colossus our Josh is. You can't keep a man like that down. So you think it might be someone with a grudge? Someone jealous of his stellar career, fame and millions, not to mention gorgeous wife?"

"That's what the detectives will be trying to figure out, Martin. Let's all just hope that the man himself wakes up and can tell us exactly what happened."

19

USUALLY HOME WAS A HAVEN. Reilly loved her Ranelagh flat. It was on a quiet street of beautiful redbrick Victorian conversions, and walking distance to almost anything she needed.

For the last few years, coming home was like a big warm hug.

Except these days, it wasn't the bastion of comfort that it had been since she'd first moved in. Now, it had become the place where she'd first found out her life was about to change forever, and where lately she just couldn't manage to sleep.

Maybe it was the pregnancy—or, specifically, the fact she hadn't exactly come to terms with the reality of a new life growing inside her.

Or that, despite a few failed attempts, she hadn't yet plucked up the courage to tell Todd about it.

She told herself she kept putting it off because the first trimester was so tricky. So many things could go wrong, and it didn't make sense getting everyone worked up about it until the baby was further along.

But now the baby was further along, so there was little excuse.

She knew she was also still dealing with the after-effects of that previous investigation, still plagued by thoughts of what Tony Ellis might have done if Chris hadn't saved her. While she'd been in such situations before, the fact that her baby's life had also been in danger was sobering.

Perhaps even more sobering was her life in general, and how it was supposed to work when the baby arrived.

What kind of future could she offer the kid when from day to day its mother was repeatedly embroiled in murdered faces and sadistic criminals?

It takes a certain someone to get into crime investigation, she knew, and it takes another type of person to stay with it.

The best ones are, in their hearts, scientists. They want to apply a scientific method to catching bad guys. To doing good work. Regular science isn't enough for them. They are not the teaching or "conducting a study" types. They are genuinely altruistic and want to do some good with their skills, something beyond the prison of academia.

Others are, in their hearts, detectives in the true sense of the word.

This breed of crime scene investigator wants to move the needle beyond reasonable doubt to catch bad guys. Not an altruistic position per se, but rather, a way of stemming the bleeding tide of the horror of what humans do to other humans.

This breed of crime scene investigator is not in it for the science, but rather uses science to be more precise than the police can be.

It is more than a hunch. It is that sound of a jail cell closing for good. It is the feeling of 'we got the bad guy' and we *know* we got the bad guy. Not only did we catch him but justice was served. She knew Chris had always struggled with that, the idea of justice. It was one of the things that actually made him a great detective.

But for Reilly, the case ended with catching the bad guys. As far as she was concerned, a trial was only a formality, because the evidence doesn't lie.

For her, the science was a means to the end, not the focus.

Julius—he was all about the science. If he had his way he would never leave the lab, and rarely went out in the field to visit a crime scene, unless absolutely necessary.

He would just happily take whatever was found directly to the lab and unleash his arsenal of test tubes, computer analyses and mathematical equations. Whereas Gary and Lucy were in Reilly's camp.

They wanted the bad guy—with or without science. It seemed the team was lopsided in that direction, which meant they always worked well with detectives, but it also meant they used hunches, personal experience and worse, often their own opinions to guide investigations.

That was what Reilly was doing now in the Morrison case and she needed to knock it off. Not only for this thing, but forever.

She'd seen what happened to forensics people that were secretly detectives. They burned out—each and everyone one of them.

It was the scientists who got gray-haired and retired. The rest of them—the Reillys, Garys and Lucys of the world can't break science to meet their ends, and so break themselves trying.

Reilly had a long history of frustration, false leads, and a roller coaster ride of emotions while on a case, and knew there would be lots more of the same in her future.

Was this what all her life was about?

Was she really going to introduce this child into a world full of violence and hatred? A world where its mom had a front-row seat, and sometimes - like in the Chef investigation - even a starring role.

If Reilly could default just to the science, she could better distance herself from atrocity and stay on the straight-and-narrow.

Like Julius, she would not internalize these cases. She'd have a healthy disconnection with the victims, and a marriage only to the evidence.

In that paradigm, her child would be fine. Motherhood would be fine.

But how would things fare if she continued to take on the weight, guilt and anger of every case she worked on?

She needed to talk to Todd about all of this, she knew. First and foremost he had the right to know. And being in the same line of work himself, would understand better than anyone her thoughts and fears.

Better than Chris? her subconscious taunted, and she tried to brush the thought away.

There was no point in discussing any of this with Chris.

They'd already decided that ship had sailed, to say nothing of the fact that it wouldn't be fair to burden him with any more of her personal problems.

But what did she truly know about Todd? How could she anticipate how he would react to the news? She was confident that despite being on the other side of the Atlantic, he would want to be involved somehow. It was the kind of guy he was.

What she was doing wasn't fair, Reilly realized now. Todd had the right to know. It would be unconscionable to not tell him.

But it would be so much easier not to…

She knew that many women in her position would have considered alternatives. For her, there was no alternative. This baby was her responsibility, and she would see it all the way.

Maybe it was the universe's way of humbling her—or grounding her even.

No matter what, it was an earth-shattering event for which she would have to realign her worldview in order to accommodate.

Whatever the case, Reilly would not look at it as a mistake, and she would not allow her obligations—work or otherwise—to interfere with her baby's life.

Thinking all of this through did little to help her state though.

She paced, drank herbal tea. Paced some more and at some point in the early hours, fell asleep on the living room sofa.

20

THE FOLLOWING MORNING, REILLY PULLED into the GFU, rolling her eyes at the presence of media there now too.

Hardly the crime of the century, she thought to herself. It wasn't even a homicide for Chrissakes.

Gathering her things, she quickly made her way upstairs to the lab, but was joined in the elevator by none other than Inspector O'Brien. Her boss's sudden appearance in the building was so startling, she dropped her case.

A hard-lined man with salt and pepper hair and shrewd eyes, the chief quickly helped her gather her things and apologized.

"I was hoping for a word," he said.

"Of course, sir. What is it?"

Getting out of the lift, he walked along with her towards her office. "I know that your team will be - as always - turning over every stone."

"Goes without saying."

"But there's a lot at stake here as I'm sure you know. I really want you to pull out all the stops. The world is watching."

"I know," she said barely suppressing a sigh.

"The headlines, you've seen them? They're making us sound inept, provincial even. We can't have that, can we?"

"Of course not," she said.

"So we'll see some progress soon then? Glad to hear it."

Reaching Reilly's office, he gruffly patted her on the back and continued back to the lift. He'd come here specifically to see her then…She gulped.

Then as a parting shot he added, "Oh, and Steel?"

"Yes?"

"I have a press conference later this morning at eleven. I hope you and the detectives can deliver a preliminary report before then. Need some time to prepare, you understand."

She nodded, but couldn't say anything. Instead, she watched him go back into the elevator and toddle off back to headquarters. A place where he didn't have to do anything except wait for the GFU to make him look good.

A report by eleven?

Let's hope the chief believed in miracles.

She shook it off, heading straight to the lab, where she found Julius looking over her assessment of the victim's lacerations.

"Morning," she said, noticing that he had those horrifying pictures of Josh Morrison's knife wounds cast about on the workstation. He was viewing them with a magnifying glass, double-checking and cross-referencing.

"What are your thoughts?" she asked.

"Probably not the wife anyway," he said, his tone slow and deliberate.

"How so?" she challenged shortly, still a little rattled by her run in with the chief.

"Firstly, we're surmising that the initial incised wound occurred from behind, which I'd agree with."

"You're absolutely sure?"

"Yes, because the edges of that laceration are straight, clean and comparatively shallow," he said, pointing at the photo of the incised wound on Josh Morrison's shoulder. "Whereas the edges of the other deeper injury - the one to the stomach - looks torn and irregular."

She nodded, "So the blade was damaged a little upon first striking harder tissue on the victim's shoulder."

"Possibly the scapula."

"OK, so it seems we're right about the perp coming up from behind, probably while the victim was making tea."

"Yes, and based on the margins and angles I'm seeing here, particularly on the frontal wound to the stomach, the perp would need to have been about the same height as the victim, give or take a few inches. The blade went in at a straight trajectory, no upward or downward angle, and the slash to the shoulder blade again went from top to bottom."

"So you're saying it's unlikely that someone of Annabel Morrison's height and stature could have inflicted these injuries. Not even in high heels?"

Julius gave her a sideways look. "There are other factors too, such as the depth of the blade and ferocity of the thrust, and trajectory of withdrawal. Also the position of the defensive wounds help calculate an overall picture of the attacker's approximate height and weight. Impossible to be absolutely certain of course."

Reilly nodded. "OK. Let's try that scenario on iSPI, see how it plays out."

Taking out the 3D reconstruction tablet, she set it on the counter and Julius plugged in the relevant data so that the app could reconstruct the scenario.

It took a few minutes but the software finally clicked into place.

Already programmed in were the dimensions of the crime scene, approximate distance between markers, and the relevant blood spatter based on their initial findings, along with the countless other variables that made iSPI such a helpful little piece of technology.

"If we're right, the blood spill should concur with what we're thinking," Julius said, looking on.

"Okay, so let's start there—we can assume Josh was standing somewhere on this side of the island, filling the kettle and setting it on the hob maybe. Then, perp comes up from behind…"

Julius nodded.

She moved across to Lucy's workstation, where the younger girl was busy analyzing blood pattern.

"You're looking at blood spill?"

"Yeah, a little tricky. Sharp force wounds, so it's not like the blood will splatter—not a lot of arterial spray from the first one. But still, it's coming along."

Julius came up from behind, iSPI still in hand.

He entered Lucy's information along with the wound stats, and reloaded the program, and when the new scenario loaded, he added some contrast to better make out the blood patterns.

"What's that?" Lucy asked, but they were all thinking it.

iSPI was displaying barely visible impressions amongst the blood spill on the inside of the kitchen island.

"I think I know."

They followed Julius to another part of the lab and moving a table aside, he rolled out some plastic.

"Can you grab some mix?"

Lucy took a bag of simulated blood from the below-counter fridge and handed it to him. Carefully checking the crime scene photos, he scattered some of the liquid in an approximate pattern on the plastic.

"Look about right?"

Reilly nodded.

Julius knelt down, knees pressing onto either side of the blood. Then he stood up, having completely ruined his clothes.

"Of course. So the victim gets slashed on his right shoulder, maybe staggers a little, then falls to his knees. Perp tried to straddle him? Maybe tried to go for the throat?"

"But Josh pushes him off, turns round and goes to grab the knife - which is where he gets the defensive wounds. They struggle on the other side of the island for a bit, before the burglar goes in for the kill, stabs him in the stomach and Josh collapses back onto the glass table, smashing it and everything on it, before bleeding out amongst the glass."

Reilly's eyes widened. "Sound like one angry burglar."

"Then the wife comes home minutes - seconds - later?" continued Lucy, "Spooks the doer and calls in it. Just in time too."

She stood still for a moment as the narrative began to unfold in her mind. Josh Morrison was viciously attacked—likely from behind while he prepared to make himself a pot of tea. He tried to fight off his attacker at first, but was eventually overpowered and brutally stabbed.

And the strength of that attack…

No, Reilly decided once and for all. Annabel Morrison could not have done this.

Such a struggle would surely have shown itself on her person, and when Reilly had talked to her yesterday, there were no scratches or nicks on the woman's arms and hands - even her nails had been flawless.

"OK, so working with that narrative, let's take a closer look at prints, trace, anything in that kitchen that doesn't belong. You have the first responder info for elimination?"

Lucy nodded. "Sent through last night. And a couple of early reports from the detectives too, along with Annabel Morrison's official statement."

Statement? If you could even call it that, Reilly thought remembering. Despite the new findings in relation to Morrison's attacker, she wondered again why the wife had seemed so reluctant to answer questions without her solicitor, and hoped the detectives were following up regardless.

Why would any woman who'd happened across her husband at the centre of the scenario they'd just described, hesitate for even a second about helping them?

21

LATER THAT MORNING, THE INVESTIGATIVE team met up to compare notes and cobble together a preliminary report in time for O'Brien's all-important press conference.

"We've interviewed Josh's business associates and staff, Annabel's TV colleagues as well as the family's weekly cleaner and landscaping company," said Chris. "We'll send over the transcripts later."

"You're talking about the interviews, but you aren't talking about suspects. O'Brien won't like that."

"Or motive - unfortunately," he said. "I think we need to just focus on the notion that the attack on Morrison was indeed just a robbery gone wrong."

Reilly snorted and then grew serious as she realized he wasn't joking. "What? No intruder alarm, or physical evidence of any such break-in, never mind that there was nothing stolen. And that whole thing with wiping the phone messages?"

"We need more from you then," he said tersely. "The DPP is already down my throat fighting for space with O'Brien. I just got a voicemail from Phoenix Park. We were a headline on the *The Journal* this morning. Do you know what it said? NO TRY. Big picture of Kennedy smoking outside the house, and a series of articles about how we're scratching our arses and don't know what the hell we're doing."

"I don't get it…"

Kennedy who looked suitably shame-faced, went on to explain to Reilly that the headline was a pun on a term for a rugby score.

Way over her head…

"Lab results should be back later, maybe something will turn up in the trace. Also Rory is still going over Morrison's phone."

"Weird that his messages were deleted. Wonder if that happened before or after the attack?"

"No way to know unless we can establish a firm timeline."

The lab was calling, so she quickly picked up. It was Gary.

"Got a partial for Marlboro man."

"Seriously? That's great news."

"Running it now, will let you know if anything comes back."

"If you could make it happen before O'Brien's press conference I'd love you forever."

"Try my best but you know as well as I do how long these things can take."

Hanging up, she filled the detectives in. "Gary got a partial from a cigarette butt in the garden."

Kennedy frowned. "Seems a bit reckless. I'm off to rob this gaff, but first let me finish this fag?"

"Unless you weren't planning on hurting someone when you went in there—and in the aftermath you'd forgotten the fact you had a cigarette earlier," she pointed out.

"Or, you're just a sociopath," Kennedy bantered. "Don't forget the random element."

"You don't forget the random element, I'll keep working on the evidence."

"Deal," he said with a half-grin, before getting up to use the men's room. When he was gone, Chris paused a little before turning to Reilly.

"I was thinking about what you said yesterday, about being swayed by Annabel Morrison's celebrity, and honestly, that wasn't it. Yes, she's famous and on TV and puts on this perfect face for her show and the media. Everyone always talks about how elegant and poised she is. And seeing her like that, so vulnerable, I think it caught me off guard a little."

Ever the knight in shining armor.

"I don't get it. I don't adore anyone unless they've proven they're worth adoring."

"Must be where I'm going wrong then," he said and she smiled.

He shrugged. "I'll tell you one thing for sure though, burglar or not, we're going to find the bastard, make sure that woman and her family are safe."

"You got your white horse parked out front now, too?"

"Just for once, I'd love to see you without cynicism."

She winked at him. "You'll be waiting a while."

22

"WELL ONE THING'S FOR SURE," Gary informed Reilly later, without looking up from the microscope. "Josh Morrison and Annabel Morrison were definitely in the kitchen."

"Very funny," she said.

"I'm not joking. Eliminating first responders, I don't have anything else - *anyone* else. All the prints checked out. And if the guy was intent on robbing the place, chances are he was wearing gloves."

Reilly bit her lip. "Call the hospital, see if they can expedite sending over Josh's clothes," she told him. "If we're going to find the perp, we have to hope he cut himself during the struggle."

Next, she continued on to Rory's workstation.

"You get anything off that phone yet?"

He nodded and wiggled an iPhone at her.

"Yep, phone messages were indeed wiped. Time stamp is all I can get," he said, when she looked underwhelmed. "It's an iPhone, unfortunately. Nothing is recoverable."

"How'd you get the time stamp then?"

"Stored on Apple's systems, that's all. Can't get anything from the phone itself, it's a brick."

Reilly went back to her office and sat for a while, thinking over the findings so far.

The question remained, why - if this was a simple robbery gone bad - would the attacker go to the trouble of deleting Josh Morrison's phone messages? Of course, until they could ascertain the exact time of the attack, there was no way of knowing when the tampering had occurred.

Had Morrison heard the robbery in progress and deleted his own messages before going to check it out? That was a scenario she couldn't quite wrap her head around, unless there was some very valuable data - personal financials or confidential company information - on the device.

Unless Josh had deleted the info because he knew his attacker?

But then how did this tie into his being attacked while he made tea. Unless - and this again tied into the perp being known to him - unless he was making tea for someone who took the opportunity to lash out while his back was turned?

That was an interesting theory and one that made more sense to Reilly than the robbery in progress one, to be honest.

But the fact remained that they had yet to isolate a print or some piece of trace putting someone other than Josh or Annabel Morrison in the kitchen that night.

Next, she went through the crime scene photos and took out the ones of the sliding glass door from the kitchen and onto the patio.

It definitely looked to have been forced open from the inside. Yet Annabel Morrison mentioned yesterday that the intruder had 'slipped away' out of the corner of her eye. You'd think she'd remember someone forcing the door open to escape, but if she was tending to her husband, her back would have been to the patio doors, and her attention obviously elsewhere….

The fact that the track was off had seemed suspicious to Reilly at the time because she was trying to ascertain whether or not the perp came in from the garden. But now it looked more like the door was forced open from the *inside*.

Only one reason for that; the perp was trying to leave and couldn't get it open in his haste? Maybe put his shoulder against it and knocked it off the track. Then he'd jumped the perimeter wall and escaped back onto the street via the lane way before vanishing into the night.

No prints to be had from the sliding door unfortunately, but like Gary had pointed out earlier, if the guy was intent on robbing the Morrison place, chances were he was wearing gloves, so it was unlikely they'd happen across his prints in the usual places.

As always, during this stage of an investigation, nothing seemed to be adding up. Like with all crime scenes, there was a story in here—a narrative.

But the team hadn't yet uncovered all of the pieces, so they couldn't attempt to put them together.

23

"WITH US THIS EVENING, IS former criminal justice barrister, Elaine Thompson. Elaine, thank you for joining us."

"Pleasure to be here, thank you."

"Now Elaine, there has been much in the press over the past day or two about the fact that the Gardai have made very little progress on the Morrison investigation. And many voices have expressed a concern that if it takes much longer, they may not solve the case at case at all. That Josh Morrison's brutal attacker may well go free."

"Well I suppose it's easy to forget, since there has been so much press, that they are really only in the very early stages of the investigation. In clean situations, detectives often have a list of suspects and it takes time to reach them all, interview them and begin to build a case."

"So what is DDP's office up to now?"

"Staff from the Department of Public Prosecutions would be working closely with the investigative team, reviewing all evidence assembled from the crime scene.

Remember, the DPP's job isn't to find the person who stabbed Josh Morrison, that's the job of the detectives. The prosecutor's office is simply looking to see if any evidence the detectives have against a suspect will hold up in court."

"But unless something has changed, or Store Street is not releasing information, the case has yet to see a suspect, doesn't it? Would the DPP still be involved at this time?"

"Absolutely. Even without a suspect, the detectives need authorization from the courts for search warrants and eventually arrest warrants. At this point, the DPP will be reviewing evidence that may require legal authorization for further investigation. Unfortunately the victim in this case remains incapacitated, and the authorities have no choice but to conduct their investigation without his input. The only witness arrived after the attack had taken place."

"Annabel Morrison."

"Yes, and from what I'm aware was only able to provide a very limited physical description of the perpetrator."

"So if this crime against Josh is random—and it certainly appears that way, what chance do the investigators have in finding a suspect for the courts to prosecute?"

"These cases are never easy to muddle through. There are entirely too many variables. Random cases rarely see resolution and certainly if the investigation goes too far into the next week or so, chances are any viable, yet undiscovered physical evidence will be lost."

"Thank you Elaine, for that interesting insider scoop on the legal aspects of the Morrison case. Are you available to stick around and take questions from our listeners?"

"Of course."

"Great, well stay tuned and we'll take your calls. You know the show, you know the number! Be back right after this."

24

THE FOLLOWING MORNING, WHILE THE team continued combing through the evidence from the Morrison attack, Reilly was still thinking about the timeline.

They had the 999 dispatch time, but nothing from the other end of the spectrum. The taxi firm the TV station used hadn't yet come back to Rory with details of the car or driver that had dropped Annabel home after her night out in Ballsbridge.

Reilly reckoned more precise information was needed about what time Annabel had left the pub. 'About one am' wasn't good enough as far as she was concerned.

Getting a handle on when the wife actually arrived back at the house would go a long way towards understanding when the attack on her husband had happened.

And more importantly, if there was something off about her story, the timeframe would reveal it.

The Gate House pub wasn't open at when she arrived at 10.30 am, so she waited in the car and thumbed through her emails.

After about half an hour, Reilly saw a fifty-something heavy-set man opening up, so she got out.

"Hey there," she said, showing her credentials. "I'm with the GFU, are you a manager here?"

"I'm the owner, Paddy Barrett," he said extending his hand. "Is this about the Morrison thing? I already told those detectives everything."

"I know that and thank you. But I'm from the GFU, and I just need to ask one or two questions. Hope you don't mind?"

"Forensics? My place isn't a crime scene is it?"

"Of course not, we just need to ascertain a firm timeline in the investigation. Do you have security cameras here?"

"Yep. Gave 'em to the detectives."

Good. Seemed the guys were following up on Annabel's story then.

"Well, do you happen to keep your till receipts? For accounting purposes. I'm looking for Friday night in particular."

He shrugged. "I might have them—if they're credit card transactions. Cash ones get input each night. Why, what do you need those for?"

"They might be no use at all, but like I said, I just need to follow up."

"Come in," he said, leading her through to the bar. "I was working that night. The TV crowd come in most

Fridays, actually. Nothing unusual to report. Same rowdy bunch, blowing off steam after a hard week. You would be too, if you had a job like theirs."

"I'm sure," she said raising an eyebrow. Yep, her job was a picnic compared to the trials of make-up, hair and pieces-to-camera.

He went to the back office behind the bar and rifled through some folders, "Yeah, I have Friday's receipts. Here it is, they usually set up tab."

Reilly looked it over. Hefty bill—over four hundred quid. Nice tip. Then she snapped her gaze up to the owner. "This receipt was processed just after 12 am."

"Yeah, we don't have a late license. I know it's a little bit on the late side, but…well they're good customers. I usually let them out the back on the quiet. You won't say anything will you?"

Reilly knew that Irish pub owners routinely flaunted the liquor laws and if it didn't have a late license, by rights The Gate House should have served last drinks at 11.00 and closed its doors shortly thereafter.

But Paddy's concern had given her an edge. "Sure I won't report you, but I will need to take this."

"No problem - it's all yours."

Outside, she picked up the phone and called Chris.

"Did you know the Gate House doesn't have a late license?" she said without preamble when he picked up.

"You're joking," he sounded suitably muted.

"So Annabel couldn't have left the pub at one am like she said. Not when the place closed its doors an hour before that."

She told him about the till receipt and the bar owner's assertion that he hadn't let his patrons stay any longer past midnight, and had let them out the back door.

So it was unlikely they'd see Annabel leaving on CCTV.

"Shit. OK, I'll talk to Flanagan, see if we can bring her in for more questioning."

"Great, and Chris?"

"What?" he asked tersely, obviously kicking himself for taking the wife at her word.

"Leave your white steed outside this time."

25

BACK AT THE LAB, THERE was some more news.

"Gary's isolated a print on the worktop near the knife block that doesn't check out," Lucy told her.

"You're kidding me," She headed straight to Gary's work station where he was examining the print in question.

"It's kinda weird," he said, "which is how I missed it before. At first I thought it was smudged, but looking at it, I can see that the splotch is actually part of it…"

"Show me."

He stepped back and Reilly lowered her eye to the viewfinder. The print did indeed look smudged along the side at first sight, but now she saw that there was a more definitive circular shape along the edge of the tip that appeared as a black spot.

"Callus," she told him.

"That's what I thought. You've seen something like it before?"

She nodded, excited by the find. If this belonged to the perp it gave them some very individualized information.

"And in other, possibly related news - we just got back a print hit on the cigarette butt," he told her.

She couldn't believe it. This day kept on getting better and better.

"Really?"

"Yes. Guy called Richard O'Donnell, twenty-two years old, just finished a year-long larceny stint and not long out on probation."

"You're kidding me. So it *was* a burglary."

"Presumably," he said. "I have his offender information here."

"Does it happen to say anything about calluses on his fingers? Or his shoe size?" she added, thinking about those boot impressions in the lane way behind the garden.

"Not that I can see. Oh and we identified the tread on those too," Lucy said, obviously following her train of thought. "Doc Martens, size eleven."

"This is brilliant work, guys," Reilly scanned through the report and took a note of the offender's last known address. "I'll pass it on to the detectives, so they can go and pick this guy up."

"Ah hold on boss," Gary warned, and she paused, waiting.

Always a catch.

"I've run comparisons, and there are no definitive similarities between the partial on the cigarette butt and any prints found inside the house."

"Including the callused one?"

"Yes, so tell Batman and Robin to hold their horses; we can't match the smoker with the doer just yet."

Without connecting prints on the cigarette to those found in the house, the detectives didn't have enough cause to bring in Richard O'Donnell.

Yet.

The cigarette butt could have blown in on the wind, or even been dropped in the garden by a passing bird - Reilly could list in her head the various arguments spurious or otherwise, any defense solicitor worth his salt would use if they tried to pin this on the guy without being able to definitively put him in the Morrison kitchen.

Still, the fact that the cigarette had led to a known thief was more than enough reason to check Richard O'Donnell out.

26

"NICE LEAD," SAID KENNEDY, AS he and Chris made their way to the address listed on Richard O'Donnell's probation information. "The guy fits the breaking and entering theory at least."

"Wonder if he fits Annabel's description too," Chris said, deliberately caustic, as they both knew that description was about as generic as you could get. 'Normal height and weight, dark clothes, and a hoodie,' could be used to describe the majority of the Dublin male youth population.

"Well if O'Donnell is our guy, chances are he's already taken off by now," Kennedy continued. "And if he hasn't, at least we have enough to bring him in for questioning. How many reasons would a guy like that have for smoking in the Morrisons' garden?"

In front of the house - a small former corporation three-bed evidently converted into flats, was an older woman out watering flowers. She looked to be in her early sixties, but with good posture and a wry look about her.

"You the landlady here?" asked Kennedy.

"Who wants to know?"

The detectives showed her their badges.

"Who is it this time?" she said sighing.

"Richard O'Donnell, we just need to ask him a few questions."

"That's the new boy, but I haven't seen him."

"Seen him for a while, or all?"

"At all. His rent is up to date though and that's all I care about."

"Do you mind if we try the buzzer?"

"If you like, but as I'm sure you know, I can't let you into the flat without a warrant."

"Of course," Chris said, ever courteous. "Thank you."

As expected there was no reply at O'Donnell's flat.

"So can you tell us anything more about your tenant?" Chris asked the woman. "How long has Richard O'Donnell been a tenant here?"

"About a month now I'd say. He signed the lease and everything, but most of that is done through Mountjoy."

"Do you typically work with the prison services then?"

She nodded. "Yes, it's me bread and butter. Everyone here has a past. I let them stay for as long as they want, and then they get themselves right and move on. Or they don't. Either way, I get paid. Not by them of course, but by the Social. Better than having to worry about squatters or troublemakers. I don't see much of them either way."

"You don't live at the house yourself then."

"God no, this place is just my pension. I live on the Northside. The house was my sister's and she left it to me."

"So you said you don't have all that much communication with your tenants?" Chris continued.

"Suits me down to the ground. These fellas, they just want to hide away in their holes like they're used to. Don't seem to see much daylight. Most of them work small jobs, night shifts and all that. I let them mind their own business. I mind my own too."

"OK Ms…"

"Mullins. And it's Mrs actually.

"Mrs Mullins. Thanks very much for your time. Here's my card. If you do happen to see Mr O'Donnell, I'd appreciate it if you could give me a call."

27

"LOOK, I'M VERY SORRY FOR the Morrison thing, I mean really I am, but come on, this is starting to become a circus."

"Are you saying that…"

"No listen, I mean come on. *Every* radio show. *Every* news broadcast. How can they possibly satisfy the media's bloodlust?"

"No, I can't…"

"You come on here…"

"Don't interrupt, I'm in the middle of…"

"It's what people want to know!"

"Since when do we provide news based upon what people want to know? We're journalists!"

"A man is attacked in his own home…"

"In a rich suburb like Killiney Hill. Come on! This is not a public threat! The only reason we're all so interested in this is because his wife has a nice arse!"

"That is completely unacceptable."

"Is it? He's rich, his wife's a babe. That's why they care. It's an episode of Beverly Hills 90210. It's reality television. And the media is feeding it."

"The media is reporting on a heinous crime…"

"Oh save it!"

"Cynicism isn't even a…"

"And look, did you see this headline? By…I don't even know who this is…some sort of fanciful retired cop, calling the cops clueless."

"We're into the second day, they don't have a single suspect…"

"How many suspects do you think they get in an average day? They have to investigate don't they? What? Do you want them dragging in every idiot they come across? They have a job to do. The media just needs to back off and let them do it."

"The media's job is to make sure the public is aware…"

"And they're not aware? Do you think camping out in front of the Morrison residence day and night is absolutely necessary? We have major world problems going on at the moment. The Irish economy is falling into the toilet, entire countries are defaulting on debt, genocide in Africa—and here we are, every major story is about on a stabbing in some rich Dublin backwater? This is insane, and sensational."

It's TV. We all want to know what happens in the next episode and get incensed when that plot point doesn't hit soon enough. Then we call our police force clueless and parade around their crime scenes like some indignant teenagers, completely detached from the reality of the situation. A man was stabbed. That's it, that's all. Can we move on please?"

"Well, no. Clearly we cannot."

Chris and Kennedy were pacing in the hallway at the courthouse.

The waiting was always the worst part. Who knew if that cigarette butt would be enough to convince the DPP's office to give them a warrant for O'Donnell's flat?

Chris guessed the suspect would not be there in any case, but as this was about the only decent lead they had on this so far, they needed to check it out.

Helen Marsh suddenly appeared in the hallway. Chris didn't notice where she'd come from or how she approached. The woman was like a ghost. Or ninja.

But most importantly she had that all important pink warrant slip in hand.

He grinned and snatched it from her.

"I have to say, the forensics isn't great," she said. "The only reason we're allowing this at all is because we want the public to know we at least have a suspect. If you do bring this guy in, let's hope for a stronger case than a cigarette butt."

"The cigarette proves he was at the Morrison residence that night, Helen," Chris assured her. "I'm sure it won't be long before we can get the rest."

28

THIS TIME, MRS MULLINS LET the detectives inside without complaint and, as expected, no one was there.

By the looks of it, no one had been there for quite sometime. The small room was bare-bone empty, impeccably cleaned but not the least bit lived in. The fridge was empty, cabinets bare, wardrobes empty. All of the furniture looked unused. There wasn't even a TV to be found.

"Do you rent the flats furnished?" Chris asked Mrs Mullins.

"These places are usually halfway houses between prison and jobs. I only keep them stocked up with the essentials."

He nodded and looked around. He could already tell this was a cold lead.

"The guy's never even stepped foot in here."

"Quite possible," Mrs Mullins agreed. Then she shrugged and left them to it.

The GFU team arrived shortly thereafter to sweep the flat. Reilly walked slowly around the perimeter, then crisscrossed the small room, only looking and not touching.

Once that was done she would walk along each wall and look inward, under furniture or at the lower parts of the opposite wall, hoping to find something that might further implicate Richard O'Donnell, footwear so they could ascertain his shoe size, or a definitive print that would put him inside the Morrison household.

On the first pass, she found nothing of interest. There were no trash bins, or trash. The refrigerator was completely empty. There were no pictures on the walls or on the shelves, no books, records or personal objects of any kind.

The place was simply not lived in.

Lucy and Gary swept the area with UV and didn't find anything of note that way either. No hair fibers or skin flakes in the bed, no prints on the windows or door knobs.

They went through the empty closets, drawers, cabinets. Nothing.

Reilly fell into a quiet state, which often happened in times like these. To the average observer it almost looked like she blanked out, or had begun daydreaming even.

But really she was just finding an internal silence.

Putting all thoughts aside in order to be completely empty and receptive. Sometimes in those moments there were strikes of inspiration or wisdom.

Or something occurred to her that hadn't before.

But this time, nothing. It was like trying to prove the existence of a ghost.

29

BACK AT THE GFU, SHE tasked Rory with investigating the magistrate's records on O'Donnell, specifically for family members or friends with close ties to the suspect.

The guy was holed up somewhere, he had to be.

In the meantime, Gary went to the hospital to expedite the transfer of Josh Morrison's clothes to the GFU, in the hope that examination and analysis of the bloodied garments might tell them something else about the person who'd so viciously attacked him, be it O'Donnell or otherwise.

There was one other thing niggling in her brain. Who had deleted the data on Josh Morrison's iPhone and why?

According to the timestamp, this had happened six minutes *after* the 999 call, so it had to been Annabel, as Reilly couldn't imagine a scenario whereby the attacker would have hung around long enough to do so, with the cavalry already on the way.

Which, for the moment at least, put Mrs Morrison right back in the spotlight.

She dropped by Rory's workstation on the way back to her office.

"The iPhone, I presume you took prints from it?"

"Of course. Before I hooked it up. Got both husband and wife."

She supposed that wasn't at all out of the ordinary, spouses often used each other's phones.

She bit her lip, thinking hard. "Any way to tell if it was reset locally, or remotely?"

He stared at her. "To get that information we'd really need to get a subpoena."

"Why don't we, then?"

"Reilly, we'd have to subpoena Apple. The courts would have to subpoena…Apple Computers."

"OK, I get it," she sighed. That should only take…oh about eight months or so.

Back in her office, she saw that she had two missed calls from O'Brien. She returned the call right away, realizing that she might as well just get the inevitable dressing down over with.

"That wasn't a report yesterday, Steel, that was a mockery! The man was stabbed in his own home. The best the GFU could come up with is that the wife didn't do it? That his twelve year old daughter, didn't do it?"

"I understand, sir. It's very frustrating."

"Frustrating? No, it's embarrassing, that's what it is. Do you know how many calls an hour I'm getting from Phoenix Park? Do you have any idea how many government offices, civil servants, media representatives and

God-knows who else has called this office over the last forty-eight hours?"

"A lot?" she attempted meekly.

"That's an understatement. And what do I tell them? Three days in, and you have nothing. Absolutely nothing..."

"With all due respect sir, we do have a suspect."

"Well let's all have a party...what? What do you mean you have a suspect? Where in this report is a suspect mentioned?"

"Something came to light today, sir. The detectives are working on it. Looks like it was indeed a robbery gone bad."

"I don't care if it was a Satanic ritual gone bad, book the man and let's close this out, do you understand me?"

"Yes sir, I want it closed too, every bit as much as you do. Believe me."

"Good because there's more. And take this however you want. But if there isn't any progress by tomorrow morning, Steel, I have to mix things up, do you understand? I need to move the investigation around to somebody that can get results. That'll be even more embarrassing than what's happening now, so don't make me do it. I don't want the GFU to look incompetent. It can't happen. So do your bloody job."

He hung up the phone.

Well that was fun....

Such a fuss, she thought. And all over an assault on some trumped up celebrity. She could understand the pressure the chief was under, with all the media pressure but this wasn't even a homicide.

Just as she suspected, Jack Gorman was next to pay her a visit. Obviously he was getting his ear bent from Phoenix Park too.

Closing the door behind him, his aged face looked worn and tired, and his eyes glazed with exhaustion. Reilly wondered what he'd been through that day. How many media interviews, how many interdepartmental calls, how much pressure from O'Brien.

The whole country had blown this case out of proportion and the GFU were at the epicenter of it.

He sat down and regarded her for a while.

"I know you, Steel," he said at last. "You usually don't show your hand until you know you have a royal flush. Maybe this time, you don't need to play it so close the chest. Be honest with me, what do we have on this?"

She sighed. "A cold suspect, Jack. We can place him at the scene, but we can't directly connect him with the crime. If - when - we find him though, the pieces should come together."

"You sure about that?"

"One hundred percent sure."

"Because if you bring this guy in and it doesn't come together. Where does that leave us?"

"Back at square one," she said, just above a whisper.

When Jack left, and the notion was still playing at the front of her mind, Reilly realized that deep down, she didn't truly believe this O'Donnell guy was the one.

Her gut was telling her otherwise.

From the very beginning she'd thought that something about this robbery thing didn't ring true.

So why, in the face of weak evidence, was she willing to pursue that angle now?

Was it pressure to close the case? Pressure from O'Gorman and the media? An attempt to prove to Chris that she wasn't being irrational?

Was her judgment cloudy? And what about her instinct?

30

DESPITE HER BEST INTENTIONS TO keep him at a distance, Reilly couldn't deny that Chris Delaney was a handsome son of a bitch.

Now, as they met up for a bite after work under the auspices of catching up on the search for O'Donnell, she tried her best not to be distracted by it, as she had so successfully ever since their first case together over two years prior.

The hard lines that had in the meantime appeared on his face from sleepless nights and tough cases day after day, only contributed to his brooding exterior. He'd seen stuff, been through stuff. He had regrets, empathy and wisdom. They'd all seen too much.

And mostly, they saw it together.

This whole thing was a mess. Reilly didn't want any of it. She didn't want her pregnancy to get in the way of her work, her friends. Her colleagues.

Yet here she was, having a catchup with Chris after work in the guise of catching up on the investigation.

She knew she needed to clear the air and get over the stupid personal stuff that had been affecting their interactions lately. They needed to be the well-oiled machine they always had been.

There he was at a corner table, eating French Fries… chips, she corrected herself, and drinking Guinness. iPhone out, thumbing through who knows what.

She slipped into the chair opposite him.

"Hey you," she said like a teenager who awkwardly needed to discuss a fight she'd had with her best friend.

"Hello yourself."

They both stared at each for a moment and then started speaking at the same time.

"I know I've been weird," she began.

"Look, I'm sorry if…" he said.

They stopped at the same time, both chuckling nervously.

Chris stepped up. "Just…just let me, okay?"

"Okay."

"You're a good friend Reilly. At this stage, probably my best friend. And I don't like being an arm's distance away like this. Lately, I don't know…it's been hard work. Is there a way we can reset all this somehow? Start over?"

She paused for a time, collecting her thoughts. This wasn't about friendship, she knew.

It was about something much more than that. He knew it. She knew it. They'd been on a road together when suddenly a massive construction zone had popped up out of nowhere, forcing their paths apart.

"Starting over means we have to scrap all the stuff we learned, doesn't it," she stated, refusing to meet his gaze.

Chris fiddled with a chip. "Maybe not start over but…try again?"

Still she didn't look at him. "Try what again?"

He went quiet. "Do you really want me to say it, Reilly?"

Something stirred inside her and she didn't think it was the baby.

"Chris, you and I have been very close for a long time, there's no doubt about that. And recently…I guess that was about to turn into something more…That was until…well you know as well as I do that things are a lot more complicated now."

"Of course I know that," he said. "I'm not an idiot. But like you said yourself, we've been through thick and thin together. It's just…I don't know, it feels like you're pushing me away altogether now. A bit like I'm only getting a drawing of you instead of the real you. Even though I told you before I'd be there for you, support you in any way you want…instead you just put this wall up, and I can't handle it. You're just so…cold."

"It's not just you, Chris," she admitted softly. "Maybe I just can't let anyone in right now."

"Lookit, I know I can be an asshole sometimes too…" He shook his head. "Oh I don't know, this whole bloody thing pisses me off."

"What pisses you off, Chris?" she said, hackles rising instinctively. "The fact that I had the audacity to sleep with someone else instead of you?"

His face changed. "This is what I'm talking about, Reilly. You never used to talk to me like that. I'm not your enemy here. We're in the same boat."

"Easy for you to say."

"Is it? Since when have we not been in the same boat? I thought we had an understanding. When we're on a case together we're a team. We have the same agenda."

"That hasn't changed."

"Come on. We've been butting heads ever since this Morrison thing kicked off. We can't see eye-to-eye on anything lately. You're not letting me in. We're not working on this together. And we're losing it, Reilly. We are losing it because of that. The case is slipping away and there's not a thing I can do about it. You won't talk to me."

"I don't have anything to say," she said quietly. "I know the case is slipping. But it has nothing to do with you and me. There just isn't enough evidence…"

"What about this lead then?"

"I hope it's him, I *think* it's him," she added trying to convince herself as much as Chris. "I'm just not sure we can directly connect him to the attack."

"There's more you're not saying," he said, looking down at his food.

"Chris…honestly it's not worth saying, not now anyway."

He sighed, clearly holding back. Taking a deep breath he leaned back in the chair and did his best to soften his demeanor.

"How's the baby?" he asked gently.

She shrugged, a little taken aback by the sudden change of subject. "Everything seems fine."

"Have you told Forrest yet?"

"Not yet. I still need to figure out if…"

"If what?" He stared at her. "If you're going to go back to Florida, is it?"

"Is that it? You think I'm giving up on the GFU?"

"I don't know. There's no doubt that things have changed since you got back from that trip in more ways than one. You've changed, Reilly. The passion and drive and sheer tenacity you used to have just isn't there any more. Anyone with half a brain can see that." Chris gripped the stout with both hands, absently looking into it.

What the hell…?

Frustration welled up. He really did view her as unstable, unpredictable.

Not dedicated to the work. Her very judgment was in question, yet it was her judgment that made her a good investigator.

It was the single quality that made her who she was.

Yet Chris seemed to be doubting that now, doubting everything about her. He couldn't even tell for sure if she would stay with the force. What sort of trust did that represent?

Or lack of it.

She couldn't look at him. Instead she found a place on the wall to look at. Wood paneling with a portrait of some random Irish chieftain from the 19th century, complete with top hat and mustache.

"I don't know what to say to that," she said at last. Emotion welled up against her will. She pushed it back, but it had to be obvious. If not tears, then anger. Or both. "I thought we understood each other better than this," she said finally.

"So did I. But what am I supposed to think? You leave, you come back—and you're this completely new person."

"I *am* the same person, Chris. I actually think that's what's bothering you. Even though I'm pregnant, I'm still the same person whereas you expected something different. That time, during the Ellis thing when my hormones were all over the place, you enjoyed my being this kind of…damsel needing rescuing, didn't you? And then when I figured out what was going on, you didn't expect me to just go off and do things on my own. Take control of my own responsibilities…"

"Control of your responsibilities? Reilly, you haven't even told the father."

That stung. The temperature at the table decreased several degrees.

"I'm sorry, look I didn't…I'm sorry."

"There's nothing else to discuss." She stood up and began to walk out, but then stopped. "I want you to know something," she said just above a whisper, as Chris quietly waited. "It might be easier if we were friends, but we don't have to be either. I have a job to do. So do you."

And she left him, halfway horrified at the words that had come out of her mouth. She didn't know in that moment if she meant it, or just wanted to cut him deeply like he'd cut her. She couldn't even say objectively who was right or who was wrong, or even why they were fighting like this.

But her hackles were up. Her claws were out.

Her only recourse now was to bury herself deeper. To get the job done.

Do the job right, catch the bad guy and find the missing piece of evidence no one else could see.

To be ahead of the game. Smarter. And whether or not Chris Delaney was supporting her, Reilly would soldier on.

31

AFTER THAT, SHE KNEW THAT if she went home, there was no chance she'd be going to sleep. There was hardly any point in trying.

So instead she kept driving and went straight back to the GFU.

The crew was all gone by this point, and only minimal power-saving lights were on.

She holed up in her office and started to blindly go through case files other than the Morrison investigation that needed her attention.

Then later, against her better judgment while having a coffee break, she started checking out news headlines on the internet. That was a mistake. Apparently this whole investigation was a fiasco, if the press were to be believed. Golden-boy Josh Morrison's attacker was still on the loose and no one knew anything.

She shut down the browser in disgust and started rifling though some paperwork the team had left on her desk earlier: a brief analysis from Gary of the victim's bloodied clothes…and from Rory, a print-out of Richard O'Donnell's all known associates and relatives.

She skimmed the list, and nearly fell out of her chair when she saw the address jump out at her like a slap in the face.

With barely a breath, she dialed Chris, completely forgetting their harsh words of earlier.

"Get a patrol car, you're going back to Killiney Hill."

"What? Why?"

"Ted O'Donnell lives right next door to the Morrisons. And he's Richard O'Donnell's brother."

Damned media, she thought, as half an hour later, she tried to discretely find a place to park away from the news coverage mayhem.

By now, even Sky News was involved, along with God knows who else. The never-ending news cycle.

Reilly had to believe that something more important in the world was going on, but apparently not.

A domestic attack on a has-been Irish athlete who happened to be married to a C-list celebrity TV presenter, was clearly of most importance to the national media, broadcast or otherwise, to set up permanent camp in an affluent Dublin suburb.

If humanity had some sort of "worthwhile" barometer, the weather would be looking pretty terrible right now, she thought tiredly.

Partly cloudy and raining assholes.

She quietly skirted the perimeter of the media gathering and looked down the street to the O'Donnell property.

Something told her that they wouldn't need to wait long to move forward on this investigation now.

The chances that the brother of a known larcenist was living next store to an attempted larceny were so nil, that O'Donnell *had* to be the guy.

They just needed to find him, bring him in for questioning and connect him to the scene, then they could go back to normal and the media could stop this ridiculous grandstanding about the value and worth of the force.

She scanned the area looking for the detectives. They would likely be coming in stealthily as well.

In any event, the prospect of finding the suspect on site was not very good. If Richard O'Donnell had in fact attempted to rob his brother's next door neighbor, ending up stabbing him the process, then he was surely in hiding somewhere.

The best they could hope for was a lead from the brother, who based upon the convertible BMW parked in the driveway, looked to be home.

Only snag was, they didn't have time for a warrant.

But if Ted O'Donnell was at all co-operative, much could be gained from the initial interview, Reilly knew.

That was why she wanted to be there. She hoped to get an inkling of something - however tenuous - to connect Richard O'Donnell to the evidence from the Morrison scene, and get that ever-valuable pink slip of paper.

Something the brother might be hiding, hesitant about, or simply unable to withhold. These sorts of interviews always gave something away.

A hunch leading to another before connecting the dots and with luck, all the way to the arrest of their prime suspect. And the more the suspect ran, the guiltier he looked, until finally forensics just needed to fill in the gaps and make the prosecuting case even stronger.

"Hey," said Chris from behind, startling her so much she jumped.

"Nice catch, Goldilocks. Any bets on whether or not the suspect will be there?" Kennedy said.

"Doubtful," said Reilly. "But his brother is by the look of it."

"OK, let us ask the questions, OK?" Kennedy warned, rather unnecessarily "the last thing we need is you barreling in head-first with your UV lamp."

"Ha."

The three approached the gated entrance to the O'Donnell house as quietly and discreetly as possible, but inevitably they were spotted.

It was a journalist from TV3 who noticed first, then the rest followed, moving en masse down the street from the neighboring house.

"Detective, what's happening?" the woman asked as they approached the intercom. Other journos snaked in around, and nearly mobbed them before Chris brushed them off.

"Um, lads…you know that's the wrong house don't ye?" another smart-ass scoffed.

Flashes were going off, cameras were circling around. Mayhem soon ensued.

"Just routine guys. Nothing worth firing up the breaking news banner for."

There were mumbles of uncertainty in the crowd, but generally this explanation was accepted and the crowd thinned. Reilly overheard someone mutter something about keystone cops.

The electronic gates opened even without Chris needing to announce their arrival via the intercom, and the front door was open by the time they walked up the driveway and reached the house.

Ted O'Donnell was middle-aged, probably approaching late-forties. He was gray around the temples and had a beer paunch, but looked healthy otherwise.

He was wearing a Leinster rugby jersey, and his tracksuit bottoms were obviously meant for lounging, not exercising.

"Can I help you detectives?" he asked, looking surprised. "I've already been questioned extensively about…"

"Need to know if you've seen your brother about recently?" Kennedy asked.

The man's eyes widened. "Richard? No - why would I?"

"I understand he's on release from Mountjoy."

"I wouldn't know. Needless to say my baby brother and I don't run in the same circles…"

"Any chance we could talk inside?" Kennedy asked. He threw a head back towards the gate. "Get away from that lot for a minute."

"Of course. I apologize."

The three stepped inside, Reilly grateful for once for the media presence that had facilitated their entry, and for Kennedy's quick thinking in making it happen.

The O'Donnell house was another mock-Georgian laid out much in the same way as the Morrison's, with some of the same finishes, and she guessed that many of these houses on this particular patch of Killiney Hill, were built at the same time, and by the same developer.

The same large entryway led through to an open plan kitchen diner, but their host didn't lead them any further than that.

"Are you married Mr O'Donnell?" Chris asked.

Ted shook his head. "Separated. I'm here by myself."

While the detectives continued to pepper O'Donnell with bland questions surrounding the incident on Friday night, Reilly tried to figure out a way to look around a little without appearing suspicious or invasive.

Suddenly she had a brainwave.

"I'm so sorry," she said to Ted O'Donnell, looking pained. "This is really embarrassing but...I'm pregnant and I wonder if..."

The man looked baffled for a moment (as did Chris and Kennedy) but then realization dawned.

"Of course," he said. "Guest bathroom is upstairs, first on the left."

Delighted that she had played such a master stroke, though a bit guilty that she had used the blob to do so, she hurried upstairs, aware that she only had a few minutes until O'Donnell became suspicious.

But she was barely at the top of the stairs when she realized she didn't need to look any further.

Ted O'Donnell was lying through his teeth. Richard O'Donnell had been here all right, she didn't need physical evidence to prove that.

Reilly exhaled.

The DPP probably wouldn't be happy, but...needs must.

32

"LOOK, MY BROTHER MIGHT BE a lot of things..." O'Donnell was saying to the detectives, "but I know he wouldn't stab a man like that. Richie is just a kid, involved with petty stuff mostly...TVs, stereos or jewelry; things that are easy to sell on."

"Can you think of anywhere your brother might be so that we can clear him?" asked Chris. "Right now, I'll be frank—it's not looking very good."

The man paled a little. "How so?"

That was Reilly's cue. "Are you a smoker, Mr. O'Donnell?"

"Used to be, but I gave up about ten years ago, why do you ask?"

"A cigarette butt with your brother's fingerprints on it was found on the Morrisons' property. That seems a bit odd, don't you think? If you haven't seen him for some time."

Ted O'Donnell's face suddenly closed.

"I'm afraid I can't talk to you any further without a solicitor."

"Are you sure that's necessary? If we could just take a quick look around…"

"Goodbye detectives," he said pointing toward the door.

Chris looked past Ted's shoulder at Reilly to see her expression, and read enough to know she that had something.

They left the house, Ted slamming the door behind them.

"Well," Chris urged as they headed back down the driveway, into a cacophony of cameras and media people.

"You didn't get it?" she asked, toying with them a little.

"Get what?"

"The heady smell of days' old Marlboro."

While Chris and Kennedy tried to persuade a judge that Reilly's nose had given them enough to at least charge Ted O'Donnell with obstruction, Reilly started playing things out in her head to see if she could make the brother fit into the suspected scenario.

Richard, fresh out of a short spell in Mountjoy, goes to his well-off big brother's half-empty McMansion to lay low for a while, instead of the crappy court-assigned address. In direct violation of his probation, but not enough to raise any eyebrows.

But the pull of the famed, (and loaded) Morrisons next door is irresistible, and after a while he starts to learn their comings and goings. Starts to figure out where certain things might be stashed, like Annabel's jewelry or shoe collection, easy pickings for a low-level thief.

Decides to make a play late one night, while nobody's home. Annabel is usually out late on Friday nights and the daughter stays with friends. Clearly doesn't expect Josh to be there.

But Josh is home, and O'Donnell is caught red-handed, flips out and takes off.

This would all likely have happened without Ted's knowledge, but surely the man would be suspicious about his brother's sudden and coincidental disappearance?

So realizing it was only a matter of time before the cops came calling, Ted decides to play dumb and deny all knowledge that his brother was ever there.

All well and good until Reilly and her famed nose steps inside.

All they needed now was something solid enough to connect Richard O'Donnell with the crime. Sure she had the partial from the cigarette, but that only told them that O'Donnell had smoked a cigarette that somehow ended up in the Morrisons' garden.

Based on the data stored on him in the PULSE system though, Richard O'Donnell only loosely fit the brief profile they'd built up of Josh's attacker; he was five foot nine, and described as 'wirily built'.

There was no mention of his shoe size, and nothing at all in the file about any calluses on his fingers. And as his larceny sentence was below the three years or more required to necessitate DNA sampling, they couldn't try match any existing trace to that.

But if they brought him in, *when* they brought him in, Reilly clarified to herself, she was sure the evidence of the bloody struggle with Josh Morrison on Friday night would be visible for all to see.

33

LATER THAT SAME NIGHT, CLOSE to midnight, they were once again all standing outside Ted O'Donnell's residence, the media once again circling the heights of Killiney Bay like bats in a cave, and the detectives clutching an obstruction of justice warrant conjured by the courts.

"What is it now?" Ted O'Donnell said, from the intercom.

"Open the gate please, Mr O'Donnell."

He didn't open the gate; instead he opened his front door.

At the entrance, some cameramen had perched themselves on the gate pillars, and as the flashes went off, Chris could see Ted standing in the doorway, shielding his eyes from the onslaught.

"What the hell…?" he shrieked, as the gate buzzed them in.

The audience of journalists went ballistic, shouting out a barrage of questions and throwing flashes of light from their cameras.

"We have reason to believe you lied to us earlier about your brother's whereabouts," Chris told him tersely when they reached the doorway. "As a result you are being charged with perverting the course of justice."

"I'm not saying a word until my solicitor gets here."

"You don't have to," said Kennedy as they escorted the man through the throngs of ravenous journalists and into a patrol car.

Finally being so close to reaching a suspect in the case that had been tearing everyone apart for the last few days, Reilly was more than happy to go along to Store Street and listen in on O'Donnell questioning.

Inside the observation room, she was surprised to see Chris, Kennedy and a tired and unkempt Helen Marsh there.

O'Donnell was alone, sitting on the other side of the two-way mirror, waiting.

"Won't let us start the interview without his solicitor," said Chris exasperated.

"I wouldn't either," said Helen.

"Well, it's two in the morning, so good luck getting anyone to come out at this hour," grouched Kennedy. "And of course, we're not just waiting for any old solicitor, oh no - we're waiting for a big-shot solicitor, the kind you get when you live on Killiney Hill."

"Maybe he and Steve Buscemi should get together and go bowling," Reilly quipped, though no one else in the room seemed to get the joke.

They fell quiet and waited for some time. After about half an hour or so she got up and decided to get everyone some coffee. Could be a long night.

When she returned she saw Chris and Ted O'Donnell in the interview room with a gray-haired older woman.

"Big-shot just arrived," whispered Kennedy. "This better end well."

"Has the DPP's office decided on a plea?" she asked Helen, knowing that they would likely need to cook up something to get O'Donnell to talk.

"Not yet, let's just hear Chris opening salvo."

But Chris didn't talk first.

The solicitor immediately started in. "You're holding my client as a proxy for your real suspect and it is a waste of time and further, a violation of his rights."

"What rights? He lied to us about his brother's whereabouts."

"Your evidence relating to Kevin O'Donnell is at *best*, circumstantial. There is nothing to prove that my client's brother was at the Morrison residence at the time of the attack. Unless your evidence can connect my client to Richard's presence in his home, then I think it is time to let him go."

"Look, we can make this a lot easier if he'd just be straight with us. Instead you are talking him out of options."

"Okay," said the solicitor. "Fire away."

Chris straightened himself and turned his attention to O'Donnell.

"How long was your brother, Richard staying at your house?"

He sighed heavily. "About two weeks,"

The solicitor jumped out of her skin and reeled on him, grabbing his arm, but she knew it was too late.

"I have nothing to hide," he shrugged.

"Seems you did when we asked you earlier," said Chris.

"I thought that maybe harboring him would get me in trouble," he explained.

"It did you get you trouble. Look where you are now."

"I know that, look—I don't know where Rich is. I'm sorry I lied, can we move on now?"

"I'm afraid not. Obstruction is a very serious charge."

The solicitor spoke up. "What are you offering?"

"Offering?" O'Donnell repeated, eyes widening. "I'm not...wait, am I going to prison?"

"That all depends on your level of cooperation," said Chris.

"The Department of Public Prosecutions would be inclined to overlook some of your...indiscretions," he said. "We'd only need to know where your brother is now, so we can take him in for questioning. You understand, we aren't even looking to arrest him at this point. Really, from your perspective, we're just ruling him out—if as you say he couldn't have possibly committed such a heinous crime."

"What's the offer?" the solicitor asked.

"With full cooperation? We'll drop the charges completely. The DPP isn't interested in punishing someone for a brief lapse of judgment."

Of course 'obstruction' was such a loose term, that Reilly knew it wouldn't get very far in court.

This whole thing had only ever been about leverage.

The solicitor would be a fool to refuse, but she'd seen enough of this stuff to know that legal people were not always the best judges on what was reasonable. For them it was sometimes like a game of poker. Whomever was the best liar would win those bouts.

Certainly the detectives did the same thing, they would often hold inconsequential or irrelevant evidence over the heads of the solicitor so that they would be intimidated into advising their clients to take a plea or particular deal.

In this case, there was no doubt Chris was playing it up, and it also became clear that the solicitor was taking the bait.

Though the wheels were still turning. The game could flip around with the upcoming conversation.

"All right," said O'Donnell. He lowered his eyes and wiped some sweat from his forehead. The solicitor whispered something to him and then took some notes on her pad.

"But listen, you aren't going to get anywhere with it. The only reason Richard took off in the first place is because he guessed you'd suspect him. He's not your man, I promise you."

"What makes you say that?" Chris asked.

"Because he's not some hardened criminal. He's made a few mistakes certainly, and got caught up with a bad crowd and involved in a stupid situation that didn't end well for him. That conviction…it was a one-off."

That was true, Reilly thought recalling the guy's offender record. But it was typical for family to suggest that their flesh and blood had got 'caught up in a bad crowd', as if that somehow diminished their responsibility for their actions.

The fact remained that they'd found evidence relating to Richard O'Donnell, a known thief's, presence on the Morrison property at some point during or before a reported robbery.

And whether or not the guy did it, they needed to find him so they could see if the other components of this crime fit.

"He's working now, getting himself sorted out. He only stayed with me because he got a part-time job in a nightclub in Dun Laoghaire, and could save time on the trip to work. He's changed."

"Of course, he has," said Chris. "Where is he?"

"At his girlfriend's house."

34

CHRIS'S CAR WAS QUIET EN route to the address Ted O'Donnell had specified.

They only had circumstantial evidence with which to bring Richard O'Donnell in for questioning, but it was enough.

Reilly was confident that once they found the guy and established his whereabouts at the time of the crime, that everything else should fall into place soon after.

A big giveaway would obviously be any tell-tale indications of a struggle on his person, whether or not his physical attributes coincided with any of their findings, and most pertinently, if any of his fingers had developed calluses in the two years he'd last been fingerprinted following the larceny arrest.

In the good old days, not two months ago, Reilly and Chris would have been bantering and quipping the whole way. Now it was all very awkward.

The car was stone silent. They couldn't even make eye contact.

After a while she said. "You don't have to act like this."

"Act like what?" he said. "I'm just thinking."

"Well, I can feel your thinking."

"Not the time, Reilly. I just want to focus, okay?"

"Okay," she said, sighing and so she turned her head to look out the window.

Accompanying them was Kennedy in another patrol car with a couple of uniforms she recognized. She had seen them working on the night shift generally and so she only came upon them once in a while. The night crew was always a bit sullen and a little too focused, but she supposed you would have to be to pull a shift like that.

They each parked a little way down from the address to avoid arousing suspicion. There was a chance this guy would try to run, so the cops wanted to mitigate that as much as possible.

Chris looked at the crew before proceeding, making sure each was alert and ready for anything. Then he rapped heavily on the door.

No answer.

Chris tried again. "Store Street Detective Unit, we have a few questions for Mr O'Donnell please."

There was something of a commotion inside, but no response.

"Open up please, or we will have no choice but to come inside."

Still no answer.

Chris nodded to a uniform, who promptly kicked in the door.

Reilly heard a young woman scream in the bedroom before she saw her. She wore only a t-shirt and was curled up on a bed, horrified at the invasion.

The small flat had very few places to hide, and sure enough they saw the scampering figure of Richard O'Donnell, wearing only boxer briefs, as he bolted toward the back window. He wasn't fast enough. The uniform easily caught him and wrenched him back.

"Get off me, pig! I didn't do nothin!"

"That'll be for the detectives to decide. Will you accompany us to the station for questioning please?"

But a single look at a near-naked Richard O'Donnell's thin body, pitifully scrawny arms, and small sized feet, was enough to convince Reilly that this couldn't be their man.

35

"A MAJOR DEVELOPMENT IN THE Morrison investigation broke last night, just days after a brutal knife attack put former Irish rugby captain Josh Morrison in intensive care.

Gardai arrested nearby neighbor and successful property developer, Ted O'Donnell on a charge of obstruction of justice, but in an unexpected turnaround, he was released in the early hours of this morning, accompanied by his legal team and some very strong words about the force.

'This is not just an innocent mistake, it is a complete miscarriage of justice. The Gardai recklessly interfered with my life, tarnished my reputation, and attempted to pin a crime on me because of their complete inability to do their jobs. The arrest was nothing more than a publicity stunt and a waste of taxpayer money. And rest assured, these so-called detectives are no closer to finding Josh Morrison's assailant than they were from day one. My solicitor and I are discussing our options at the moment, one of which will certainly include legal retribution.

"Mr. O'Donnell! Mr. O'Donnell! Do you have anything to say to the victim and his family?"

"The Morrisons and I have always had a great neighborly relationship. I've known Josh and Annabel for almost two decades. I'm deeply, deeply sorry for what's occurred in our midst, in our locality, in their home. I pray for Josh's speedy recovery. And I hope that the Gardai get their act together and attempt to catch the person who did this."

"Mr. O'Donnell, why were you released?"

"Because there was never any evidence. Our police are bumbling idiots, keystone cops, tripping over themselves to get any indictment they can. Make no mistake, this is not about justice, the authorities simply want to close this case and stop the media attention. And they want to do it at all costs. It's a complete failure of Irish law enforcement, not to mention a huge embarrassment."

"Mr. O'Donnell! Why was your brother Richard also brought in for questioning? Is he a suspect too? Is it because of his nefarious background?"

"My brother might have made mistakes, but rest assured he is every bit as responsible for these stabbings as I am. Which is to say, not at all."

"Ladies and gentlemen, that is all. My client has had a very long night, I'm sure you understand. Thank you for your interest."

36

REILLY STOOD IN HER KITCHEN in the early morning light, drinking her fourth coffee of the hour.

She'd skipped sleeping altogether, knowing her insomnia would prevent her anyway.

Since the release of the O'Donnell brothers, the force and courthouse had fallen into utter mayhem.

Phones rang off the hook, text messages flew around, accusations made, the top brass yelled, the whole place came unhinged.

Yet even O'Brien conceded there was probably little else they could have done differently.

That didn't change the court of public opinion, though. At some point, very soon, Inspector O'Brien would be forced to take the detectives off the case.

As it turned out Richard O'Donnell had an alibi - he was working at the nightclub on Friday night, but because he didn't know what time Josh Morrison was stabbed, he'd taken off in case anyone would point the finger.

The force was embarrassed and scorned, and the powers that be in the Phoenix Park would soon look to apply their own agenda and interrupt the system.

They had to turn this around.

Chris and Kennedy had both gone home for a couple hours' rest before starting afresh and taking another look at alternative avenues of investigation.

The GFU team was asleep, so now it was just Reilly, and a very large pot of coffee.

She was stumped, looking at the Morrison crime scene photos again. She'd envisaged the scene over and over. They'd been over every inch of that house. Worked on the evidence. Analyzed the injuries, the blood spill, the shoe impressions, prints…

There was something they were missing—there had to be.

And once again she returned to her instinct, her gut feeling that the attack wasn't a robbery gone wrong - it was a crime of passion.

That sort of crime - an unintentional one - always yielded mistakes, didn't it?

The doer isn't prepared for what he's going to do. So he's messy.

He leaves prints on surfaces before the incident, trace transfer on the victim, shoe impressions as he escapes, maybe injures himself in the process….

She'd already finished another mental walk-through, studied some more photos, rechecked the trace analysis.

Waited, thought. Drank more coffee.

Drank coffee…

Tea, she remembered. Josh was making tea when it happened.

When it happened.

Plugging into the GFU database via her laptop, she sought out the recording of the 999 call Annabel had placed at 1:39 am and listened carefully.

"Oh God, Oh God—he's been stabbed! Josh...I think he's dying, there's so much blood...please God somebody come here now. Hurry!"

The sound of the handset dropping as the dispatcher tried and failed to get further information from her.

Reilly stopped the recording. There towards the end, was something - another sound - in the background, behind Annabel's voice. Sort of like a child crying or keening.

What was it? Had Annabel lied about her twelve year old daughter being at friend's house? Had Lottie been there the whole time and - heaven forbid - witnessed the attack on her father?

Reilly checked the time. 7am. She and wondered if Rory was at the lab yet. If not, he would be soon.

"Rory, hi," she said, when he answered his mobile. "Glad you're up."

"I am now," he replied groggily.

"Are you at home?"

"Yeah, they still let me go back there sometimes."

"Do you happen to have any of your sound software there?"

"Well, obviously nothing as good as at work, but I've got some music apps I use. Basic stuff though, why?"

"Can you pull up the 999 call on the Morrison thing? Maybe try to tune out Annabel's voice? There's a sort of…high-pitched sound in the background I'm trying to focus on."

Rory grunted and said, "Okay, hold on a sec."

Reilly could hear his laptop powering up, and after a moment of keying, he fiddled around with files until she once again heard the 999 call play on his side.

"Okay, I'm importing it into a minimizer. This will isolate the various frequencies. Stand by."

Reilly paced the floor of her living room, waiting impatiently for him to do his thing.

A few more minutes passed until he came back on the line.

"Just listened back. Sending the file to you now. You have three guesses on what the mystery background sound is, but the last two don't count."

When the audio file popped into her inbox, she quickly clicked on it and turned up the sound.

It took less than a second. "Kettle whistling."

She breathed out, immediately relieved that it hadn't been a young girl crying.

"Yeah, but it only starts about two-thirds of the way through the call. Before that is just the sound of the water getting ready to boil."

"You're right."

They'd already suspected that Josh Morrison had been about to make himself a pot of tea right before he was attacked, which was why his back had been turned.

Now they knew he'd gone so far as to start up the gas hob.

So, Reilly realized now, the attack had happened throughout the time it took for the Morrison kettle to boil.

Later at the lab, having taken a brief detour to Brown Thomas department store on the way, Reilly set up the GFU's brand new Alessi kettle for its dummy run.

She knew that it usually only took a couple of minutes for a typical electric kettle with an in-built element to reach boiling point when full.

But for this, they needed to be more precise.

Checking the information they'd recorded from the corresponding model at the Morrison house, she filled the kettle to the exact same water level, then took it to a gas burner and switched it on.

It actually took longer than expected for the designer kettle to boil, likely down to the absence of an inbuilt electrical element.

Two whole minutes and 45 seconds before the little plastic bird on the spout started to whistle, announcing that it had reached boiling point.

As it was safe enough to deduce that Annabel Morrison hadn't come in, found her husband bleeding out on the floor, and decided to make a nice cuppa before phoning 999, it seemed they now had a very firm idea of the time the attack began.

About two minutes before the 999 call.

They would need that audio file analyzed further with equipment considerably more sophisticated than Rory's home kit, but still, it was now pretty obvious that the kettle had reached boiling point, while Annabel was making that call.

The call…

Immediately her thoughts segued to the phone, and she called across to Rory.

"What was the time on Josh's iPhone message wipe again?"

"1.45."

That was six minutes *after* the 999 call.

A number of new scenarios were presenting themselves now: Annabel had in fact committed the attack, called it in and deleted Josh's messages afterwards because of incriminating data—such as a marital fight, accusations of infidelity….whatever.

Or she was completely innocent of the attack, and had deleted the data on the phone after calling in the incident, because she realized there could be data on there that could incriminate her in *something*.

In either case, and just like Reilly had suspected from the outset, Annabel Morrison wasn't telling the whole truth.

37

WANDERING AROUND THE LAB, DEEP in thought, she mulled over everything in her mind before deciding to consult the detectives about the discrepancies regarding the timing.

After what had just happened with O'Donnell, she knew she couldn't go off all guns blazing, and especially not with Chris, since he'd already accused her of having some kind of beef with Annabel Morrison from the get-go.

"Do we still have those accounts from the first responders?" she asked Lucy.

"Should be in the file. What are you thinking Reilly?"

"I'm not sure. The wife, she was just in from a night out, wasn't she? So it's likely she was wearing high heeled shoes…"

"Yep, very nice ones too. Prada."

Reilly very quickly realized that she didn't need the police report for information on what the wife was wearing, not when they had an Annabel Morrison fan-girl right here in the lab.

"But those bigger tread impressions around the island clearly aren't women's Prada heels…"

"No," Lucy confirmed. "Understandably enough, there were lots of Annabel's footprints immediately around the dining room table, where she found him…"

Reilly thought hard again. They'd already established that it was highly unlikely the wife could be the attacker.

"What are you thinking?" Gary asked.

"I'm wondering if maybe the attacker wasn't alone," she said vaguely.

"Two robbers? How'd you arrive at that?"

"Not two robbers. An attacker *and* Annabel."

He gave a low whistle.

"Better be pretty sure about that one, boss. If you get it wrong, the media will have your guts for garters. No one pisses off Queen Annabel."

She bit her lip, thinking hard. "I know."

She looked again at the kettle on the gas hob, trying to play various scenarios out in her head.

But maybe it shouldn't be in her head at all, maybe they needed to play this possibility out - for real.

"Get a dummy, and that glass coffee table from reception," she told Gary.

"What?"

Lucy smiled, understanding immediately. "Play time."

Julius went to fetch the GFU's hapless dummy, and by the time Gary was back with a glass table, the kettle had been refilled and set up afresh on the hob.

Cross-checking with the crime scene photos and iSPI's 3D visualization, he went about setting up the table in a corresponding position the correct distance away from the hob.

"Lucy, you record this and time it. Gary, stand in front of the hob and go through the motions of making tea. I'm the perp."

He sighed. "Of course you are."

They took their positions. Lucy set up the shot, filming from a tripod and Gary mimicked filling the kettle with water and setting it on the hob.

Just as he switched on the flame, Reilly came up behind him, and using a ruler as a 'knife', feigned a slash corresponding to Josh Morrison's shoulder injury. Gary dropped (dramatically) to his knees at first, and as Reilly stood over him and tried to control him while down, he then stood up and tried to shield himself, grabbing onto the ruler with his fingers.

The two struggled for a bit, around the countertop, until Reilly went in for the kill and made a final thrust at Gary's stomach. He stumbled backwards a little before Julius rushed in with the stuntman dummy, and let it crash back against the table.

Lucy stopped the timer.

"Minute and a half." The kettle was still only halfway to boiling point.

More than enough time for the wife to come home, spook the attacker and make the call. Assuming everything had played out much the same as they'd envisaged it.

"Okay. Take two."

This time they constructed an alternate possibility in which Josh managed to fight back for longer, and even get a hold on his attacker.

They went through the incident five times altogether, each attempt using different scenarios and reactions that could be expected from a man being surprised and injured in such a way, yet in accordance with the existing crime scene reconstruction.

Each and every attack situation - even one that was implausibly slowed down, took less than the time it took for the kettle to whistle.

"Looks like the perp could easily have come and gone, not only before the kettle boiled, but even before the wife arrived back and made the call," Gary said. "Nothing to say that Annabel Morrison was there when the attack happened. Her story checks out."

Except for the part that she left the pub at one am, Reilly thought, when the barman insisted it was just after twelve. So where had she been in the meantime?

And did that single inconsistency in her story necessarily have anything to do with the attack on her husband?

But then why the deleted phone messages...

If they were in agreement that the attacker had taken off when Annabel arrived, and there was nobody else in the house at the time, then it stood to reason that she was the one who had deleted the messages in the ten minutes or so it took for the paramedics to arrive.

Ten minutes would surely feel like a lifetime when your injured husband is bleeding out on the floor. While she had made an attempt to stem the blood, surely Josh's phone would have been the last thing on Annabel's mind?

What was so important about the information on the phone that, in the midst of so much trauma, she'd go to the trouble of seeking it out?

Unless whatever was on the phone was directly related to the attack and as Reilly suspected there was no robbery at all, and the person who'd attack Josh was someone they both knew.

What (or perhaps who?) was Annabel trying to hide?

While she was more convinced than ever that there was more to this than meets the eye, Reilly couldn't officially cast suspicion on the woman until she had something more solid.

Not after the O'Donnell fiasco.

And certainly not while the entire country - including the Irish police force - were so firmly positioned up Annabel Morrison's butt.

38

"THANK YOU SO, SO MUCH for coming on the show today, Annabel. Really, with all you're going through - we so appreciate it."

"I feel like I needed to, Tara. There's been such a huge response from the public…such a huge outpouring of love for Josh and our family. So I wanted to come here - my home away from home - to say thank you from the bottom of my heart, and I suppose, to just let everyone know that we're doing okay."

"None of us can imagine for a second what you must be going through, sweetheart. It's really brave of you coming on this morning."

"I suppose I don't think of it as brave, but thank you."

"So…how is Josh?"

"Oh it's not…it's not great to be honest. He's stable but…they've induced a coma until his liver is functioning."

"As soon as he wakes up, I'm sure he can help the detectives."

"That's what we're praying for. The doctors say the prognosis is looking pretty good, thank God. Although you wouldn't know to look at him…all those tubes and machines…"

"I know this must be so hard, honey, but do you mind talking with us about some of the details of that night? I'm sure you've gone over it a million times with the detectives…"

"No, it's fine. I mean I do mind…it's just so hard to relive the horror, but talking it through helps a bit too."

"You were the one who found him."

"I…yes, I found Josh…just lying there in our kitchen. It was horrifying. I mean, here you are going through your life, and then all of the sudden everything you know falls into a tailspin. It still seems like such a nightmare, and I keep…I keep wondering if I'm ever going to…wake…up."

"It's okay sweetheart. It's okay. Take your time."

"Sorry, I just…"

"It's okay. Why don't we take a break."

39

REILLY GUESSED THAT IF SHE wanted to get to the bottom of the wife's story, she would have to rely upon old fashioned detective work.

Yet conversely at this point, she wasn't going to inform the detectives of her latest strand in her thinking.

Not for the moment.

No, she was thinking detective work in the literal sense.

So she decided to begin where her investigative peers of years gone by would have.

The archives.

But just as she was about to get started, the GFU receptionist buzzed her.

"Dr Corcoran here to see you."

Damn, the shrink. She'd forgotten all about that.

And it seemed if Mohammad wasn't going to come to the mountain....

A few minutes later, the mountain, who was actually an affable middle-aged psychologist, appeared in her office doorway.

"I know how busy you are, and guessed coming here might take up less of your time…"

"Is this really necessary? Here, now of all times? Like I said, I'm in the middle of a major investigation…"

"Just a quick chat, I promise. Enough to tick the necessary boxes at HR."

She rolled her eyes. He wasn't really giving her a choice, was he?

"Pull up a chair then."

"How is the case coming along?" Corcoran asked.

"Not particularly well. It's been frustrating, stressful and largely fruitless."

"Lots of eyes on this one," he said nodding.

"*All* eyes seem to be on it. And every last one of them have an opinion on it, too."

"Are you sleeping much?"

"Much?" She almost laughed.

"You're getting a few hours at least?"

She shook her head.

"Ms Steel, how can you possibly expect to take on this kind of responsibility - at nine weeks pregnant - if you are not properly rested?"

Reilly shrugged. "Goes with the territory."

"I can prescribe a very gentle sedative if you like …."

"A sedative? I can take something like that?"

"It's quite gentle, no risk for you or the child."

She shrugged again.

"Are you irritable? Impatient?"

"You have drug for that too?"

"Well, of course. But it is far too early in this process to suggest medicinal therapy. In fact, I think what you are going through is quite natural and very healthy."

"Healthy?"

"Your recent encounter with Mr Ellis was a very traumatic experience, Ms Steel. Your mind needs to play out all of the new barriers that have been put up. Defensive barriers, you understand, that were placed to protect yourself psychologically. When others overstep these barriers, you strike out and they, presumably, strike back. I say this is healthy, because you likely have identified a comfort zone within which you are willing to operate. Now you are in the process of training others on where that comfort zone is. The more they intrude, the more hostility you display."

Reilly had automatically started to zone out, but a little of what he was saying made sense, especially in relation to how she'd been dealing with Chris.

"Wouldn't you normally advise against hostility?"

"I'm sure that you have little choice. For you, this is merely a defense mechanism. A way to protect your new worldview, and more importantly, protect your unborn child. Since the pregnancy, you are adjusting to a new world of possibilities. Such a new realization can dismantle some people psychologically, and they must rebuild their worldview."

"Obviously, in this line of work, I kinda get that danger is a possibility."

"Certainly. But what the mind knows and the heart understands are two very different things. Unless you have truly experienced something, the mind does not take it as part of your world."

She sighed inwardly. "Okay. Got it. Anything else? I really do need to get back to -."

"One more thing, I'd like to talk a little more about sleep."

"I'm not sleeping."

"Precisely. What is the origin of the insomnia?"

"What do you mean?"

"For some people it is simple anxiety. There is just too much to think about, too much to do, and too much to worry about. So the mind fixates on these things in a permanent repeating cycle until exhaustion takes over. Then, there are those who are anxious about sleeping. They have night terrors that keep them up, and are afraid to close their eyes. How would you describe yours?"

"I don't know, simple anxiety I guess. I just can't sleep."

"You aren't having nightmares? Residual fears from the incident at the restaurant?"

"Hey no offense, but I really don't think that incident impacted me as much as everyone thinks it did. I'm not some special snowflake doctor, I'm a trained law enforcement officer who just happens to be pregnant. So no, I'm not getting night terrors."

"It's nothing to be embarrassed about."

"I'm not saying it is; I'm just telling you that's not happening with me. I have too much on my plate. This is a major case with a lot of pressure. I'm somehow keeping an embryo alive every day aren't I?"

"Embryo? That's an uncommon way to refer to your unborn child."

"I was making a joke," she growled.

"Further symptomatic of your irregular detachment. The more detached and isolated you are, the less support you get and the more you lash out."

"Well, then, my life should continue to stay interesting. I have no intention of making friends. I have a case to solve."

Dr. Corcoran smiled, and stood up. "I think that should do it for now. I'd like to see you again next week."

"Next week? You mean this is going to be a regular thing?"

"It would be good to meet again and truly explore if you've internalized any latent trauma issues. Issues that could perhaps grow into problems."

Taking a moment to glare some more, she finally assented. "Fine."

"Take care of yourself, Ms Steel."

She didn't want to hear it, so didn't respond. This whole thing annoyed her. His assertion that the incident with Tony Ellis had in some way damaged her permanently just because she was pregnant was annoying enough, but then to talk about the way other people's behavior was somehow reflective of her own…

Reilly wasn't repelling people to become more isolated, she was just going to do things her way if no one else seemed to be stepping up.

Grumbling under her breath, she stopped off for a coffee before heading downstairs to the GFU archives.

At least she could be alone and quiet there.

She could bury herself in data and research and focus on the case, the only thing she truly wanted to do.

She needed to resolve this thing, and she needed to do it to prove to herself that the pregnancy didn't mean she'd lost her edge, and that she wasn't the loose cannon everyone seemed to think she was.

She was fine.

40

I'VE KNOWN JOSH MORRISON FOR twenty years. During that time there was more than one moment in which I thought he was immortal.

He'd managed to break through so much adversity and create a harmonious support unit, dripping with success and stability long before most of us even left college.

That's why moments like these can be so hard for the public, and garner so much attention from the press. Here is someone that did everything right. He took superstar fame and turned it into a practical and healthy enterprise.

Of course as athletes we are trained to be the best, to push every limit and to train tirelessly to do so. It is so ingrained that we may find ourselves feeling invincible. Especially those that make it to the top of the sports world.

For people like Josh Morrison, the sky isn't even a limit.

I played with Josh for Ireland and in the Lions team, too. There was no achievement outside of his reach. No opponent that could cause him to buckle.

AFTERMATH

He has such a tremendous life force that allows him to break through any obstacle and rise above any challenge.

It pains me deeply to see him in this state. When I saw him in the intensive care unit, with tubes coming out of him, eyes closed and chest breathing in a rhythmic pattern, I didn't recognize him.

This was not our fearless Lion who rose above all adversity—who excelled in the face of failure and triumphed on the field.

This was not our captain, the man who toed the line for our team, who took us from being champions to legends.

Yet there he lay. As fragile as we all are. The myth now deflated and returned to the reality of man. His imperfections, his losses, his scars. All there for the world to see.

Does he still dream of excellence? When trapped in his mind, does he think of the sport? Does he see the victories? Or does he see a vicious, thankless world prompted by horror, pain and suffering?

Josh Morrison reminds us that we are all human. That a single moment in time can unseat your entire life. Redefine your legacy. Change your world to such a degree that you find out what truly matters in life.

And taking a breath, inhaling, exhaling. Hearing the sounds around us, the voices of those who love us, the sky, the scents and colors of our world. All of these things matter so much more than achieving.

No matter the mythologies we create, none of us can measure up.

Our task is to collect those things that are truly important in life, that define us as human beings, and embrace them. We should do this whether or not there is adversity.

We should do this all the time, every day and without fail.

Because when we are the ones on the hospital bed, then it is too late to pay attention to the things that really mattered.

Irish rugby loves you Josh Morrison. We are all praying for your recovery. Come back to us.

Be the man who propped us up so many times in the past.

Remember your strength and remember your tenacity. Your will alone can get you through this.

41

ONLY BRAVE SOULS THAT HAD memory of how things worked before 2000 would brave down the concrete steps into the sheltered and locked concrete-floored basement room that held the microfiche.

A gray hair sprouted on Reilly's head when she recalled that these machines used to be a permanent companion at Quantico, but here in the GFU she only thought of using one when needing to unearth something truly ancient.

They were so infrequently used, in fact, that many of them had fallen into disrepair and were not kept clean. Some of the microfilm had been destroyed by the elements because detectives neglected to return them.

And others were not carefully re-filed.

Someone in the admin staff would do a round of the place every few months to make sure things weren't a complete mess, but it wasn't like anyone supervised that activity and they could easily be phoning it in.

It would appear, upon arrival, that they were. Film was left askew here and there, boxes open, and some joker had left an unfinished latte in the corner that had started its own miniature ecosystem.

Holding her breath she trashed it—but in the hall where it was more likely to be disposed of by the cleaners.

The GFU had tried to get a grant a number of years ago to transfer the film into digital archives.

But something political happened and the grant was denied. They then dispatched a couple of Garda trainees to handle the task, but that didn't pan out either, because trainees were inevitably redirected to more important mundane tasks.

So there it was, nineties-era technology and Reilly was now forced to use it.

First, she had to go to the index. With some quick calculations she figured she needed to be looking sometime around the late eighties to mid nineties - before the age of the internet.

Rifling through the massive tomes of meticulously indexed references she zeroed in on *The Independent* and the *The Times*.

The dust made her sneeze, and the index volumes towered over her working table like mountains.

It took about an hour of working through the index, but she found six possible newspaper clippings that referred to Josh Morrison.

Working through the filing cabinet, she laboriously thumbed through the alphabet and pulled out the microfiche then fired up a machine.

Its bulb was burned out, so she turned on another one. Placing the film in, Reilly hunkered down for a night of scanning articles and making print copies.

Researching data like this always appealed to her though. She was an introvert at her core and was always most comfortable, isolated, doing her own thing in a hermit cave somewhere.

Since the internet, the magic of research work had somewhat dissipated. There was an art to archiving. People would spend entire careers perfecting the art and for every archivist, the technique was different.

Now algorithms measured complex queries against the relevance of digitally listed content. It was all mathematics. Much of the technique was lost.

But going back in time, as she was now, Reilly was able to feel the art again.

The particular queries chosen, the cross references. The rabbit hole of references. Books piled higher and higher the more she researched, before she was buried behind a wall of tomes, each uniquely pointing to something that was pointing to something else that was pointing to the thing she needed.

As the night wore on, a sketchy picture started to assemble and she was relegated to some more tabloid style publications, which weren't exactly known for their reliability.

But hey…

Josh Morrison's rise to stardom happened fairly early on. He excelled in Blackrock College, a Dublin institution famed for its rugby - a sport which Reilly knew absolutely nothing about, other than what she caught on TV now and again.

She guessed it was the closest thing to American football in these parts, only they had no pads and much more contact. Definitely the more hardcore.

Being an outsider, she didn't have that innate understanding of domestic team sports. Certainly in the States, she felt the winds of the soccer World Cup when it was happening, and in her younger days even participated in some of the revelry that went along with it.

But that was nothing like in this part of the world. Sport here, particular Gaelic games was like a religion. Entire weekends would be on hold because a team from one part of the country was matched with another from somewhere else.

And the violence on the pitch was like nothing she'd ever seen. Head wounds dripping blood from hastily applied bandages, while the players soldiered on as if it was just a tiny nick, and concussion was just a state of mind, while an American player would have been long airlifted to the nearest hospital.

So it was no small estimate to say that Josh Morrison earned his stripes.

According to the papers, the guy had been nothing short of a superstar, and by university had become a rugby legend.

Following third level education, he began playing for the Leinster team, had been a Lion (whatever that meant) and went on to captain the Irish International team to a rugby world cup in 1995.

Pretty amazing story, when all pieced together.

A celebrity athlete here was hard to compare to the ones in the U.S. Sure, Americans showered money and praise on their athletes, but few ever reached the level of demigod that Morrison had achieved.

As powerful as fame was for athletes in the States, they were just flashes of light. Though with a few exceptions, typically the fame rarely last pasted the athlete's prime, no matter the length of the glory at their peak.

But with Josh Morrison, the halo had been maintained - had grown even.

He managed to stay in the positive atmosphere of Irish public consciousness for decades, and as a result, remained very successful and very well regarded in all circles.

His influence stretched from sports straight into business and from there, philanthropy.

The interesting part, Reilly realized now, is that even as far back as secondary school - the Irish equivalent of high school - Annabel had been part of that narrative. She'd known they were childhood sweethearts, but hadn't really thought all that much about what that pat phrase truly meant.

Annabel's own rise to fame also seemed to run in parallel with her husband's. When Josh took the lead in charity work, so did she.

When he excelled in business, so did she. Before long, Annabel's bright star matched, but then likely outshone his as she conquered the airwaves, and became a household name in fashion and celebrity.

Like those superstar quarterbacks in the US who retired and opened up used car lots, Josh had in this case, opened up a coffee chain.

She knew she would be able to locate that story without the hassle of microfiche and the miracle of the internet.

The most interesting titbit of information Reilly found that she didn't already know, related to an incident Josh had been involved in 1992.

He'd been playing for Leinster Rugby Club and had just been named captain, when he'd been involved in a drink-driving car accident with one of his team mates.

Josh had been a passenger in the car, but the driver, a guy called Ian Cross was killed at the scene.

The article stood out because it was an interesting vignette, but also because of the accompanying photograph.

The car was completely smashed into a wall. It looked like a horrific accident and by Reilly's estimate, was a complete miracle anyone had survived. And even from the photo—the resultant injuries surely couldn't have been good news for Josh's sporting career.

But yet, almost as by sheer force of will (who was this guy - Thor?) he'd managed to pull himself out of the car by the time help arrived, and following months of rehabilitation, returned to the rugby pitch, and eventually went on to lead the national team to a world championship title.

Whoah. She'd heard the word 'colossus' bandied about more than once in the same sentence as Josh's name but this…this was pretty incredible.

The timing of the tragedy was something that had again fueled the Morrison bittersweet media-darlings narrative, as at the time, Annabel had just given birth to their first-born, Dylan.

Sighing, Reilly turned off the microfiche.

It was late and she was tired and she didn't think she had the stomach to read any more fawning articles about the Morrisons and how after the incident, Josh had turned determinedly teetotal and was outspoken about the dangers of drink-driving in Irish life…what?

Josh was teetotal. At the hospital, the doctors had confirmed that his blood alcohol levels were nil at the time of the attack…so who was drinking from the JD bottle that smashed along with the table?

Josh didn't drink. Annabel was out with friends. And Reilly thought it was pretty safe to assume that most families didn't just randomly keep bottles of bourbon on the dining room table…

Either Annabel lied about the timing of her return, had been drinking the bourbon and was there at the time of the attack. Or someone else was there - a third party, and not some random burglar.

Someone Josh knew well enough to have a drink with - even if his own choice of beverage was a harmless cup of tea….

This had to be it, Reilly thought excitedly.

But then, where was the corresponding drinking glass? Had it too been smashed following Josh's fall?

She'd take another look at the glass samples first thing. The team had managed to isolate remnants of the Jack Daniels bottle from amongst the broken glass of the table, and now those samples would need closer analysis. If they could somehow even manage to pick up a partial…

Now Reilly was buzzing. Her theory about Annabel covering up something, was slowly but surely gaining ground.

For her, the burglar thing had never truly stood up.

But that little snippet about Josh's abstinence had thrown significance over the JD bottle, and this, taken with the deleted iPhone messages, all seemed to point towards something else. And she needed to figure out what.

She'd had it up to here of reading about how Josh and Annabel Morrison had been together forever, had been through thick and thin, and still come out smiling.

Despite their devoted happy-ever-after public persona, something wasn't quite right with that couple, she was sure of it.

It was all *too* perfect.

The archives had given her a history, allowed her to get a better sense of the Morrisons, and a true sense of the hold they seemed to have over the Irish public.

But it was only giving her one side of the story - the glossy aspirational side, and in order to truly explore what exactly Annabel had been covering up on Friday night, Reilly needed more.

In short, she needed dirt.

42

THE FOLLOWING MORNING, SHE PHONED Kennedy and asked him to meet for breakfast at a nearby greasy spoon she knew he loved.

She waited for a good twenty minutes before he arrived, going through two cups of coffee, but at least it gave her the time to figure out how best to play this.

Finally he appeared, typically disheveled, and collapsed in the seat opposite her.

"Sorry I'm late, traffic was mental. Have you ordered yet?"

Then without waiting for an answer, he hopped over to the counter and ordered a large fry-up with extra sausages.

Sitting back down, he licked his lips. "Hope it doesn't take too long; I'm starving. Josie made me eat that granola shit this morning, looks like something you should be feeding to chickens if you ask me. So, where's Chris?" he added, as if noticing for the first time that it was just the two of them.

"This is kind of…delicate."

He stared at her. "Oh no, don't even think about getting me involved in this stuff, Goldilocks. I've been out of that game for years - not that I was much good at it in the first place, ask Josie."

She couldn't help but smile. "It's nothing like that. Well, maybe it is…but the point is, I'm sure you've noticed things are a bit…weird between us."

"Yeah, I didn't want to say anything, but yeah."

"It's hard to explain without going into too much detail, but let's just say this pregnancy thing hasn't helped."

Kennedy looked mortified. It was fine to tease her about the idea of it, but actually *discussing* it…

"You do know it has nothing to do with Chris, don't you?" she asked, suddenly concerned that he'd gotten the completely wrong end of the stick.

"Yeah. Don't want you to think we were talking behind your back or anything, but…he told me about… some fella in America."

If his face flushed any darker it would soon be the same color as the fried tomatoes on the plate - that with fortuitous timing - the waitress had just laid on the table in front of him.

Reilly nodded. "So again, I just think that it's best that Chris and I keep our distance for the moment, let things calm down a little. I know he's been getting the brunt of it from the chief after the O'Donnell thing, and I don't want to make things worse."

"Reilly, this is something you really should talk to him about, yeah?" He looked as if he was about to bolt out of his seat, but didn't want to abandon the fry-up.

"I know and believe me, I'm not asking you to intervene in anything personal. Just…can you hear me out for a minute - let me tell you what's going on? It's to do with the Morrison case."

He exhaled a little, obviously relieved to be back on more familiar ground, and she had to smile. "Yeah, of course, what is it?"

She took a breath. "I'm currently exploring an alternate scenario about Friday night, one that concerns Annabel Morrison."

"Ah Jaysus, not this again."

"Just listen, please."

"Right, I'm listening."

She went on to explain about the whistling kettle in the background of the 999 call, and the mystery bourbon drinker, as well as the iPhone messages.

"Josh's phone was wiped six minutes after the call."

"OK," he said. "And why would you not want Chris to know this?"

"It's not that I don't want him to know. It's just, I think I need something a little more concrete before he'll listen. Especially given what's just happened."

He nodded, and she was relieved he could see her point.

"It could be she only erased the phone because there was something private and perhaps incriminating on it. Maybe Josh found out about an affair, or something along those lines?"

"Or it could be that the phone might give us an indication of someone who'd actually attacked him," said Kennedy, mulling it over.

"Right. So...I think we need to turn the focus of the investigation away from the burglary angle and more towards the Morrisons personally - friends, business associates, that kind of thing."

"We already interviewed many of those, and nothing stood out as suspicious," he said, reaching down to fish out a folder from a satchel alongside him. "I still have the reports here."

When Reilly gave him a questioning look, he shrugged. "Josie types 'em up for me afterwards. I'd be there till Christmas otherwise."

Reilly pulled an empty table over alongside theirs, and spread the reports out on the table, out of the reach of Kennedy's greasy cutlery and toast crumbs.

She picked up the transcription of Dylan Morrison's Skype call, which she'd already seen on video.

The interview had indeed seemed bland and nondescript, but taken with the new information, she wondered if there was anything that might have been missed.

How long have you been in California?
Almost a year.
You see much of your family in that time?
Not really, no. I mean, for holidays and all that.
Are you at all familiar with your parent's professional life?
They kept work at work. I mean, I've met a couple of dad's business partners once or twice. And mom's friends at the studio would come over for barbecues and all that. But I mean, no, they

never really talked to me about business. Why - do you think someone from work stabbed him?

We're just trying to get a sense of where there might have been recent tensions. Maybe a situation where someone would have been mad at your father.

No one was mad. My mom and dad are a really great people. I mean yeah, they fight, but who doesn't? They've been together their whole lives.

OK, but I mean outside the family. Anyone have any grudges against your father that you are aware?

Not that I can tell. I mean he's super successful. His employees love him. Investors get lots of money. They all seem okay.

"That's a little strange, isn't it?"

"What?" Kennedy scooted over to see what she was reading.

"He goes on a bit of a diversion here."

"Where?"

She pointed at the transcript. "Chris says that you're looking for points of tension. Areas where someone might have been upset with Josh. And Dylan immediately talks about Josh and Annabel. He even closes out with the assertion that 'everyone fights.' But Chris wasn't even talking about that."

"So you think it was a slip?"

"I'm not saying that Dylan thinks Annabel might have stabbed his father, but he may well be hiding something—something that could incriminate his parents somehow. That's the same suspicion I'm getting. We're missing out on something here. There's something the Morrisons aren't telling us."

She continued skimming through the file. "Did you interview the daughter?"

"God no," he barked. "She's just a kid."

"I think we should talked to her, find out more about day to day home life."

"Aw, come on Reilly, we can't do that. She's twelve, it's too invasive - and Annabel would go nuts."

"We could get a shrink to do it. Make it less scary for her."

"And what? Have that Flanagan guy there too? Or worse, Annabel?"

"I suppose. If we have to."

"Reilly, then this line of investigation won't stay under the radar. If you're sniffing around the wife for this then everyone - including the media - will very quickly cotton on to that. Never mind Chris - O'Brien would lose his life. I really don't think that's a good idea."

He had a point. "Well who else could tell us if they'd been having problems? Annabel's colleagues, maybe?"

"That'd get back to Annabel too."

"There has to be a close friend—someone who goes way back with both. With them married so long, there has to be."

"Gordon Ryan? Teammate of Josh's when he was playing for Leinster. We interviewed him."

Reilly flipped forward to that interview.

Thanks for taking the time to talk to us, Gordon.

Happy to help, of course.

So how long have you known Josh?

I'd say, well…let's see probably about twenty-five years now.

How did you meet?

We were in Blackrock together. Good mates back then, especially considering he stole my spotlight. All about the game, all about the team. Well, the team AND Josh Morrison.

So you were good friends?

Pretty close, yeah. I was at his and Annabel's wedding. Me, Ian and…oh bloody hell, what was his name…Gerry Duffy I think it was, yeah. And Josh was at my wedding too. Annabel too.

Have you kept in contact with him over the years?

Yeah, barbecues and what-not. We went to each others kids' birthday parties and all that. Saw Dylan graduate too, but my girls are still a few years' off that yet.

Did you notice anything causing stress to the family recently? Any quarrels or problems?

Annabel and Josh never fought. Not like the rest of us. No, they were right as rain.

What about outside the family?

Not that I know of. Truth be told, Josh keeps to himself on business matters. Really we only talk about rugby. These days, we meet up for matches mostly.

Were there any other people in his life, apart from work or home, that would be angry at him? Some third party with a grudge, maybe?

Nah, nothing like that. Josh's got no enemies. Everybody loves Josh Morrison. Everybody's always loved Josh Morrison.

Okay, well I think that's about it Gordon, thanks for coming in.

That's it, then? I hope Annabel's OK, anyone taking care of her?

She's distraught understandably, which is why want to get to the bottom of this and find her husband's attacker as quickly as possible.

Course. She loves him more than anything. Bet my life on it. All right, thanks. See you later, mate.

"Didn't see any red flags there," said Kennedy.

"I don't either," Reilly admitted. "All a little too clean. Do people usually gush this much about their friends' relationships? Seems like everyone - along with the media - keeps on insisting they are this perfect couple. I mean, come on…all couples fight."

"True, that."

She bit her lip. "Were all the people amongst the Morrisons' inner circle the same? All insistent about this perfect marriage?"

Kennedy thought about it. "Yeah, now that I think about it. Tara Murphy especially."

"Right, Annabel's co-presenter. Is she as annoying in real life?"

Kennedy smirked. "I wouldn't know," he muttered, which Reilly took for a "yes."

She thumbed through the file and found Murphy's transcript.

Ms Murphy, thanks for coming in.

Anything I can do to help. The poor soul. What monster would do this to Josh? You are hot on his trail, aren't you?

We are putting all available resources into this case, I assure you.

That's good. That's good. It's just such a tragedy. I can't even get Annabel to answer the phone. Not that I'd expect her to, but I just want to see how she's doing. You're taking good care of her, aren't you? She's okay?

Understandably upset of course, but being very brave.

Of course. Yes, she would be. Always so brave.

Have you been around Mr. and Mrs. Morrison over the past few months? Socially?

We've had dinner once or twice.

Can you attest to their overall temperament?

Happy as Larry. They always are. How they can keep themselves together after so many years in such a healthy way, it's really a kind of…magic. I can't fathom having so much patience and dedication. Of course, that's probably why I'm divorced.

Did you hear from them about any sort of recent stress on the family, or issues that were of concern?

No, not at all. Everything seemed to be fine. Better than fine really. Of course with only one kid left in the house, what would they have to argue about? Well, not that they argued. As a matter of fact I don't think they've argued in all the years I've known them.

I was referring to outside the home. To your knowledge, was there anything happening outside the home that might be causing stress or concern for the family?

No, not that I know of. Everything seemed to be going brilliantly for them - always is.

Reilly stopped reading and clicked her tongue.

"What is up with that? Someone, again unprompted, harping on about the fact that this perfect couple never fight."

"I suppose when you look at it like that…" said Kennedy.

"What about on Josh's side then, anyone from Perk?"

"His right-hand man, Fred Hegarty. Not a lot came from that either."

Reilly went to the transcript.

How is he?
Alright…well, not alright, but stable.
Did you see them? I mean…the knife wounds?
Afraid so.
It's unbelievable this could happen. That someone is capable of that. I mean it had to be

someone he knew doesn't it? This sort of thing doesn't happen at random, does it?

Well, that's precisely what we're trying to sort out. Now, you're fairly close to Josh?

Very much. We work side by side every day. Trust him with my life, and he mine.

Did you know if Josh was having any problems at home?

No, not especially. I mean everyone has their problems, I suppose. Annabel and him seemed to be getting along well. I mean, at least when she was in a good mood, ha. Ah, that's not fair, what do I know. Annabel's a gem, you know that. But yeah, they had a good marriage, as far as I could tell. Not that I'm one to talk.

What about at business, everything good there?

Yeah, Perk's doing great. Unprecedented growth.

Anyone at work have it out for him? Any grudges? Someone he pissed off or let go?

No, no nothing like that. He's a great boss. People love to work with him.

Wholesalers, he may have pushed a bit too hard…competitors, maybe?

Believe it or not, Detective, Josh's is salt of the earth. Never did anything. To anyone.

"A bit of a different tune," she said.

Kennedy nodded. "I remember thinking at the time that he sounded like a cynical kind of bloke."

"Any chance we could have another chat with him?"

"Be a hell of a lot easier than Annabel's twelve year-old daughter, anyway. Look Reilly, I want to help you, and I'll do what I can. But if you do find something, you know we'll need to bring Chris in on it."

"Of course. Goes without saying. But not just yet, OK?"

He sighed. "I'm not crazy about it, and he'll have my guts for garters if he finds out, but…"

"Thank you." She stood up and gave him a quick peck on the cheek.

Reddening afresh, he packed up the file and left.

She stayed on a while, poking at Kennedy's toast crumbs.

She was onto something, she was sure of it.

Every couple had disagreements and they didn't so adamantly deny that. Nor did their friends.

It was like everyone was going out of their way to ram home the long-prevailing notion of Josh and Annabel's oh-so-perfect marriage.

43

"WITH US NOW IS HELEN Marsh, official Garda liaison to the Department of Public Prosecution. Ms Marsh, thank you for joining us on Prime Time this evening."

"You're welcome. Please, call me Helen."

"OK, thank you Helen. It has been now four days since the heinous attack on Josh Morrison was reported, and the general public are becoming concerned that his attacker has not yet been detained. Can you tell us a bit about what is going on behind the scenes with the investigation?"

"As you well know, it is not our job to arrest just anyone. It is our job to arrest who we believe committed the crime. It is crucially important that our detectives find evidence that can prove a suspect committed the crime."

"OK yes, I don't think anyone expects the Gardai to arrest just anyone. But there is the expectation that suspects are referred to as such because the evidence suggests as much. What I'm saying is, shouldn't you have a suspect by now? How long before this crime becomes just another to add to the list of unsolved serious crimes in our city?"

"Naturally, we will do everything we can, and take as long as necessary to ensure we find the person responsible. But we can only do so entirely within the confines of available evidence."

"Sure…and again, no one is suggesting you should just arrest someone without cause. I suppose what I'm saying is, don't you have enough evidence by now? Surely there are leads. Surely there are suspects."

"A crime of this nature has many variables and investigating those variables takes time. It's that simple. This cannot be rushed simply because it is a high profile case."

"Okay, perhaps we need to move on at this point. You say you have more work to do, fine. Can we please though, talk about the recent detentions you did make in the Josh Morrison investigation - Ted O'Donnell and his brother Richard?"

"The GFU found an indication that a known larcenist had ready access to the Morrison household, along with - it turns out, circumstantial - forensic evidence relating to his person there. However, the investigative team subsequently concluded that the suspect was not involved in Mr Morrison's attack, so he was released. This kind of unfortunate incident can be quite common during the early stages of an investigation, which is why we must be so careful."

"So you were entirely convinced that this man, Richard O'Donnell attacked Josh Morrison in his own home on Friday night, and within a few hours' became entirely convinced that he did not."

"Again, we must defer to the evidence…"

"It sounds like our detectives are flailing. Where are the interviews? The suspects? Frankly, where is the sense of urgency? Josh Morrison is in a coma, you are his only hope for justice."

"This investigation is not about justice, Miriam."

"What is it about then?"

"Evidence."

44

"GOOD MORNING DUBLIN, IT'LL BE a sunny day today, reaching a sultry 23 degrees, its 6:35 and you are listening to Breakfast with Shelly Frost. We have a great show for you this morning as always.

First up, we have novelist and screenwriter Rita Dowling in to talk about her latest book, *Hot Mustard*, released this week. Also look forward to our segment following the city council protest that has taken place over the past few days, as locals try to force local government's hand on better funding for north Dublin schools.

"In other news, a pedestrian was struck by a motorbike in Rathfarnham, a Facebook rant puts Tesco's bacon under the spotlight after a video goes viral, and plans are revealed for a yet another pedestrian bridge across the Liffey. New photo of the adorable baby Princess Charlotte has the entire world saying 'awww' and Dublin's truck drivers should expect more delays as roadworks continue on the M50.

"Of course our biggest headline story this week is still weighing on all of our minds as we try to make sense of this horrible tragedy that has befallen Ireland's golden couple, Josh and Annabel Morrison.

For all listeners out there thinking about hero Josh lying in that hospital, and about his gorgeous wife trying to stay strong through this tragedy, this one's for you..."

Reilly tried to resist. Waking up in this state was much akin to waking up after a paramedic brings one back from the light at the end of a tunnel with a defibrillator.

The light was so beautiful, so peaceful. The body so cold and full of pain. Fogginess slurped through her waking eyes. The world spun a bit and her eyes clenched in retaliation.

There was little to do about her buzzing iPhone except to pick it up and throw it.

Fortunately for her, it was tethered to the charging plug and just tumbled its way softly to the floor. Unfortunately for her, it continued buzzing. She slapped at the floor, futilely finding the noisy perpetrator and when she did at last, consciousness signed in.

It was time to get up.

Reilly lurched out of bed and pried her eyes open. The clock on her phone said 6:39. She had to look at it several times before it registered what that meant. She had about twenty minutes to shower, get to her car and head to the GFU.

Wait, no…less than twenty.

So no shower then, she thought. After brushing her teeth and pulling her hair back into a tight ponytail, she put on some sport-strength deodorant and her wrinkled clothes from yesterday.

The sun was long up, and that cutting morning briskness common in Dublin at this hour, tickled her nose.

The weight of sleepiness began to subside and tiredness soon morphed into its uglier step cousin, grumpiness.

She was intolerant of the cold temperatures, of cyclists, of drivers who took too long to turn. She was especially annoyed at the email alerts appearing on her phone.

That radio program was also irritating her; those chirpy DJs talking too loudly and energetically. Their moods were unnaturally cheerful. No one was this cheerful every morning. These morons were phoning it and had been for years.

She shut off the radio.

The GFU building was humbly lit from morning light. It took too long for the car ahead of her to get into the garage. Once there, it took long for that person to park. Then she whipped her car into a spot, but misjudged the lines, so had to redo it.

Stomping out she marched her way to the lift. It took too long for the lift to come. The woman next to her was wearing too much perfume. Bvlgari *The Blanc*.

She liked that one actually.

Looking up, the young woman had a friendly expression and greeted her. "Good morning!"

Great, more chirpiness.

Finally, she arrived on her floor and made her way toward her office.

The team wouldn't be in just yet, so she had a bit of time to kill before the arduous work of sorting through the shattered glass they'd taken from the Morrison place, hoping to isolate the mysterious Jack Daniels drinker.

Reilly turned on the computer, and started going through Josh's emails while she waited, this time looking specifically for correspondence with the wife.

She clicked on a few and scanned though them on the preview window.

To: Josh Morrison
From: Annabel Morrison
Subject: ???
I guess you've never heard the adage "never go to sleep on an argument." Because I'm still annoyed and you're acting like nothing's wrong.

To: Annabel Morrison
From: Josh Morrison
Subject: RE: ???
Stop being so dramatic. I had to work early and you knew that. Talk tonight.

To: Josh Morrison
From: Annabel Morrison
Subject: RE: RE: ???
I won't be in tonight. So now you get to wonder where I'll be.

That was it from that thread. Not exactly loved-up, but still not far off from the mark, she supposed. Couples fight.

No matter what the friends all insisted, Annabel and Josh weren't special non-fighting marriage unicorns.

She kept going. Most of the exchanges between them were mundane, or they were sharing links—talking about weekend plans. There wasn't a lot, really.

She supposed they texted too, but fat lot of good that would do her. According to Rory none of Josh's texts were retrievable from the Cloud. And there was nowhere near enough evidence to subpoena Apple for them.

The further back she went, the less she found and then after a time started to believe she was wasting her time.

Sitting back, she took a breath and then scanned absently through the subject lines. One caught her eye. It was from Cormac Flanagan the solicitor, with the subject 'Documentation.'

To: Josh Morrison
From: Cormac Flanagan
Subject: Documentation

Josh,
I know you are avoiding me and I know you received Annabel's documents. You can't ignore this forever. Please respond asap.

To: Cormac Flanagan
From: Josh Morrison
Subject: RE: Documents

Cormac,
Fuck off.
Josh

Her eyes widened. Well now, what was that all about?

Printing the email, she then dialed the Dublin City Clerk's office.

"This is Reilly Steel GFU, I'm working the Morrison case."

"Okay…oh right, of course, what can I help you?"

"Can you see if there was a court action of any kind filed by solicitor Cormac Flanagan…" she checked the email date, "in the past sixty days?"

"Let me check. Can you hold?"

"Sure."

A couple minutes later the voice returned. "Yes I have a record. Should I fax it?"

"Please do, you have the number?"

"Yes, it's in the directory."

"Thanks, I'll wait for it."

She hung up and waited.

Annabel's documents. Certainly sounded like the D word didn't it?

What else could it be? If Annabel had recently initiated a divorce or separation, then that certainly put things in a whole new light.

The disingenuous assertions that they had the best marriage in the world really stank on ice now.

And if they were heading for the courts, was it such a big deal? Really, who cared? Reilly was no PR expert, but she couldn't imagine there being some sort of collapse of the Morrison brand just because they were separating.

If Tom and Nicole could do it, so could they. Why hold it so close to the chest? Unless there were details they didn't want the public to know. That could very well be likely—especially if there were children involved, affairs, bad business investments, who knows. Divorce brought all skeletons out of the closet.

The fax came in. She went over it about thirty times, but it revealed nothing at all to do with the Morrisons.

So if Flanagan had in fact been talking about legal separation documents, they were never processed.

She decided it was time to talk to Cormac Flanagan. No time like the present.

She dialed his office, of course there was no answer as it was red-eye-thirty in the morning, so she left a message and sent an email saying she needed to discuss something urgent.

Surprisingly, he responded right away from his iPhone. *"On my way into office, meet me there?"*

At first she wondered why he was so responsive, but she supposed it made sense considering his client was under the microscope.

Perhaps he could use his wiles to sway everyone away from suspicion. But then, what would they have to be suspicious about?

The whole think stunk like yesterday's laundry.

Reilly grabbed her jumper and headed out.

45

SHE ARRIVED AT HARCOURT STREET inside of thirty minutes. Parking was for once easy, so she walked briskly to the modern office building, signed in at security and took the lift to the third floor.

Flanagan's firm occupied the entire floor. Even at this early hour there was a secretary present, perked up with coffee and smiling broadly. At least a dozen others were in the office already, shuffling around, eating pastries and making phone calls.

"Hello, may I help you?"

"Here to see Cormac Flanagan."

"Hold on."

She escorted Reilly through a maze of cubicles and finally to a glass-paned corner office where Flanagan sat, feet on desk, shirt untucked and coat and tie hanging from a chair.

"Come in," he said and gave her a shudder-inducing Steve Buscemi smile. "We start early sometimes," he explained. "Our firm has a lot of Japanese clients."

She nodded. "Thanks for seeing me on such short notice."

"How's the investigation going?"

"I wish I had more to report," she said, shrugging.

"Annabel's a mess, I'm sure you understand. And I know her account of the night isn't as…helpful as you'd hoped."

"We're getting there," she replied, trying not to betray her annoyance.

"So, what can I help you with? Anything at all of course."

She handed the email over and let him read it. "Can you tell me what this was concerning?"

Flanagan looked visibly annoyed and put his feet back on the floor.

"This is an ongoing criminal investigation," Reilly said, before he could fall back on attorney-client privilege. "We can wait for the DPP to request the information, or you can just tell me and keep things hidden from the public record."

He sighed. "Josh wanted a separation," he said after a moment of thought. "The documents in question were provisions in the paperwork concerning disclosure."

"Disclosure?"

"Annabel didn't want to proceed without assurances that Josh wouldn't blab about their marriage."

"That's kind of odd, isn't it?"

"Not really, I mean you've all seen the tell-all books hit the shops after high-profile divorces. She wanted to stop that before it even became an idea. She has a reputation to protect."

She nodded, "Okay, so they were going for a legal separation…what happened?"

"Well, we never got past the initial negotiations. As a matter of fact, we had a meeting planned next week where we were going to go through all the finances, amendments, and disclosure provision."

"I see," she said, satisfied that he was telling the truth.

"In any case, what does it have to do with the investigation?"

"I'm just trying to get to the bottom of what's going on."

"They were having marital problems. That didn't mean they wanted to stab each other."

"Of course not," Reilly said. "That's not what I'm suggesting. Anyway, thanks for your time."

"Let me know if you need anything else," he said.

"Now that you mention it…"

"What is it?"

"Would it be possible to speak with Lottie?"

"I really don't think that's a good idea," Flanagan said, darkening.

"It would help our line of investigation."

"What line is that precisely? Lottie wasn't even at the house when it happened."

"Our team is trying to clear up some inconsistent accounts. We think she could help."

He shook his head, "The only way you interview Lottie Morrison is if she is served."

Reilly nodded and offered an apologetic smile. "Let's hope it doesn't come to that. Thanks again."

She mentally kicked herself. Now he was going to be on high alert, and this would inevitably get back to Annabel.

She needed to go further down this road in any case.

But she would have to do so much more carefully now.

46

LATER THAT DAY SHE HAD another appointment, one that she'd have completely forgotten were it not for a cheerful iPhone diary alert that popped up earlier this morning.

She paced in the obstetrician's waiting room, willing her to hurry the hell up so she could get back to work.

"Reilly Steel?" a nurse called.

Relieved, she rushed in. The nurse took her temperature and blood pressure. Then retook the blood pressure. Then said, "Mrs. Steel, take a breath and calm down please. Your pressure is far too high."

She swallowed took a breath, remembering her yoga. The nurse shook her head. "Well I suppose that will have to do."

Dr. Friedman came into the exam room after a few minutes, set down the chart and greeted her warmly.

"How are you doing, Reilly?"

"Okay, I guess. My work-assigned shrink thinks I have blood pressure issues."

She smiled. "Indeed you do. It's not abnormal as you come to the end of the first trimester, but you'll have to start watching your sodium intake soon or it will get worse."

"How bad is it?"

"Bad enough. Stressful time at work?"

Reilly nodded.

"Try some acupuncture. Do yoga. Don't eat processed foods, you'll be fine." Then she looked up with a smile, "So are you ready to see the baby?"

Reilly flinched, not expecting this. "I guess."

"Okay, hop up there and lie back."

Friedman fired up the ultrasound and applied jelly on her bare but still flat, stomach.

Then, after a long moment of moving it around, suddenly Reilly saw on the screen above the bed, clear as day, a human being in her uterus. It looked like the baby from *2001 A Space Odyssey*.

Blob.

Then an unexpected sensation happened. Something like a boulder falling onto her head from a great height. But instead of smashing her skull, it pounded her mind to oblivion.

There was a *baby* inside of her. An actual human being. Growing. Inside of her.

The uneasy knot of tension that had been harbored deep in her gut over the last few weeks, giving her insomnia, stress, anxiety and probably high blood pressure, suddenly erupted, sending a volcanic blast of heat through her body.

Without warning she began crying. Not just tears she couldn't hold back, but a rolling-shoulder weep.

It poured out as that energy spread through, and it wouldn't stop.

Dr. Friedman waited patiently and at last she stopped, feeling raw and strangely satisfied. Calm, in fact.

But *very* embarrassed.

"Sorry," she said, sniffing, and Friedman handed her a tissue. "I never cry. Ever."

"There's a lot happening with your body now. You'll find yourself doing all sorts of things you never do." The doctor smiled, a little conspiratorially, and that made her feel better.

Reilly looked again at the ultrasound machine. The fetus was a pixelated squirmy thing, but to her it looked incredible.

She wondered about the gender and was about to ask, but then realized it was too early to tell.

Maybe next time…

Friedman cleaned off the goo. "Might be a good idea to take some time off soon, if you can. Try to get that stress under control."

"Not an option at the moment, but thanks."

Reilly went back outside. Something had changed inside of her and she couldn't easily identify what.

But the world looked a little larger now.

A little scarier. A little more mysterious and unknown.

Her senses were heightened. People talked louder, walked louder, smelled stronger. Their faces appeared exaggerated and distant, obscured by some sort of cloudy membrane.

I'm losing my mind, she thought. It was difficult to orient and ground herself again. Taking her time in the car to practice her breathing, the feeling finally abated. But there was no doubt things felt differently now.

Embarrassingly enough, it had taken almost ten weeks for her to realize that this pregnancy was *real*. Her whole life was about to change and, not only that, the very definition of what she thought was important was going to change. Now she had something beyond herself.

Above herself.

She left, feeling quite a bit better than she arrived.

Maybe that shrink Corcoran was right about things. In the movies, investigators were supposed to take threats from serial killers in their stride.

Even Jodie Foster didn't seem that worried when she was in a dark basement with Buffalo Bill.

And Detective Benson on SVU never displayed an emotion other than sympathetic loathing.

She was supposed to be tougher than this. Smarter.

She should be making Chris see her point of view about Annabel Morrison through clever witty banter, not pissing him off to the point that he refused to take her seriously.

But, Reilly thought, heading back to the GFU, just in case the whole witty banter thing didn't work, she should work on finding some compelling evidence.

Later, the team assembled in a meeting room, after another heavy day's work in the lab.

It had been a long week, and everyone had bags under their eyes, were likely unwashed and on the edge of delirium.

Danishes, bagels and pastries were pouring out of a greasy white box, and coffee and tea was being thrown back like whiskey on a Saturday night.

"Okay guys, listen up," Reilly began. "I wanted to talk about a new direction in our investigation."

"What's wrong with the old direction?" Gary groaned, and Lucy smacked him on the arm.

"I've gone over some of the witness transcripts, and looks like certain things are not adding up."

"Like what?" Lucy asked.

"I think the Morrisons are hiding something. For starters, we've heard from every one of their friends and colleagues about what a perfect couple they are. That they never fight, not ever. Not in two decades of marriage. Whereas, I just learned this morning that they were in the middle of working out a separation agreement."

"What does prove?" said Lucy. "I mean, they wouldn't want that made public. They don't want their perfect image tarnished."

"Or, they don't want to incriminate Annabel. A complicated divorce with lots of money at stake. Their solicitor told me about specific clauses they were hashing out. This process was not pretty. What if Annabel wasn't getting her way?"

"Come on, Reilly," said Gary. "Even if that's true we've already established that the wife couldn't realistically have done it."

"True. But maybe somebody did it for her."

Julius shook his head, "Too risky for someone like her. In the public eye. She wouldn't be able to trust anyone for something like that."

"Unless she was seeing someone on the side," suggested Rory.

"That thought crossed my mind, too."

She went on to tell them about the Jack Daniels bottle and how Josh was apparently teetotal. "Hospital confirmed that he hadn't been drinking it that night. So who was?"

"Reilly, that glass…it's a mess. If you're thinking prints or saliva…there's just no way we could isolate anything from that. That whole area was completely contaminated. The bourbon mixed in with the blood and all that glass…

"I know but we have to try."

Julius sighed "Just as long as you know it's a seriously long shot."

"I do. But I trust you."

He looked dubious.

"In the meantime," she added, addressing the others, "that's why we need to hit the crime scene one last time, before it's released. Except this time, we're not looking for evidence on the crime, we're looking for what the Morrisons might be hiding. The separation, affairs, whatever might give the wife motive to do this."

47

"A CANDLELIGHT VIGIL IN HONOR of former Irish rugby captain, Josh Morrison, is taking place at eight pm tonight at the Aviva stadium.

Organized by the IRFU, but open to the public, fans and supporters from all over the nation will be pouring out their support for Josh tonight.

The website TryForJosh.org will be taking donations to benefit Josh Morrison's favorite charity *Try*, which offers free after-school sport programs for primary and secondary schools.

Josh's wife, Annabel Morrison has refused a contribution to the family, and urged supporters to donate to *Try* instead.

The event is attracting quite a crowd of celebrities from the Irish entertainment and sports world. Josh's former Ireland and Leinster teammates will all be there, as well as other heroes from the sport's past and present, including Brian O'Driscoll, Jordan Murphy and Peter Stringer.

We also have word that Josh's nearby neighbor and close friend Bono, will be performing at tonight's venue with U2. Interesting to see what faves the lads will go for on this somber occasion.

Our own TVSport correspondent, Lisa Carey will be there too of course, with full coverage of the event. We're told there will be entertainment and food. Mrs. Morrison will make an appearance and speak to the crowd.

Lisa, you'll keep us up to date with what's happening down in Lansdowne Road tonight, won't you?"

"I'll be there John, looking forward to it. Though of course, this is not exactly a party. I think people just want to send their best wishes for Josh's recovery, and a tasteful vigil with a little music and some entertainment - all in the name of charity - is the perfect way to do that.

"Should be great. We're looking forward to your report."

48

LATER THAT AFTERNOON, REILLY DROVE back out to Killiney Hill to join the crew, and was surprised to see the media completely packed up and gone from outside the Morrison place.

Amazing how fickle they were. Bring a few celebs to a stadium for a party, and suddenly everyone forgets there's an attempted murder.

She came in to find Gary already upstairs in the spare bedroom. He was looking through the closets, and he stopped suddenly, startled at the sound of her voice.

"What did you find?"

"Suitcase."

"Maybe she was planning to move out."

He opened it. "Nope, unless she's started wearing boxers."

She looked over his shoulder at what was obviously a man's luggage.

"Anything identifiable in there?"

Gary rummaged carefully with his latex-gloved hands. "Not really, but we'll take his undies in and hope for the best. Gotta love our job."

She smiled at this, and made her way back down the stairs to the minimally decorated home office adjacent to the living room. A PC lay open on the desk, and Reilly began rifling through the desk drawers underneath.

Just like she thought, she very quickly found the separation documents. Josh had them stored in his inbox tray, complete with colorful sticky notes to mark where he was supposed to sign.

She sat in his office chair and began scanning through it. It was the huge complicated mess one would expect from a celebrity parting. The legalese that went into it should have been award-winning. The basic terms all seemed standard; most of it was about which assets were going to whom.

All in all, over twenty-five million euro of assets, including holiday homes in Marbella and Kerry, and cash in the hundreds of thousands.

Tough life.

They seemed to be relatively straightforward about the division though. Whomever earned the money kept the money, or as close to that formula as they could make it. Custody was even worked out with no dispute. Lottie would stay with her mother, and Josh would get weekly visitation. Dylan was a grown up, so nothing to sort out there.

Then she got to the provisions, and that's when things got a little strange. The disclosure clause Flanagan talked about was in there. They were not allowed to speak about their personal relationship or any known discretions, or they would forfeit their combined assets.

Another interesting note—if it was discovered that either one of them were unfaithful, that would also result in a forfeit.

Why would someone put that in there? If someone suspected infidelity and intended to prove it, then it would show their hand. Conversely, if someone was sleeping around, why in the hell would they sign this?

What a bizarre provision.

And it was possibly one of the reasons Josh hadn't signed it yet. Annabel was asking for a lot there. A thought jumped out at her.

"Rory," she called out, and he duly scurried down the stairs.

"Yeah?"

"Can you sync to Josh's emails from here?"

He nodded. "Yeah, the files are on the database. What do you need?"

"I want to see if he had a solicitor, other than Flanagan."

He fired up the iPad and scrolled through the database.

"Well he has one in his contacts, hold on…" he said and thumbed some more. "Yeah, recent correspondence too. I'll forward it to you."

"Thanks."

Reilly pulled it up on her phone and read. It was actually dated a week previous.

To: Josh Morrison
From: Cynthia Robertson
Josh,
I've finished reviewing the papers and agree there are some concerning provisions. Let's meet at my office first thing Monday to go through. Say 9am? Hope to see you then.

Well, he missed that appointment.

Reilly called the number in the email.

"Hi, I'm looking for Cynthia Robertson."

"May I ask who's calling?"

"Reilly Steel, with the GFU. It is regarding an investigation concerning one of her clients."

"Please hold."

Elton John started playing, and Reilly paced around the room, as she waited for the solicitor to pick up.

"This is Cynthia, I'm glad someone from the gardai called actually. I wasn't sure if I should get in touch."

Reilly's heart sped up. "Well, you're talking to us now. We've just discovered you were working for Josh Morrison, can we assume it was about his impending separation?"

"Yes, and while I'm happy to talk in broad terms to assist your investigation, you do know I am still bound by client confidentiality unless directed otherwise."

"I understand, but any information you can share would be helpful."

"Well, and again speaking in broad terms, there is something a little concerning about all of this. Like I said, I was in two minds, whether I should talk to the detectives…"

"What concerns you Ms Robertson?"

"Mr. Morrison was unhappy with the separation documentation his solicitor drew up, and so turned to me. They have a family solicitor whom they've used for decades."

"Cormac Flanagan," said Reilly.

"That's the one. Anyway, the direction Flanagan was advising made him quite uncomfortable. He suggested unusual provisions in the contract that would be, to the objective eye, excessive."

"We've seen those documents Ms Robertson; that's why we were looking to find if he had representation apart from Flanagan."

She cleared her throat. "Mr. Morrison believed that Mr. Flanagan was setting him up for a contract breach. That Mr. Flanagan was siding with his wife, and planning to take advantage of such a breach when it occurred."

"Strong accusations for a family friend," said Reilly.

"I can't say that he was paranoid, because the terms looked quite odd to me too. The infidelity one, in particular. Mr. Morrison assured me that he never went outside his marriage, however whether or not he did was besides the point. Any indiscretion could point to that, and he'd be on tough legal grounding to protect himself."

"What about this disclosure provision?"

"Yes, I was rather concerned about that too, because it not spell out what specifically should not be disclosed. Mr. Morrison would not confide with me on the matter and insisted that he wanted that provision untouched."

"What did you advise?"

Cynthia cleared her throat again, "I advised that he insist the infidelity clause be omitted, and that both clients should come together and find a way to further specify the disclosure provision. That was the last time I spoke with him."

"This was last week?"

"Yes. And now I can't help thinking that maybe they got into an argument over this. He met with me the day he was attacked."

Bingo.

"You've been very helpful, thank you solicitor."

"I hope so." she said, and then added softly. "How is poor Josh? Is he going to recover?"

"The doctors think so. It would help us all tremendously if he did."

Reilly thanked her again, and rejoined her colleagues.

Finally, she thought. Someone else that's suspicious.

Though she didn't want to look for a subpoena to disclose the separation documentation at this point. They needed to come up with some more convincing evidence first.

Lucy was waiting for her at the door. "I think you'd better come take a look at this."

Following her upstairs to the master bedroom, Reilly recoiled a little when she saw what was lying on the bed. A twelve gauge shotgun.

"Where'd you find this?" she asked her.

"Top shelf in the wardrobe. Chances are he has a permit for it - maybe game hunting or something - but…"

"Maybe, we'll check it out. In the meantime, probably best to put it back."

"There's something else. I came across a box of newspaper clippings in there too, mostly just mementos and media articles from Josh's playing days. But I thought this one seemed strange - out of place a bit."

She handed Reilly a newspaper clipping.

It was of the car accident from the 1990s she'd found in the archives. The same article in fact. Faded, torn on the edges, but preserved.

Reilly stared at it, the one dark period in by all accounts a very charmed career.

Why on earth would Josh want to hold onto this?

49

"MY BANDMATES ARE ALL HERE tonight. Josh's teammates are all here tonight, feels like the whole of *Ireland* is here tonight, for Josh.

It's a beautiful thing, looking at all these people.

Wow, there's like what, tens of thousands? Filling the whole stadium. All these candles. Josh is a symbol, you know. He represents that part of us that never gives up. That just keeps on going. All of us together, celebrating a dedication to life. He always pushed, hard. He was always larger than life, out here on the pitch, wasn't he Brian?"

"Yeah, that's it, Bono. I remember as a kid watching him play, and I'd be thinking, I want to *be* that guy. He's not just tough, but he's got this grace too. The way he plays, it was almost like scoring tries is what he was put on this earth to do."

"Yeah, breaks my heart man, him lying in the hospital tonight. But all of us are here to support him. We have our candles, and our songs and our prayers, and tonight we're urging our friend, our neighbor, our *hero* to get better. Josh, buddy, this one's for you."

50

IT WAS QUIET IN THE GFU when they go back to the lab.

Reilly could hardly believe another day was coming to a close. Half of the building seem to have taken off to the Morrison vigil, though.

Jack Gorman had popped his head in earlier and told her O'Brien had ordered him to show his face, represent the GFU.

It was ridiculous. Expecting law enforcement to go down there with celebrities, rugby players and Bono, sit and hold hands and sing kumbaya?

Fat lot of good that would do Josh Morrison.

But luckily, her team was as studious as ever, as she'd set them to uncover what, if any significance, a car accident that had happened two decades ago might have in the context of their current investigation.

They went to work on the accident photo; Lucy and Gary sitting close together, arms touching, examining the photo of the crash, and talking about vectors, trajectories and other mathematical scenarios, trying to piece together the specifics.

Rory had disappeared into the archives to find the original case files from twenty years ago. Julius was deep in glass shards, analyzing every last piece, trying to isolate that tiny piece of evidence that might prove somebody other than a random burglar, was at the Morrison house on Friday night.

"Any thoughts?" she asked Lucy.

"Well, it was a head-on collision, that part's clear. Looks like the driver just rammed straight into a wall."

"Do we know exactly where in Killiney this was?" Gary asked. "The paper just mentioned it wasn't far from the Morrison house."

"And remember it was twenty years ago," said Lucy. "Who knows what's changed since then?"

"I'm sure the specifics will be in the case file. Let's hope Rory can find it."

Lucy pointed to the windscreen on the picture. "I do think something looks a bit off there, but I can't say for sure until we get a better look. Seems to me a bit like the fracture starts on the passenger side? But that wouldn't make sense, would it?"

"I can't tell," said Gary. "Pic's too grainy."

Just then, Rory arrived with a file box containing Road Traffic Accident reports from within the timeframe.

They split the files up, and everyone thumbed through them until Lucy found the one they wanted.

"Photos, here we go," she squeaked and laid them out on the table.

Reilly grabbed one and looked closer at the windscreen to see what Lucy had been talking about.

The younger girl pointed. "Yeah, look. The impact definitely started there; the glass break fanned from here. The deceased was launched out through the windscreen all right, but he was in the passenger seat."

Reilly sat down and studied the photograph taken at the scene of the crash, comparing it with the specifics on the report. It was plain as day that something was off here.

The deceased, Josh's Leinster teammate Ian Cross, was drunk driving, no seat-belt, and Josh the passenger, was mercifully buckled in. That's what the paper said, anyway. He survived only because he was buckled in.

And - ever the hero - was able to drag himself out of the car.

But the break pattern on the windscreen suggested this was not what had happened at all…

Reilly immediately started digging through the rest of the file, looking for more crime scene photos, and stumbled upon another of the victim. It was shocking in its gore.

The guy had been thrown against a stone wall at high velocity, smashing his skull and most of his upper torso. The bloody mess that was left over was barely identifiable as human.

"This is awful," she said. "No wonder the accident made the papers."

"A miracle Josh survived at all," said Gary.

"Miracle, or plan…" Reilly mumbled distractedly. Her mind was doing cartwheels.

"What do you think happened?"

"Not sure, but something's up, whatever it is. Find the transcripts. We need to know the entire story."

Rory thumbed through a file and tossed out a stapled stack of paper, "Witness interviews," he said.

Reilly snatched them and began reading, her heart sinking as she started to jump into another case. This would either explain everything or send her down a rabbit hole.

Possibly both.

51

Donner: Were you at the party last night?
S. Ward: Yeah.
Donner: Did you see Ian Cross and Josh Morrison present at the party?
S. Ward: Yeah, it was Josh's party, at his house.
Donner: How many were present at the party?
S. Ward: I don't know, ten, twenty maybe?
Donner: Did you see Ian Cross drinking?
S. Ward: Oh yeah, he had way too much. He and Annabel got into a fight.
Donner: Annabel Morrison?
S. Ward: Yeah. She wasn't happy.
Donner: What was the fight about?
S. Ward: Who knows? Knowing Ian, he probably grabbed her arse or something.
Donner: He was inebriated during this time?
S. Ward: Yeah, Josh took him out front, said he was going to get him some air.

Donner: *That's when they left the house in Josh's car?*

S. Ward: *Must have been, we didn't realize they were driving off anywhere. Assumed they just went to the chipper or something.*

Donner: *Was Josh Morrison inebriated?*

S. Ward: *Yeah, probably.*

SHE READ THROUGH SEVERAL MORE witness transcripts; they all had basically the same story.

Ian and Annabel got into an argument over something, and Josh took his mate out to get some air. Everyone seemed equally surprised they'd gone off in the car. It was a good story.

But a little too good.

Not one detailed account over what the fight was about? The investigation, lead by Detective Larry Donner, interviewed twelve people who were at that party. All twelve gave pretty much the same story.

Reilly had heard of Donner, he was a bit of legend throughout the force, and considered as a thorough and meticulous detective. There were a few detectives that had been personally mentored by him, and they were some of the best.

Even Chris would tone it down or notch or two when dealing with one of detectives who worked with Donner.

According to the investigation summary, the RTA involving Josh Morrison and Ian Cross, happened sometime around 12:30am. The cops arrived at the Morrison home at 1:20 am. The party would have certainly dwindled by then. Donner did put together a list of others who'd attended, collected from the twelve interviews. It was an incomplete list, and he didn't have full names for every witness. Additionally, he likely had enough supporting eyewitness accounts to avoid having to go through the pain of searching out any more.

Things were a little easier these days. Now the force had networked databases like PULSE, and sophisticated search engines. She brought the list to Rory.

"Cross reference these names and see if you can get any matches in the system. I don't care about criminal histories so much, just want to check connections to Josh or Annabel. Or Ian Cross."

Rory took the report and started thinking, eyes glazing over.

"Will that be a problem?" she asked.

"No, just figuring out search queries. I can run a script to match…never mind, just give me a few minutes."

"Thanks."

Reilly went back to a lab where Lucy and Gary were reviewing enhanced photo projections.

"The trajectory is interesting," commented Lucy when she saw Reilly.

"How do you mean?"

"Look, the car is evenly smashed across the front. Consistent with a direct head-on collision."

Gary nodded, "Right, not typical, is it? A drunk driver driving head-on into a wall."

"I suppose it depends on the circumstances. Look for tire marks in the old photos, that'll help figure out trajectory and speed," she said.

"Yeah there are some here, I think," said Gary distractedly.

Reilly went back to her office and opened the RTA report again, flipping through it for anything that might grab her. It was always difficult looking through older cases. There were things the GFU automatically looked for, were accustomed to collecting, that another team wouldn't be.

Back then, there was no GFU at all, and would have been a very different team, with different ideas, agendas, leadership and technologies.

The climate would have been different too.

She tried to put herself back there at the centre of that incident.

Given Josh and his teammate's stature as Leinster Rugby players, it would have been high profile like this one, but a tragic road accident that left a man dead was a very different dynamic to finding a bad guy.

Not that investigators all thought that way of course, but the distinction did exist.

The core reason this current investigation was such a problem was because no one was willing to consider anything much beyond Annabel Morrison's story about a robbery gone wrong.

But Reilly's early suspicions, coupled with some of what they were finding now, definitely made a suggestion to the contrary.

The only way at this point to bypass that obstacle, was to find stronger evidence or testimony that brought such suspicion to another level.

Forensics was built for that. It was the objective, cold, hard truth of science that defense solicitors could not easily rebuke.

The frustrating part was that they had the forensics, but it was increasingly looking like the top brass did not have the patience to let things play out. For starters, it seemed Josh Morrison was going to survive, and that once awake could either identify his attacker, or give an account that would either corroborate his wife's story or contradict it.

Of course, by then, the attacker could be in Texas or Timbuktu or some other damned place, far from their reach. It had already taken far too long as it was.

So she was taking unusual measures.

And she didn't want Chris in on this yet, because she truly thought he would shut the whole thing down and send her back to ground zero with nothing.

The folder also contained pictures of Ian Cross. First were the accident scene photos, and it made no difference how accustomed she was to seeing these, this one was particularly gruesome.

The guy had careered head-first through the windscreen, into the broken stone wall, his head buried underneath stone debris.

The coroner's photos were even worse. His face was crushed under the stones, leaving little. Much of his skull had caved in and the features left were distorted and buckled.

The autopsy notes were grisly and difficult to read. Major points were consistent with the scene.

Cross had several lacerations from the windshield glass and contusions from his impact with the wall. The impact caused an avulsion of the cranium and several depressed skull fractures.

There was no doubt, according to the coroner, that the crash killed him. BAC was at .27. He was completely intoxicated, a stumbling drunk at that level.

Another report showed that Josh hadn't been too far behind.

Gary came in, interrupting her thoughts. He spilled a pile of photos on her desk showing prints of the wall, maps of the road on which the accident took place and tire tracks.

"I did the math."

"Good for you."

He twirled a top-down print out of the road.

"To have impacted that wall head-on after ricocheting out of control, and glancing off something else first, the car would have had to be doing over a hundred kilometers."

She squinted at the street. "On that road?

"It's possible," he said with a shrug. "But. There would be tire marks. A turn at that speed and at that quick of an action—there would be tire marks."

"Aren't there?" she asked pointing to another photo.

"Yes. But those marks are not in the middle of the road, indicating a sharp turn. These tire marks are straight ahead and diagonal."

"I don't follow."

"The only way the car could have made these marks is if it was speeding at the wall from across the way."

She dropped her pen and closer examined the photos.

"Wait, are you saying Cross *aimed* the car at the wall, backed up to the far side of the street and drove straight at it?"

"That's my guess."

It was unbelievable. The evidence was suggesting Josh had to be driving. And it was suggesting he had deliberately directed the car at the wall.

His best friend was launched out through the windscreen, and into the wall. And by the time the cops came, he'd dragged himself out of the wreckage.

No one thought to check the windscreen break pattern or the tire tracks, because why would they? Who in the hell would do something like this?

It might never even have entered their consciousness. The only reason the team had spotted it today, was because they were *looking* for something inconsistent.

And more to the point, Reilly reminded herself it wasn't a criminal investigation, it was an RTA. A road traffic *accident*. Involving two of Leinster rugby's star players.

But looking at the same evidence, over twenty years later through a new lens revealed much.

It revealed things Donner should have seen.

The thought suddenly occurred to Reilly that being a crime scene investigator wasn't just about the evidence. It was about being able to see the woods from the trees.

About detaching yourself from the events and the narrative, and focus entirely on what the scene was telling you.

Easy to do in hindsight, and she couldn't say with any amount of certainty she would have seen anything in Donner's situation either.

So, even if it turned out they'd uncovered something insinuating Josh Morrison of being a murderer at worst, or of manslaughter at best, that didn't really help them much now.

The guy didn't stab himself.

Certainly he would have to answer some hard questions when he regained consciousness…but what about this case?

Was it related in some way? Could this incident be the thing Annabel wanted kept quiet in the separation documentation?

But why?

If anything, Josh would be the one to want to hide it—if it was something Annabel had found out about, and was holding over his head.

But it seemed all backwards now.

She found herself pounding the table in frustration.

"What?" Gary asked. "I thought you'd happy about this."

"Well, if we were trying to solve a twenty-year old RTA puzzle, then yes. But we aren't."

Rory appeared then, holding some papers, "I was able to find a few people who might have been at the party that night."

"Well, that is very good news," she said, raising a smile.

"And I have their phone numbers."

"Even better."

52

REILLY WAS NOT IN THE least a religious person, but it was a miracle of God that Kennedy agreed to leave the candlelight vigil, and meet with her in the car park outside Lansdowne Road stadium.

It was even more amazing that he agreed to do so without Chris.

"What's going on?" Kennedy said pacing a little, as he drew on his cigarette, clearly uncomfortable with this.

She opened the twenty-year old RTA report and pointed to the photograph of crash scene.

"The Morrisons have been hiding something about this accident from twenty years ago. We've looked into it and their story doesn't check out."

"Ah Jaysus, Reilly," Kennedy said losing his patience. "So what if it doesn't - it was twenty years ago."

"It matters because they are about to undertake a legal separation, and whatever they are holding back is at risk of being exposed."

"What does that have to do with our case?" he said, frustrated.

That was the hard part. In order to get him on board, she had to convince him there was a direct connection between this and the current investigation.

"Kennedy, listen, if Josh was planning on outing some kind of secret that could implicate Annabel—that's motive."

"But didn't you yourself already agree she didn't attack him," he said, rightly puzzled.

"Forensics suggest she didn't physically attack him, yes. But they don't rule out the possibility of her being there at the time. Now we know she might have a reason to have been there. To orchestrate all of this."

"I don't know about this," he said under his breath.

That was a stalling mechanism, she knew.

Kennedy was thinking about it, weighing the argument against what he'd already learned. He was waffling now, trying to figure out a retort, which Reilly knew he didn't have. So she decided to press him on that point.

"What other possibilities do we have?"

The detectives were just as immobilized as the crime unit. There was no more evidence and there were no more leads.

Reilly knew well that this was the only alternative avenue presented. It might be the more undesirable avenue, fraught with difficulties and stumbling blocks, but still it was the only one.

Kennedy knew this too. She just had to lure him into action and away from complacency. She knew how it went. He and Chris were likely in that mode where they needed to wait until something new presented itself.

Something new had presented itself.

"I need you to check out a couple of people, people who knew the Morrison's back then, who were at the party that night."

"Witnesses? What about their transcripts?"

"Josh was Ireland's great white rugby hope remember, nobody looked too closely at this thing, they were all too relieved that the guy had survived."

Kennedy looked at the folder and then skimmed the transcripts. "What makes you think the reports don't add up?"

"Josh was supposedly the passenger, and Ian was driving under the influence. The story was that Ian drunkenly swerved, the car ricocheted and then hit a wall. He wasn't wearing a seatbelt, Josh was. But we looked at the report and did some fresh analysis. Whoever flew out the window came from the passenger side."

"So you're saying Josh lied?"

"Maybe. But without question, that's what happened. We ran the scenario through iSPI. Furthermore, the windshield fracture could not have happened from the driver's side. Josh had to have been driving that car, not Ian."

Kennedy was in. He would have to take this seriously now. He flipped through the photos. "

Well, that's very interesting."

"Will you talk to the witnesses?"

He took a moment to think about it and then said, "OK, give me the details and I'll take a look. But now I'd better get back…"

"I've taken the liberty to call ahead, two of them are available right now."

"What? You can't just expect me to take off…"

She pointed at the stadium, "They're in there."

He rolled his eyes. "Of course they are."

53

SAM HURLEY WOULD HAVE BEEN a linebacker if he was American.

As it was, in his early fifties, he looked well out of place from the other attendees at the event, enjoying the music of U2, and the cuisine of some local celebrity chefs.

Josh Morrison's 'tribute' looked more like an outdoor festival than a candlelight vigil, and the party had been going on now for at least a couple of hours.

Media was heavy in attendance, and based upon the temperament of the crowd, they intended to stay all night.

At some point, Reilly knew, the speeches would start and candles would light, but at present they were celebrating Josh. For rugby fans, this was the best way to wish him well.

Kennedy didn't really need to know much before approaching Hurley.

In fact, the less he knew the better. Just talk casually about the party and whatever memories he had of that night, and Reilly hoped his detective spidey-sense would take over and drill down into the information—if there was any.

Anything could slip at this point—sometimes things that were long ago buried and forgotten about, turned fresh and raw when stimulated.

Interviews with people in these situations always revealed something.

They were not guarded or aware of the topic, so had not worked to position things like they had during the initial details. If there were lies, it would be hard to remember them—it would also be hard to remember the reality of the truth.

Memories faded, but case files did not. They were equipped with details witnesses wouldn't have.

"Thanks for meeting with us, Sam," said Kennedy.

They'd found a quiet area in the stands away from the music and crowds. "No problem," he said, looking past them at the crowd. "Ideal place too, wouldn't have wanted to be anywhere else."

"Yes, quite a turn out," Kennedy said looking back. "Okay, Sam—well you might be wondering why we wanted to speak with you."

"Not really," he said, shrugging. "Josh got stabbed. Figured it wouldn't take you guys very long to start asking around about the accident."

Reilly tried not to exchange looks with Kennedy, but found herself doing it anyway. This guy was about to let them in on something, only because he assumed they figured it out already.

"I always said the cops covered it up, no offense. But of course, no one wanted to believe the truth."

"What truth is that?"

"Josh was driving that car. We all knew it. No one wanted him locked up, so they went along with the idea that Ian did it. He was dead anyway, so what difference did it make? And he was very very drunk. We all were."

"Tell us about the party."

"It was a big bash; the lads had just finished the season so were in the mood to let off steam. All of us drank too much that night, even Annabel, though she'd not long had the baby. Probably the reason actually. I remember her yelling at Ian like a mad thing."

"Annabel and Ian were arguing?" Kennedy asked.

"Yeah, I think that was the whole reason Josh took Ian home. Or tried to."

"What was the fight about?" Reilly asked.

"Who can say. We all thought they were having it off on the side, but you never know. Anyway, Josh didn't think so. He and Ian were close. Best friends. But see, that's what I've been thinking about, ever since this happened. I've been thinking about that night. I don't know what you found over there, but I can tell you this much, Annabel Morrison is off her rocker. I've never seen anyone lose the rag like that. The kid's the same."

"Kid?" Reilly asked, interested.

"Seriously? Don't you guys do your research, or what? Dylan Morrison is a mental case too. Half the reason he's in the States is so Annabel and him don't tear each other's heads off."

Reilly frowned at him, "How do you know that?"

He tsked. "Everyone knows that."

Kennedy stepped in, "Can you tell us anything else about that night, Sam? Any more about the argument?"

"Can't remember much more to be honest. Annabel went upstairs in a huff and Josh went to drive Ian home. No one saw them after that. Next thing I know, the accident's all over the papers the next day."

"What time did they leave the party?"

Sam chuckled. "I may remember it well, but not that well. It was late. I"m sure your lads have a record of that."

"Have you been in touch with the Morrison's recently?" Kennedy asked.

"No, they don't really talk to any of us now. Basically anyone at that party. Especially afterwards when Josh went all out on his teetotal crusade. I think they like to pretend it never happened."

Kennedy nodded. "Cheers Sam, you've been helpful. We'll be in touch if we need anything else."

"Glad to help."

54

THEY FOUND A QUIET PLACE to sit at the back of the stadium, behind the crowd. Kennedy got some chips from a nearby food van, and sat down, offering some to Reilly who refused.

"What do you think?"

"Interesting account," he said, mid-bite. "OK. Let's assume the fact Josh was driving that night is this big secret they don't want to get out. Why should it matter at this stage? The thing happened years ago. It wouldn't do that much to destroy his reputation now, and as for her—it has nothing to do with her."

"I know."

"And here's another thing," he said in between licking his fingers. "Let's assume, just for a second, mind - that it was Annabel who attacked Josh the other night, or for argument's sake, had somebody else attack him. Why would she be crying on the telly, or here at a candlelight vigil, when at anytime he could wake up from a coma and incriminate her?"

Reilly bit her thumbnail, "I know. I can't figure it out either. If the road is leading to her then it wouldn't make sense that she's still around. Or that Josh isn't actually dead by now."

"Unless," reasoned Kennedy. "Annabel's not worried that he'd say it was her, because it *wasn't* her."

Reilly sighed. "But then, who?"

"Aren't you lot supposed to tell me that?"

"We're trying," she said.

"You said there was someone else here to have a chat with?" he asked then.

Reilly nodded and thumbed a text to Tricia Sullivan.

She was another friend of the couple who'd been at the party. A childhood friend of Josh's apparently.

They found her sitting alone outside the stadium, smoking a cigarette.

Reilly thought that the woman, in her mid-forties, had probably once been very pretty beneath the stress and worry that since had worn out the features of her face.

She briefly wondered if that's what she looked like to others too.

Tricia saw them coming and stood up to greet them.

"You the detectives?"

"I'm from the GFU, and this is Detective Kennedy," said Reilly.

"Yeah, I'm a bit surprised you were looking for me. You don't think I have anything to do with this, do you?" she asked nervously, and Reilly immediately identified her as an anxious type who would worry herself to death about the slightest thing.

"Not at all," said Kennedy, trying to put her at ease. "We're actually looking a bit of background about something long ago."

Her eyes widened, "You mean that thing with Ian? Good God no, I don't know anything about that either."

Reilly stepped in calmly, "No one's going after you Tricia, we really are just trying to connect the dots."

"Why though? Why did this come up? What does this have to do with the stabbing?"

"Well, Tricia, that's exactly what we're trying to figure out," she replied patiently.

Tricia sat down again and took a long pull from the cigarette.

"Josh stopped talking to me after that," she said softly. "I think that was the part that hurt the most."

"What do you mean, love?" Kennedy asked.

"Annabel went nuts that night," she said slowly. "It was partly my fault. I told Josh about their affair."

"Whose affair? Annabel and Ian's?"

She nodded, fighting back more tears, "I can't believe this still upsets me," she said angrily. "It was a lifetime ago. But every day that went by since, I had to watch them together, Ireland's most adoring couple. I knew it was all a lie. It was always a lie."

"You're sure Annabel and Ian were having an affair?"

Tricia took a breath and tried to compose herself.

"The whole thing was just ridiculous. And well, it all came out that night at the party. Josh confronted Ian and he admitted it."

"Annabel went crazy. I mean really crazy," she went on. "You see, Annabel never gave a shit about Ian. She'd married the winner. The alpha. The guy who'd give her the life she wanted. She didn't want second place. She'd screw second place, but she didn't *want* him. And she certainly wasn't going to give that up."

"So this argument?" Kennedy asked, as Tricia took a moment for a few more drags of the cigarette. "It happened in front of everyone at the party?"

"Not really, the party had pretty much broken up by then; I think there was only a few of us left. But Annabel… she was…unhinged. She went for Ian…I never saw anything like it. He was down on the ground and it took a couple of the lads to drag her off him."

Reilly was trying her utmost to imagine the cool and collected socialite losing control like that.

But it wasn't too much of a reach, all the same.

"They finally got her off him, and she stormed off. But Ian…he wasn't responding. She must have knocked him out or something. To be honest I couldn't really see. But there was blood. Josh picked him up, and said he was going to take him to the hospital. I wanted to call an ambulance, but he didn't let me. He didn't want the press to find out."

She started crying again, but Reilly couldn't console her, she was too busy looking at Kennedy with bewildered wonderment.

"You could have gone to the authorities anytime since then Tricia, why didn't you?" Kennedy asked.

"Who the hell would believe me?" she said weakly.

"Tricia," Reilly said, her brain kicking into high gear. "Would you testify in court about this now?"

She looked terrified. "I don't know."

"Please, it might be important. And if you and Josh Morrison were ever truly friends, then he may need your help."

Tricia nodded reluctantly. "OK…maybe."

Reilly left Kennedy to take her details and to let Chris in on this new avenue of investigation.

They had her, she realized, her mind reeling with the possibilities.

Annabel Morrison was a fake, possibly a murderer too. Now all they had to do was prove it.

55

"THIS IS SUCH A BLESSING. I can't believe how many faces I see here tonight. So much love. So much goodwill. Thousands paying tribute to my wonderful husband. I'm just…I'm just so…overwhelmed. Thank you, thank you so much. I love you all.

"The candles are beautiful. I've always loved candles. But let's not forget that this isn't about someone we've lost. Josh is a fighter. He's the strongest most ferocious fighter I've ever known. He will get through this, and when he does, he will tell us what happened to him.

"We are not here to mourn Josh, we are here to urge him on. We are his fans on the pitch, his cheerleaders in life. We want him to win this, his biggest challenge yet. We need to spur him on, let him know that we are here and we want him to make it through. We must resurrect those old chants from the Ireland matches, shout his name from the stands, let him know we support him!

"So many times I saw him on this pitch, a warrior beating a path through his enemies. Well now his biggest enemy is a coward. Someone who struck him down with no motive. Well, that monster will get his just rewards, mark my words. I will not rest until Josh's attacker is brought to justice.

"And none of you must rest, either. Don't stop believing. Don't stop hoping. Give him your cheers, your support. And when he comes back to us, when his eyes open and he rises from the depths of the darkness, he will see what I see here tonight. An ocean of angels.

"Thank you all so much for this event and for your kind words, your music, your wonderful food. Thank you for being here for Josh. Thank you for being here for me.

"My prayers are with my husband now. I know he will return to me strong. As strong as ever. And just like always, I'm sure he will have an amazing story to tell.

"Thank you all, you've been so wonderful. I think…I think that's about all…that's about all I can say. Thank you."

56

IT WAS LATE, SO REILLY ordered pizza.

The team was grateful, but having unloaded Tricia's story, they were eating it with sullen expressions. Maybe she'd misread them—it could have been thoughtful expressions? Sullenly thoughtful, perhaps.

She ate silently too, letting the scenario dance in her consciousness a bit. Truthfully if Annabel Morrison had killed Ian Cross it made a lot of sense, and would explain why Josh felt the sudden need to drive his friend through a wall.

To cover for what his wife had done.

This scenario also worked with the separation documents. Annabel was likely holding this incident over his head, but needed the legal standing to make sure he wouldn't squeal.

So the connections were starting to come together, but where was the evidence?

That was what the team was thinking about, while slowly eating pizza which had long since gone cold.

Moments like these weren't particularly unusual. Often at the climax of any major investigation the crew would be completely lost in their own worlds, trying to process everything through a sort of mental osmosis.

Sometimes making evidentiary connections required a step back in order to just let the information flow. Many of Reilly's own major breakthroughs had been a result of quiet contemplation.

All of them, while eating the cold pizza, were on that track. They hoped for some inspiration. Some missing link they hadn't yet noticed.

Backtracking through the whole process and trying to uncover that one thing that was missed.

But with this, it was so much more difficult, because they had to rely upon someone else's evidence. Draw conclusions based upon decades-old assumptions. And they had no access to a crime scene. No access to witnesses.

Even the data preserved from all that time was incomplete, aged or completely missing. They had a Herculean task ahead of them, trying to connect things that really had no obvious relationships. The act of solving one crime, so as to drive another one forward was not new for them, but that didn't make it any easier.

She drifted in and out along the ebbs and flows of thought, and then snapped to consciousness. The others were staring off into space, apparently lost in their own ebbs and flows.

"So what are you guys thinking?" she asked finally.

There was no immediate answer.

Julius finally spoke, "There's no way to prove that she killed that guy. Any physical evidence relating to that crime is long gone."

"Wait…" Gary jumped up so quickly, his pizza fell on the floor.

"What?"

"Did you get a specific account from that witness about where the argument happened? I mean in the house?"

"Yes," said Reilly.

"Limestone."

"What?" Lucy looked blank.

"Of course," Reilly said, sitting up. The material's famously porous properties meant that they might still be able to pick up latent blood stains via fluorescence.

"Or urine stains," said Gary, when he explained. "They have a cat. Or did have. Apparently."

"Even better, we should have Cross's DNA on file," said Julius eagerly. "We'd have to, they'd have taken blood samples on autopsy."

"Twenty years ago? Do we keep lab samples that long?"

He nodded.

"And the DNA would still be good?"

"DNA has a 521-year lifespan," he said solemnly. "We just need to make a positive control test and use a barrier filter."

"Brilliant," Reilly said, snapping into action. "Lucy, can you look over the coroner files again, and see if there's anything in the autopsy that concurs with the witness's theory?"

"Sure," she said, jumping up along with Julius who had an atypical bounce in his step at the prospect of a DNA-related challenge.

Reilly took Villa Azalea's blue print and looked it over, going over Tricia's account of the time.

The argument had taken place in the hallway, she'd said. With a surface like limestone, it shouldn't be too difficult identifying latent bloodstains.

She hoped though, that the Morrison's hadn't replaced the flooring or remodeled extensively since then, but by her recollection the same Moleanos limestone had also been present in the O'Donnell house the other day, suggesting this had been the builder's original finish.

She wondered too how much fluorescein they would have to use to find the precise spot. If they found nothing, it wouldn't necessarily disprove Tricia's account, but would leave them with little to go on if they wanted to bring Annabel further into the frame.

She was once again grateful that her team included guys like Julius who seemed to have an endless volume of knowledge on forensic technology.

As she thought more than once, she didn't have enough scientist in her sometimes.

She marked the general area on the blue print and drew markers around the possible parameters for investigation.

They only had one more chance to do this before the crime scene was released tomorrow.

A while later, Lucy called Reilly over to look at the coroner photos again.

"So anything stand out as different, now that you've heard Tricia's story?" she asked.

"Yes, unfortunately."

Reilly looked the report over and immediately saw it. "Sharp force patterns," she said above a whisper. "Those didn't come from rocks."

They were speaking about the punctured lacerations all over Ian Cross's face and head. Taken all together, it looked like blunt force trauma from the brick walls, but in the context of Tricia's interview, it seemed clear as day.

There were several small puncture wounds surrounded by contusions.

"Stiletto heels it looks like," Lucy said, looking a bit green at the thought that her style-hero could have used her enviable shoe collection for such a purpose.

"Is that even possible?" Reilly asked.

"Why not? They're certainly strong enough. The heel is sharp. If was down and she was wailing on him …."

"How many times was he hit?"

She shook her head, "I really couldn't say. A lot."

Reilly felt nauseous. This was too much. She'd had about all she could take from these people. In her view there was plenty enough evidence to bring Annabel in on suspicion of stabbing Josh.

No doubt the woman was capable of such an atrocity, mostly because she had too much to lose if that more heinous crime ever came out. They both did. More than money and a ruined career. Life in prison. A daughter taken into care.

It was a long time before Reilly could think straight again, let alone talk.

She thought about the baby just then, a thought that was becoming increasingly paramount.

Would she be able to do this kind of thing with a child in the mix? If she couldn't handle the realities of people now, what would she think when she was raising a kid that had to live around them.

She felt depressed, angry, scared.

"You okay, boss?" Gary asked.

"Yeah. Yeah, I'm fine. Let's head for the Morrison place now. You drive. Do you have the fluorescein prepared?"

"Oh yeah, I'm ready for this."

"Great, then let's do it."

57

THE FIRST THING THEY FOUND was the cat.

"Hope someone's been feeding it," said Lucy.

Reilly knelt down and scratched its ginger tabby ears. It offered a friendly meow and then rubbed against her legs. She checked to make sure the food bowl was filled and it was, then she handed Gary some of the fur.

"There, now you can eliminate the cat."

He laughed and began preparing the fluorescein.

"Where do you suppose we should do this then?"

Reilly gave him the marked blue print. "Tricia said Ian and Annabel were arguing in the hallway."

The rest of the team stayed outside the area and watched while Gary put sterile wraps over his shoes and equipped himself with a mask. Very carefully he mixed a solution in a spritz bottle and then sprayed down the area Reilly had indicated.

"Now we wait," he said.

They did so quietly for about ten minutes as they waited for the solution to set in. When it was about time, Gary stood up and grabbed the UV lamp from his kit.

"Okay, we need this place completely dark," he said. "Draw the curtains, kill the lights."

Lucy did so until it was very dark inside. Gary turned on the UV light and swept it over the floor.

They saw it immediately. A latent blood splatter that went a couple of inches around the floor.

"An argument?" Reilly said. "This was a homicide."

"How the hell did they miss this?" Lucy cried sharply.

"They weren't looking for it. As far as they were concerned Ian Cross died at the scene of a drunk-driving accident. Why would they come here to look for a covered-up crime scene?"

"Okay, stop staring," said Reilly. "Get the pictures while the solution's still fresh. Nail it."

Gary did as he was told, meticulous about the photos and the positioning of the blood spatter trajectories. There could have been more, but the clarity was obscured by the limits of the solution. The process took quite some time, and when he was finished, Lucy turned on the lights.

"So," said Gary. "What now?"

"I think it's high time we brought in Annabel Morrison in."

Annabel had been staying at the InterContinental Hotel in Ballsbridge - handily only a stone's throw from Lansdowne Road.

Reilly guessed she'd be going back there after the vigil, which judging by the time - almost eleven - must be very nearly over.

She'd called Chris, but had only managed to get his voicemail, Kennedy's too. She guessed things must be getting pretty loud at the event…ah heck, it was a goddamn concert.

It was truly now or never. They needed to get this woman in for questioning once and for all.

While there, Reilly knew the truth would come out. They now had far too much evidence that would incriminate her, and so she'd probably insist on making a deal.

Then it would all unfold from there.

She knew she would likely take some heat for this, especially from Chris, but that didn't matter.

In spite of the obstacles, she'd done the right thing. And in the process uncovered a momentous cock-up under the nose of one of the force's most respected detectives. They needed to close off this case and turn the tide of public opinion. They needed to turn the media spotlight off the investigation and towards a trial.

Reilly knew to her core that Annabel was behind this and finally, after everything, she would make sure that the woman had to answer for everything she'd done. Answer for Josh Morrison. Answer for Ian Cross.

Answer for two decades of manipulation and cover-ups.

Certainly Josh would have things to answer for too—but in Reilly's mind, Josh's crime was reactionary.

Sure he'd be investigated for what he did to cover up his wife's murder, but the real villain in this story was Annabel Morrison.

She was the prize.

The person who needed to take an account of what she'd done and be put away for life for doing it. This wasn't just an attempted murder; this was so much more. This was manipulation of the highest order. The woman had been imprisoning Josh Morrison for decades, and now her reign of terror was over.

Who cared, at this point, about curious fingerprints and mysterious liquor bottles? About construction records of the accident site. She didn't even need a weapon. She had everything she needed.

Except, Reilly realized - biting her nails as she tried Chris and Kennedy's numbers again, to no avail - a detective.

58

A MINUTE OR SO LATER, Kennedy called.

"Can't keep doing this, Blondie," he said. "It'll look like we're having an affair. Especially as everyone knows you keep looking at my bum."

"You still at the stadium? Something's happened. We need to talk to Chris, tell him what's been going on…"

"Already have. He's gone home."

"But - "

"Leave it be, Reilly. It's been a very long day and the man is exhausted. He was at the doc's earlier so I hope everything's OK, but you know Chris, won't say a word. And I know my darling wife - who *will* - and she's expecting me home in half an hour."

"The vigil's over? Where's Annabel Morrison?"

"Gone to Lillies with Bono and Ryan Tubridy, I think."

Reilly bristled. Typical that the callous witch had the audacity to head off to a celebrity nightclub with her famous friends, while her husband fought for his life in a hospital not far from here.

Shaking the thought away, she quickly filled Kennedy in on all that had happened in the meantime.

"Christ alive..." he said sounding shaken. "You're sure?"

"The team's taken everything back to the lab, trying to get all our ducks in a row so we can go pick up Annabel."

"Reilly where are you?" he asked, suddenly suspicious.

"At the Intercontinental."

"For football's sake…"

A few minutes later, she got through to Chris.

"Reilly, it's almost midnight…what's going on?"

"You need to arrest Annabel Morrison."

He sighed. "So I hear; Kennedy just got me up to speed. While I think it's an…interesting avenue of investigation, I'm still not sure why something that happened over two decades ago is relevant to our case."

"The team just made it relevant - we found latent bloodspill at the Morrison house. Lab's testing it now for a match with Ian Cross."

"What? You were back at the house tonight…? Hold on, slow down a little. Kennedy just said the two you were talking to a couple of people…"

"Yes, we were trying to get the job done. And as of now, the job's gotten much bigger, Chris. We have forensic evidence of a 20-year-old homicide in that house. This is way bigger than any of us thought. Josh and Annabel Morrison are not the angels everyone thinks they are."

"What in God's name are you talking about?"

"We need to bring in Annabel for the murder of Ian Cross. After that, I'm sure we'll find out what happened to Josh, straight from the horse's mouth."

The line was silent for a moment. "I'm sorry, but you sound like you're out of your bloody mind," he retorted. "Ian Cross? *The* Ian Cross? The Leinster player who died in that drunk driving accident?"

"Yes, it's a long story…"

"Then why am I only hearing it now? Jesus, Reilly as if going behind my back with Kennedy wasn't bad enough…"

"I know and I'm sorry, but speed is of the essence now. We're entering day six here, and we don't want to waste valuable time trying to get decisions by committee. I need to do my job and I need you to trust me."

"We can't just jump in with both feet either - especially after what happened the other day. Anyway, Annabel's just left her husband's vigil, it would be a PR disaster. Let's talk tomorrow, get us up to date on everything, I'll talk to O'Brien, and if there's cause enough to bring her in for a chat…"

"A chat? Chris, this bitch beat Cross over the head with a stiletto."

"What?" She could actually hear him gulp.

"That's how it looks from the autopsy photos. We don't have the specifics yet but - "

"Exactly, you don't have the specifics. So tomorrow, when you do, this will all look a hell of a lot clearer. As it is, it's midnight, it's been a long week and there's no need to rush this. We need to get it right this time."

Maybe he was right, she thought, reluctantly acquiescing. He sounded tired, and she remembered what Kennedy had said earlier about some kind of doctor's appointment.

"I guess you're right, but if nothing else I hope you're coming round to the idea that Queen Annabel is not the innocent flower you thought she was. Hey, you OK?" she added then. "Kennedy mentioned something about a doctor's appointment."

"The usual," he said without going into detail, and she figured that his condition must have been playing up.

Chris suffered from the blood disorder hemochromotosis, which necessitated him having blood exanguined when the symptoms flared. She guessed the pain could have been the primary reason behind his mood lately, and felt a little guilty for being so hard on him.

"They take much?"

"A couple of pints this time," he told her. "So you can imagine why I don't exactly feel ready to go into battle at the moment. I just need a good nights' rest. So do you. How'd your appointment go by the way? I hope you kept it."

How in the hell did he remember that, when she'd needed her diary organizer to remind her?

Sometimes Chris Delaney really did surprise her.

"Good actually. I saw Blob for the first time."

"Ah, that's great. Such a big moment. Let me guess, restless as hell and kicking like a mad thing? Sounds like someone I know."

She nodded, trying to fight back a sudden surge of emotion, and she wasn't sure if it was the mention of the ultrasound, or the gentle way Chris was discussing it.

"Pretty much."

"Well then, go home and get some rest, and come back fighting tomorrow."

"But - "

"*Tomorrow*, Reilly. I'll talk to you then."

59

"NOT EVERYONE REMEMBERS, BUT THIS is not the first time the Morrisons have faced tragedy. Not at all.

At the peak of an illustrious career, filled with championship trophies and endless medals, and Annabel's burgeoning media stardom, it seemed as though nothing could stop the couple's shooting star.

But a horrible tragedy almost upended everything. Over two decades ago, Josh was involved in a tragic drunk-driving accident. He was the front seat passenger and by some miracle of fate, he survived.

But his best friend and Leinster team mate, Ian Cross was killed. Cross was heavily under the influence, and lost control of the car. Josh was belted in, Ian was not.

Happening not long after Annabel had given birth to their first child Dylan, the tragedy affected the couple deeply, and changed them forever.

Josh became a major public figurehead for abstinence, and still works tirelessly with the Road Safety Authority to promote safe driving, and as such, has always been a wonderful role model for teenage youth.

That's why it's such a shame to see them having to confront another tragedy just now. They've raised two great kids, have become a beacon for social issues and culture in this country, and have done everything to move past that dark chapter of their life. I'm sure they haven't forgotten about it, though. Horrible tragedy for anyone to go through.

But the Morrisons have so many times proved themselves to be a tenacious team.

They won't back down from anything. They certainly won't be backing down from this either. Hearing Annabel Morrison's brave and emotional speech tonight is testament to their strength and tenacity.

I predict Josh will be on top again sooner than we expect. And Annabel will be right there by his side. An amazingly brave and admirable couple. We at the studio, and certainly everyone in the country are praying with our friend and co-host, for her husband's quick recovery."

60

THE FISH TANK NEEDED CLEANING. Not only had mildew—or algae—or whatever it was that was—collected along the corners and sides, but it started to discolor the Poseidon aquarium ornament inside.

The only fish left alive, a large goldfish Reilly called Nemo was three-weeks old and nearing the size of a tennis ball. She had to turn off the filter because the water had evaporated enough there was a gurgling sound when it was on. She didn't know when she'd have time to clean it out.

It required digging out the bucket, syphoning the water, disposing of the water, filling the tank again with pitcher after pitcher of dechlorinated water.

She began to wonder why she got a fish tank to begin with.

But it was a test of sorts, wasn't it? Something to prove that she was capable of taking care of something, thinking about its welfare, keeping it alive.

Gulp.

Now Reilly wondered why, at 2:10 in the morning she was so preoccupied with the fish tank. It really was a daylight hours sort of problem. There was actually very little she could do about it now.

There was little she could do about anything now. Yet so many things were entering her consciousness. Sure, the investigation.

But more too. The fact she needed to clean the fish tank and her car. An embarrassing amount of coffee cups had gathered in the backseat.

She also began wondering about the state of her desk at work. It, too, needed a thorough cleaning.

So many things needed cleaning at the moment. She was sure Dr. Corcoran would have a word or two to say about that.

She tried drinking some chamomile tea, but it didn't help.

Her mind was still racing, cataloging all the things she needed to do, didn't need to do. All of the things she should be worrying about.

Inevitably her thoughts returned to where they always did; the pregnancy.

It seemed if she were psychologically evaluating herself, that the pregnancy had overtaken the Tony Ellis thing in terms of traumatic things that had happened to her in the past month or so.

Of course, she was happy about the idea of a baby, but terrified about the reality of a baby.

There was so much she didn't know. How was she supposed to hold it? She remembered something about supporting their heads from behind. Should she breastfeed? Was there a knack to it? A book or something she should read?

She had no support, especially for those scary early days. Sure, she would have paid leave and all the wonderful benefits of the public health system, but what about after that? Who would take care of the kid during her crazy work hours?

Who would raise him or her to be a responsible adult? Surely that was something that was expected of her, but Reilly wasn't exactly raising-a-responsible-kid kind of material.

She was more of a forget-to-clean-the-fish-tank material. She would forget to do laundry for a week, so how the hell would she remember to do things like change diapers or sing lullabies.

Not a bad idea, she thought then. She skimmed through her iPhone and sought out Billy Joel's *Lullaby Song*. It was very soothing, but she was no more ready to sleep than before. It was past the point of looking at the time.

That would only prove exactly how desperate the situation had become.

In just a few short hours, she would have to convince her superiors to arrest Annabel Morrison for murder, and she hoped against hope that she had everything they needed. She thought of everything they'd discovered today, every connection, every scenario. Was it enough?

No point in thinking it about now. Chris was right; she needed to be fresh and coherent tomorrow. She needed to sleep.

But in order to do that she had to try and get out of her own brain.

She sighed heavily and tried some more chamomile. Then she made the mistake of looking at the clock. Three am. Almost automatically, she did some math in her head and figured out the equivalent time in Florida.

I could call Todd.

The thought entered her mind like a snake. Without the ability to block the idea, it began worming its way throughout her consciousness.

Before long it was all she could thing about.

Call him and tell him what? Hey, what's happening? You're about to be a dad by the way. No, it's all right, go ahead and get back to watching the game, just shootin' the breeze.

Reilly felt ill. Her head was pounding. She was dehydrated, tired and feeling overly emotional. It was like she had been drinking all night, which of course she hadn't. But that same sort of sick and spinning feeling rushed through her. She felt hot and then cold. Then spontaneously began sweating.

The thought was anchored and seeded. It was blossoming into a full on idea with projected consequences. It was entering actual consideration.

Then before she realized what she was doing, she was opening FaceTime on her iPhone. She went to her contacts and saw Todd's profile pic.

Kinda unshaven, dirty blond unkempt surfer hair. Dark features, light eyes. The little blue dot next to the picture was on.

Her fingers punched in a message, and before she could stop herself she sent it.

Hey

Maybe he won't see it, she thought. But right away, the dancing ellipses showed up.

Whoah, was just thinking about you! How's Dublin?
Not good now, big case.
I heard. Dublin's OJ or something?
Not exactly.

She stared at the text and wanted to add something conversational, just to let him know everything was okay, so he wouldn't know that she was flipping the hell out.

The pause took a long time apparently, because he typed some more.

It's late there now, isn't it?
Yeah, can't sleep.
Something wrong? Miss me maybe? ;)

Ugh. She hated emoticons. She didn't know what to type, but soon he typed again.

You want to talk?

And her thumbs went ahead without her again. *Sure.*

Her FaceTime alert jumped out from the phone and she stared a moment or two before answering.

As she did, Todd's tanned face appeared from what appeared to be his living room.

"Hey, you're looking…pale."

She laughed in spite of herself and tried to adjust what must have been the disaster that was her hair.

"A week of insomnia," she explained, with a weak smile.

"I'm glad you called, really. I wasn't kidding; I've been thinking about you."

She nodded, deciding to get right to it. "Yeah. Look Todd, there's something I've been meaning to talk with you about."

"What is it? Everything OK?"

"I…well I've been thinking a lot recently too and… that night—"

"I know, I know. We should have talked about it. I'm sorry, but things got so crazy…with Bradley and the case…I hope you're not saying you regretted anything. I mean I certainly don't."

You might soon.

"Listen, Todd, it's not that I'm regretting it—or anything like that, I'm just. Look, I need to tell you something?"

"What is it? Everything OK?"

"Yeah, I think so. I mean I hope so. Listen, Todd… I'm…um. I'm pregnant."

His stunned face first started bright and congratulatory, and then it sank in. Blue eyes lowered, face pale and then he blurted, "You're pregnant? Or…wait, do you mean…?"

She just nodded, trying to wipe away the rush of emotion coming from behind her eyes.

"How…wait…how?"

"The usual way," she said, in poor taste. "We weren't exactly thinking straight that night. Look, it's okay, I mean I'm not asking anything from you. I just thought you should know."

More weight came down as the news really started to sink in.

"Jesus…we're having a baby."

"Let's be honest, Todd. *I'm* having a baby."

"What? Are you saying you don't want me involved?"

"I'm saying that it's complicated. I mean, you and I - it was nice, but…I can't imagine—or didn't expect it to be a life-long thing."

"Well, it kind of *is* a life-long thing now, Reilly, isn't it? I absolutely want to be involved in this kid's life. Not just involved - I mean, I want to *be* a father."

"I don't know how that will be possible."

"We'll make it possible, OK? We'll find a way. We can do that much, can't we?"

"You shouldn't feel obligated…"

"Obligated? Reilly, you and I are going to have a child. How could I not feel obligated. I am entirely obligated. You have to know, you are not on your own with this. I won't let you be on your own. I'll find a way. I'm not saying you have to be with me or even *like* me, but I am saying we can do this together. Somehow, we can do this together."

She smiled. "That's very sweet, Todd. But we need to be realistic. We're in opposite time zones for Chrisssakes."

"I'll find a way. But for now, there's FaceTime. OK? And you can tell me everything that's happening. I want to know everything, OK? I want to know blood pressure, I want to see ultrasounds."

He was getting very excited now, a bit frantic. And that kind of worried her.

"Okay, Todd. I get it. Look, I'm sorry. I should have told you sooner, it's nine weeks and just…I guess I just wasn't ready to admit it was real. I couldn't really come to terms with it."

"You don't have do this alone, Reilly. I'll be there. In every way that I can. So will Dad."

She grimaced, pushing away the emotions. "Oh God. He'll hate me."

"Are you serious? He's going to be thrilled! He already thinks of you as family, always preferred you to me."

Her emotion subsided with a sentimental laugh. "OK, so what now?"

"Now, you keep the channel open. I know you're in the middle of this big case, but as soon as it's over, we need to talk this through. We need to start making some plans. I'll find a way to get out there soon."

"I see," she said, and fell quiet for a time. "Todd?"

"Yeah?"

"Thank you."

He kissed the camera and smiled at her, "Try to get some sleep, Steel. You look like shit."

"Oh, now the truth comes out," she laughed.

"Night, Reilly," he said smiling fondly at her.

"Night Todd."

She hung up and collapsed back onto the bed, looking at the ceiling.

The results of that call were completely unexpected, and had succeeded in overriding much of her anxiety.

That one call. Now, she could focus on the case.

And with luck, on sleep.

61

CHRIS SHOWED HIS BADGE TO the guy manning the front desk at the Intercontinental hotel.

"Detective Delaney, I need to know what room Annabel Morrison is in."

It was mid-morning and based on GFU findings from the Morrison house the night before, they'd been given authorization to bring in Annabel Morrison for questioning about Ian Cross.

The kid was pushing twenty, had shortly trimmed black hair and a baby face. The sight of the badge startled him.

"Is…is there a problem, detective?" he asked nervously looking between Chris and Kennedy.

"Nothing to worry about, we just need to take her in to ask a few questions," Kennedy told him.

"Oh, yes, of course. About the…uh…right. She's in Room 206. Should I call ahead?"

"Please don't," said Chris and the two of them went to the lift.

They stopped at the second floor and found Annabel's room.

Chris knocked without hesitation, "Mrs. Morrison, Detective Chris Delaney. Please open the door."

There was rustling inside, and then Annabel opened the door to her suite. Even though it was almost midday, she was still wearing a nightgown, last nights' make-up and holding a large glass of water. Must've been a late one at Lillies, Chris thought.

"What is it? Something wrong?" she asked, generally unconcerned but confused.

"Mrs. Morrison, you are under arrest for the murder of Ian Cross."

"*What?*" she screamed, dropping her drink. "What the hell are you talking about?"

"You do not have to say anything," continued Kennedy. "But it may harm your defense if you do not mention when questioned, something which you later rely upon in court. Anything you do say may be given in evidence."

"Are you out of your mind! My husband was brutally attacked and you're arresting me for Ian Cross? He died in a car accident twenty years ago! What in God's name is going on? I want my solicitor. Get me Flanagan right *now*."

"You have that right, of course," said Chris. "Now please get dressed and come with us without incident. I don't want to have to summon a uniform and put you in handcuffs. You are above that."

"This is utterly outrageous. I will have your head on a pike for this. You will be discharged from service. You'll be driven out of this city in disgrace."

"I'm willing to take that chance, Mrs. Morrison. Now please, let's not make this an incident. Come along."

The woman glared intensely at Chris before flicking her eyes to Kennedy and back again.

"I'll go along with this charade...for the moment, but I'm not saying another word without Mr. Flanagan present."

"I understand, you can call him from the car. Now, let's go," he said calmly.

Annabel followed them out without incident.

The car drive was deadly quiet, save for her brief and ice-cold conversation with Flanagan in the back seat, using Chris's phone.

"I'm being detained. Suspicion of murdering Cross. Yes. Yes. I know. Okay. You'll know where to find me."

Chris thought it was quite interesting and worth noting, that Annabel didn't have to explain to her solicitor who Ian Cross was.

The interview room was completely silent. It had been that way for twenty minutes. Annabel Morrison sat in a chair and glared across the table at the detectives, who had several folders piled neatly in front of them.

The interview started with, "I'm not saying a word without my solicitor."

So there they sat, the detectives on one side of the glass, Reilly and Inspector O'Brien on the other. No ordinary solicitor would do. She needed Cormac Flanagan. The one man that could get her out of this mess.

The one elusive pain in the ass Reilly had been dealing with in one way or another since she'd set foot in the Morrison house on Friday night.

And Cormac Flanagan was taking his sweet time.

Annabel didn't even fidget. She just sat there, stone-faced, still and quiet.

For a while, Kennedy tried small talk. He mentioned the heat, thanked her for her cooperation, even tried giving her the latest about Josh from the ICU, which wasn't much. Everything that was said was deflected by cold, unblinking eyes.

Cormac Flanagan at last did arrive and not a moment too soon.

"I need a few minutes with my client," he said without preamble.

"I really hope you're sure about this, Steel," said O'Brien from alongside her. "If there's nothing to book her on, we're sending her home. And then I'm sending *you* home. We can't afford any more cock-ups."

Of course that was everyone's initial reaction when Reilly laid out her suspicions as to what had happened at the Morrison house at the party that night, but the song would be very different when they were done with this interview. Annabel would be going to prison.

And they would have gotten to the bottom of not only Josh's attack, but an age old homicide. It would reveal flaws in the system.

Problems with the protocol.

No, today they were going to nail this, and reveal to the country precisely the type of person Annabel Morrison was.

Chris returned to the interview room.

A haughty-looking Flanagan was seated next to Annabel, squinting his Steve Buscemi eyes. The suspect also looked smug. Her impeccably beautiful face, exaggerated with each gesture, stared down her nose at the person she viewed as an insect, or more specifically, a pest.

She had no idea how bad her situation was, thought Reilly. Stick it to her, Chris. Get it out of her. Show the top brass—they'd all be watching later.

"Ian Cross," Chris began, opening a folder with a strategically placed photo of him posing with the 1991 Leinster team.

"No wonder you haven't found my husband's attacker yet - when you're wasting time investigating incidents that happened twenty years ago. Josh was stabbed multiple times for Christ sake!"

"I know how many times your husband was stabbed Mrs Morrison. Defensive wounds too. He also had countless lacerations from falling through the glass table, but who's counting."

"You insensitive bastard," Annabel snarled.

"Detective Delaney, are you here to upset my client," said Flanagan, "or is this an interview?"

"Ian Cross," Chris said again pointing to the photo. "You remember him?"

"Of course I remember him, we were very close."

"How close were you?"

"What is this about? Cormac, do I have to answer this twat?"

Flanagan raised his eyebrows, "Always best to cooperate. You have your innocence to maintain, of course."

"We were very close," she said gritting her teeth.

"Were you sleeping with him?"

"This is ridiculous!"

"Really, detective," said Flanagan. "How is this relevant?"

"We can come back to that if the conversation makes you uncomfortable."

"You accusing me of being a murderer and an adulteress, what else do you have in that folder? Blind submission to a genocidal cult?"

"You were with Mr. Cross on the night he died?" Chris proceeded without responding.

"Yes, of course I was. You know I was. I was interviewed by police. Two decades ago! Now I really don't understand why this is coming out now."

Chris sighed and then said dully, "You really are hung up on the fact I'm talking with you about Ian Cross."

"Of course I am! It's outrageous. You should be focused on my husband's attacker, not on this tripe."

"Mrs. Morrison, if it will help us get past this emotional block you have about talking about Ian Cross, I am happy to talk about Mr. Morrison's attempted murder and logically bring you to the point we arrived at. Which involves Ian Cross."

Flanagan outright laughed, "This is a hoax. You must be joking. Are you suggesting my client has anything to do at all with her husband's brutal attack? Annabel Morrison?"

"I'm not suggesting it no, Mr. Flanagan. Absolutely not. The evidence is."

That struck both of them quiet. Chris opened another folder.

"Since you were arrested under suspicion of homicide I had naturally assumed you would want to talk about that, but since you are so paralyzed by the topic, we can start with your husband's attack."

"I would prefer that," she said with a barely controlled rage.

"Our investigators found no evidence of forced entry and no valuables missing. Mr. Morrison was slashed from behind as he was preparing tea. The impact knocked him off balance at first, but then he tried to defend himself, and grabbed the knife. There was a struggle, but then the attacker thrust the knife deeply into Mr Morrison's stomach. This quite strongly suggests the attack was an emotional and vengeful one. That it was personal."

"That is conjecture," said Flanagan.

"No, it is analysis. A burglar would have slashed just enough to scare Mr. Morrison and then run—and, indeed would have broken into the place in the first place. The depraved and sadistic killer-for-fun would have ensured he was dead before disappearing. Only the emotionally and personally invested person would lash out uncontrollably in a fit of rage, and take off without ensuring the end result was death. Can we move on?"

Flanagan said nothing.

"Interestingly, Mr. Morrison had already started his tea. He turned on the hob to heat up the water in a kettle. We know this because during Mrs. Morrison's 999 call, the kettle begins to whistle. This presents us with one of three scenarios: Mr. Morrison started the tea after he had been stabbed - unlikely. Mrs. Morrison started the tea before calling 999. Or, Mr. Morrison started the tea, was viciously attacked and Mrs. Morrison called 999 after the attack."

"This is all conjecture, where is the evidence?" Flanagan barked.

"Furthermore, we do know for certain that someone, either Mr. Morrison or Mrs. Morrison reset Mr. Morrison's phone messages to delete all data six minutes following the 999 call. And since Mr. Morrison was on his way to bleeding to death, we can only deduce it was Mrs. Morrison who did so."

The table was silent.

"We reserve comment on that," said Flanagan after a moment.

"I thought you might, but it doesn't matter. That particular detail will not hold up the interview. As you see I have a few questions about other aspects of this case."

Flanagan sat back and exchanged a brief glance with Annabel, who up until this point had not changed expressions from the lofty narrow-eyed anger she continued to project.

"Our team understandably wondered what Mrs. Morrison might be hiding. After reviewing many of the witness transcripts, it became clear that everyone seemed to think the Morrisons had a supernaturally perfect marriage. We suspected that perhaps something was being covered up.

"Some cursory exploration of the matter uncovered the drunk driving accident twenty years ago, so we began looking at the incident. What we found was rather disturbing. You see, when the police at the time went to the accident site, they had no reason to suspect foul play. But when you look at the same case with our more informed lens you'll find some troubling details."

He pulled out a photo of the wrecked car.

"Our analysis has proven that it was impossible for Ian Cross to have flown from the driver's side of the vehicle."

"What?" Annabel barked.

"Ian Cross had to have projected from the car from the passenger side in order for the windscreen to fracture in this way. That suggests Mr. Morrison was driving this car before it crashed into the wall. That also suggests Mr. Morrison covered up the fact he was driving this car, by pulling himself from the wreckage before the authorities arrived."

"That is truly terrible," said Flanagan cutting off Annabel who was about to burst out with another exclamation. "And I commend you for your police work, but what does this have to do with my client? If what you are suggesting is true then there's an easy explanation. Josh didn't want to be arrested for drunk driving and manslaughter. It would have destroyed his career. I'm not condoning it, but that's what the evidence suggests, isn't it?"

Reilly was momentarily speechless. She had never heard a solicitor so readily incriminate his client than Flanagan did in that moment.

He'd deliberately thrown Josh Morrison under the bus with that statement and he had to know that fact. There was no reason in the world for him to provide that conjecture—well, there was one reason.

To protect Annabel. He knew where this was going. She knew it too.

"There's more," Chris said and then showed the tire tracks. "Mr. Morrison did not accidentally crash into the wall. These tracks indicate that he stopped, backed up the car and then drove at top speed straight into the wall. He drove into it on purpose. Why do you suppose he would do that?"

The two had no comment, so Chris proceeded.

"And there's more," he said, and pulled out the gruesome picture of Ian Cross at the scene. Annabel averted her eyes and Flanagan partly covered his.

"Please, detective," he said.

Chris put it back in the folder.

"The photo that is so difficult for you to look at is of Ian Cross' shattered body after Mr. Morrison's purposeful crash."

They still stayed silent.

"However, the life-ending blows to Mr. Cross' head were not a result of a high-velocity impact to a brick wall, but from something else."

"Do you think Josh killed him?" Flanagan said, squinting.

"No," Chris said flatly.

He opened up another folder and showed Annabel a picture of a high-heeled shoe.

Reilly saw it, then. Ever-briefly. Her face fell. It regained composure immediately, but there was a sliver of a moment when something broke through the hard shell exterior and penetrated.

They had her. And she knew they had her. That shoe could only mean one thing and Annabel knew what that thing was.

She was busted.

62

"OUR FORENSIC INVESTIGATORS FOUND WOUNDS on the coroner's photos consistent with blunt force trauma."

"What are you getting at, detective?" Flanagan asked.

And now for the kill.

He opened another folder and revealed the separation documents.

"Where did you get those?" Annabel yelled. She stood, completely out of control. "This is finished. This is over. I'm not saying another word. You can go to hell. Where did you get that?"

"Evidence we found in Mr. Morrison's desk. We got it from your house, Mrs. Morrison."

Flanagan didn't need to look at it, he knew quite well what it was.

"Do you recall the provision about disclosure in this?" Chris asked.

"It's none of your business."

"What were you so worried about Josh disclosing, Annabel?"

"None of your goddamned business! I don't want him all over town talking to the media about our marriage."

"About your perfect marriage? Built on affairs, murder and cover ups? That marriage?"

"Detective, you are out of line," said Flanagan. "If you want my client's cooperation, you will need to speak in a civil manner."

Annabel was pacing like an agitated panther at a zoo.

Chris began to lose his temper, "Do you remember Tricia Sullivan?"

Annabel stopped and glared at him.

Yes, that's right, Reilly thought. You know exactly who he's talking about.

Chris continued. "She was at the party, Annabel. She saw what you did, but she was prevented from telling the truth. Cut out of Josh's life, and left to stay silent because no one would believe her."

Annabel continued to glare at him, so Chris continued.

"Ian wanted you to break up with Josh, didn't he? He wanted you all to himself, but you couldn't do that. Ian didn't have the cachet Josh did. He didn't have the prospects. You were fine with an affair as long as nothing got out of hand. Well it got out of hand that night, didn't it? It was all out in the open. Your imperfect life finally exposed.

"And that put everything into jeopardy, didn't it? You'd just given birth to your first child and your perfect life was compromised. What if Josh left you over this? So you lost it, Annabel. You lost your mind. You beat Ian Cross to death and you sent Josh off to stage an accident.

"We picked up latent blood evidence in your house yesterday. Mere yards away from where your husband lay bleeding, you bludgeoned a man to death. And now that the divorce is coming, you can't risk the secret getting out, can you?

"But that plan didn't work. Josh wasn't budging this time. He wasn't going to sign that provision. So you had to get rid of him. And you had to do it in the only way you know how."

The room was deathly silent. They both stared at Chris, wide-eyed.

Reilly could feel the tension like molasses in the room watching from behind the mirror. This was it.

Annabel Morrison was going down.

Then she and Flanagan looked at each other for a moment, and in a gesture impossible for anyone to predict, they both started laughing.

Not just chuckling, full on laughter. Annabel laughed so hard she had tears running down her cheeks.

Chris flushed, anger and embarrassment rising volcanically through his voice. "I'm having a hard time seeing what is so funny," he said.

Flanagan went first. "Tricia Sullivan? We put out a restraining order on that nutcase years ago. She's been harassing my clients for years. She's a stalker, detective. There is an official track record a mile long. She's clinically schizophrenic. The courts had her in a halfway house for five years. The only five years she wasn't trying to break into my clients' house. And she didn't do it to steal, oh no.

She was caught and arrested on several occasions stealing my clients clothing, her lingerie! She was in custody for two months for stalking my client at her work, posing as a camera person.

"Detective, Tricia Sullivan is bat-shit crazy and has a long—very easy to locate—psychotic record. I'm assuming, and for your sake - hoping - you heard the same account from some other witness, before you decided to arrest my client during one of the darkest periods of her life."

Oh God…

Reilly was speechless. Check and mate. They hadn't done enough due diligence. She and Kennedy had just taken the woman's word as gospel. Especially when so much of the evidence corroborated her story….

"It sounds to me, detective, that you might have a case against Josh Morrison, and I look forward to defending him in due course. But at this juncture, I hope the next words out of your mouth are 'you are free to go,' followed by an apology."

Just then, the interview door opened and Reilly knew it was over.

It was O'Brien.

"Thank you for your time, Mrs. Morrison. You are free to go."

Annabel smiled at Chris as she left, like a spider about to lurch onto prey, "We'll meet again soon, detective I'm sure. In court."

63

"I WANT TO REITERATE THIS Pat—and I feel like I've had to say this time and time again. But the public needs to calm down about this investigation."

"Calm down, what do you mean?"

"It's great when a case can be resolved in a week. Fantastic! Everyone involved is much happier when that happens. But these things are hardly ever wrapped up so neatly. Many can take several months, even years. The public can't expect them to go tromping in and find the bad guy within days of a high profile crime."

"Why do you suppose that is the expectation?"

"We're fed it, I suppose. Hollywood taught us that crimes are solved within hours, using the best technology available. We've all seen *Law and Order, CSI*—all of these shows feature crime scenes and open and shut cases that wrap up neatly within forty-five minutes. That's not how these things work in reality. They take time. It can take weeks to get DNA results back. Months to get fingerprint matches. The expectations are way off here, Pat."

"The Gardai has so far made a very public high-profile arrest that turned out to be nothing."

"You see, that there is precisely the problem. When so much pressure is put on the investigators to close a case, they start rushing. They cut corners. They make mistakes. These things take time, Pat. We need to just shut up and let them do their jobs."

"Well, if we shut up, then we wouldn't have you on our program."

"Indeed, I understand that and I thank you for doing so."

"And thanks for joining us. Next, we'll replay that heartfelt speech Annabel Morrison gave last night at her husband's candlelight vigil. Stay tuned."

64

REILLY STOOD THERE AFTER THE Morrison interview, motionless, defeated. Deflated. She'd thought they'd had it; they were so close.

And now, after all that, there had never been a point in the case where they were further away.

All that evidence, all of those conjectures—how could she have missed it? She believed Tricia, but didn't do the grunt work.

And now it was over. She'd lost it; lost everything.

Worse, she'd taken Chris and Kennedy down with her.

She'd run away with her own suspicions and went out all guns blazing, assuming that even though the evidence wasn't yet watertight, that the detectives could break her.

No matter that she was supposed to be emotionally detached, especially with regard to suspects. No matter she had no business forcing the hand of a detective on hunches and preliminaries, before ensuring all suspicions and allegations were court-worthy.

Now the case was lost. The evidence useless. The only suspect firewalled behind an expensive solicitor. The most high-profile case in recent memory was completely blundered because of her.

This failed interview could mean her career. It would certainly mean her relationships. Her credibility. Her standing in the department. All of it was crumbling around her.

The weight of Annabel Morrison's laughter still descended so heavily in her mind, she couldn't even stand it.

How could she have been so obtuse?

The entire situation blind-sided her so much, she felt she was in her own sort of car accident. All of the things she thought to be true were now standing on their head and she was incapable of moving.

Reilly was not the crying type, but she wanted to just then. Standing alone behind the glass in front of the interview room, she looked at the empty seat where Annabel Morrison had sat. Clouds of emotion wafted through her, and her knees felt weak.

The door opened. She didn't look up. She was afraid to.

It was Chris.

He sat down opposite her and unconsciously fiddled with his phone like it was a stress toy. There was no eye contact.

"What you did. What Kennedy did. You went behind my back. And for what?"

She couldn't answer that.

"If you had a suspicion you should have told me first."

Reilly shook her head. "You wouldn't have believed me."

"I still don't. But that doesn't matter, does it? We still work as a team."

She pushed back the emotion. It wouldn't help for Chris to see her fragile. But he was right. He was absolutely right. The whole point of having a team on the case was that everyone fulfilled their specific role.

What good was it if there were no contrary perspectives—if everyone fell right in line. She was so determined to move forward with this, she never gave a thought to what the contrary position would do. It would have required her to do her job. She would have had to hand over the conjectures to the detectives and just find the evidence.

Instead, she'd bulldozed this forward like she was queen of the goddamned force, and it had completely exploded in her face.

She couldn't even look at him. She was embarrassed, traumatized and still in shock. She needed to apologize. She needed to set this right. To get out of the self-pity pit and move forward. She still had a job to do.

"Now what we have to do," he said, sincerely—not with sarcasm, "is start from ground zero."

"I'm sorry, Chris. I should have been more solid on this. I'm just—I can't explain it. Everything has been so off. I can't seem to control a single thing lately. My life is in a flat tailspin, and I can't figure out how to get it back under control. I can't even figure out why it's out of control. I thought I could bury myself in work, but the work wasn't good enough. I had to crack the case. I had to put the bad guy away. So I took risks. Made assumptions about things that weren't water-tight."

She shook her head, struggling now to keep the tears of frustration from exploding.

"Look, it's probably time for you to take some time off, OK? Maybe this whole thing with the baby, the Tony Ellis thing last month—maybe you're just…I don't know…maybe you just need some time."

"Just what, Chris? Say it. Just cracking up? Is that it?"

"Not the word I chose, Reilly."

She finally made eye contact with him. His eyes were soft. Concerned. There was an aura of helplessness around him. He too had been defeated and chastised.

"Chris," she said quietly. "I don't know, maybe you're right. It's just, I had a clear idea of the rest of my life and now everything I know about—everything I'm sure of, has been brought into question. A few weeks ago, I was at the top of my game, fresh back from Florida and ready for anything. Now I'm a mother-to-be, recent target of a psychopath, and saboteur of the force's most-high profile case in years. And us…what was going on between us—if there was anything—I don't know which Reilly Steel that belongs to. The one who could handle anything, or the one who's been dismantled and left scrambling to put together the pieces."

He carefully covered her hands with his, "I don't care which one you are, because at the core you are still you. And so now what? You're in some sort of personal crisis, so you push away your friends? Your only support network? People who rely on you, and trust you?"

"I'm sorry I…don't know what else to say, Chris."

She left the interview room and into the hallway.

The small cubicles that held the other Store Street detectives revealed many of them standing, trying not to act like they heard the whole thing.

They looked down, aside, averted their vision to anywhere but her.

She saw Kenned then, head-lowered too. He exchanged an apologetic look, and then sat down with his arms crossed, staring at the floor, deflated.

Looking back one more time at Chris, she saw that he wore much the same expression, except he was still fiddling with his iPhone.

65

IT WAS JUST AFTER ONE pm when Reilly took the short drive home to Ranelagh without music or thought, and holed herself up in the flat with the curtains closed.

She couldn't go back to the GFU and face the team after this.

It was still all too overwhelming. The severity of the situation was really too large to reconcile.

It felt like her entire life was in a flat spin, tumbling out of control.

Every thought she had lately seemed to betray her. Now all her colleagues would look at her differently, look at her suspiciously, warily.

Like they couldn't trust what she was capable of, or that she needed pity and help.

That was the worst part of this. The last thing she wanted to be was pitiful. She felt pitiful. She felt completely disenfranchised. Cold, alone and a failure.

Her life's work now lay in precarious balance.

Thoughts descended into despondency. She wanted to cry again, but what was the point?

Her emotions were raw and tangled and the fact remained she really messed up. The case could have fallen apart anyway without her and none of the weight of things would be on her.

Instead she took things too far and forgot her true role. She forgot to focus on the evidence—and only the evidence.

In a way this was worse than losing her job. She'd lost her dignity. The force already suspected she wasn't operating with a full deck. Yet, from her point of view she was only ever on the right track.

How could things have gone so far off track?

All of a sudden, she longed to talk to her father, hear Mike's chirpy voice, and maybe absorb some of that California sunlight, anything to help block out the dull ache in her brain.

But it was early afternoon here, so it would be the middle of the night on the West Coast.

Middle of the night on the West Coast...

The thought suddenly jumped out at her as if from nowhere.

She leapt off the couch and scurried over to her laptop. Quickly firing up the PC, she logged on to the database and clicked through to the Morrison witness transcript folder.

That Skype log Chris saved from his interview with Dylan Morrison. She checked the time stamp, becoming excited as she noted it, her subconscious firing on all cylinders.

She needed to watch that video log again, but it was taking a very long time to load.

Come on, come on…

Finally, it downloaded and she played it.

Dylan was on a train, and the ambient light in the picture was bright, very bright. Highly unlikely it would come from a warmer electric light.

Especially the sort of lights found on trains.

She looked carefully frame by frame.

Then after a few minutes more she found it. For just a split second in two frames of the video, when Dylan moved his head to a certain angle, there was a reflection on his glasses.

Daylight sky. And a cloud.

Dylan Morrison was allegedly in California on Friday night, and had told them he was on his way to a meeting when the detectives talked to him on Saturday.

But when they interviewed him it was early afternoon in Dublin, about the same time as now. So it should have been the middle of the night in California.

The reflections on this video showed that he was lying.

Reilly took a screenshot, wrote a quick message and emailed it to Chris. Then she dialed Gary.

"Hey, where are you?"

"Run those prints again - the callused ones - but this time use Dylan Morrison for a match. He'll be in the system on account of his US visa."

She hung up and stared at her email until Chris responded.

He did, from his mobile.

Holy shit, he wrote. *I'm on it.*

66

ALL OF THE PIECES STARTED falling into place after that, very suddenly and overwhelmingly.

It became all too clear that Reilly's suspicions were not in fact, unfounded. Annabel Morrison absolutely had something to do with the attack on her husband, and it certainly wasn't a random burglary gone wrong.

Dylan Morrison had been there that night with his father, and for some reason had carried out the attack on him.

He was the one fleeing the scene of the crime, and his mother was helping him. Covering for him. Whether or not she was there when the attack happened was now besides the point.

So the son had taken off through the back garden, jumped the wall and into the night, easily putting some distance between himself and the house - via DART perhaps, there was a station just down the hill.

At that hour of night, the trains would be quiet. And then possibly another train, somewhere else in the country on Saturday, which was where he was when the detectives had Skyped him.

She already had Rory trying to get hold of the transport system's CCTV cameras.

He must be laying low for a while, waiting for the heat to die down, or maybe until his father woke up. But where would he have gone to? Other family members, outside the city, perhaps?

Then she thought of something; the holiday home in Kerry.

The phone buzzed and Reilly nearly tackled the table in order to grab it.

"Gary?"

"Got it. Reilly, it's a match."

The velocity of her delight caused her to throw up the handset in excitement. Then she scrambled to go pick it up.

"You're sure?"

"Yep. The prints place Dylan Morrison at the scene. But wait, there's more. It seems the Americans have a file on him too, including DNA."

"What?"

"He has a record, violent offenses. Assault mostly."

"How in the hell did we not know that?"

"Why would we? He wasn't a suspect. But I mean, this Dylan—he's been in and out of medical facilities all his life. Juvvie medical records are sealed, but I have a statement from one of the assault cases in a more recent file, that says he's been diagnosed with bipolar disorder."

She started thumbing another message to Chris but it was taking too long so she picked up the phone.

The answer was quick. "What do you have?"

"Prints match and he has a history of assault. I think he might have taken off on the DART, then maybe onwards down the country somewhere. The Morrisons have a holiday home in Kerry."

"Perfect, we'll get in touch with the locals down there. Reviewed the video too, and you're right."

Julius started calling while he was still talking. "I'll call you back OK, this is Julius." She hung up and answered.

"Got Morrison's DNA, ran it through the system."

"And?"

"There's more than we first thought, the DNA is a partial match for Annabel Morrison."

"Of course, Dylan is one of their kids."

"No Reilly, you're not listening. Not one of their kids. One of *Annabel's* kids. Josh has no match."

She almost dropped the phone. "I'm coming in."

67

"FOLLOWING A DRAMATIC LOW NOTE in the continued bumbling travesty that is the Gardai's attempt at crime investigation, celebrity *Good Morning Ireland* presenter and Dublin socialite, Annabel Morrison was arrested this morning for the attempted murder of her longtime husband Josh Morrison.

In what has got to be the biggest public public relations disaster in the force's history, she was released after just an hour of questioning.

"Clearly grasping at straws, it is believed that the detectives tried to put pressure on Mrs Morrison into admitting foul play, so they could put an end to this highly public and hugely frustrating case. For more on the scene, Michael McCarthy."

"Thanks Joe. We are standing by for a comment from Annabel Morrison at her Killiney Hill home. Not much was stated as she sped away from Store Street station with her solicitor, leaving what must have been a harrowing hour-long interview with detectives. She has been released, so whatever it was they were hoping to find... here she comes now..."

"Thank you all so much for your concern during this terrible time for me and my family. I'm disheartened, and deeply saddened by the actions of the police force, and so dismayed that they would point the finger at me when my husband's attacker is still at large.

"Our family will be pursuing legal action when appropriate, but for now at this time, we are praying for my husband's recovery, giving thanks for the efforts of the wonderful doctors and nurses, and we pray for the quick resolution of this criminal case.

"And detectives, I'll forgive that you put me in that room and tried to force me into admitting a heinous atrocity, but that forgiveness comes with a price. You must find my husband's attacker. You must not let this case get cold. It is your responsibility—your duty to do the right thing. You cannot simply let this fade away, I will not permit it. You owe it to me.

"Thank you all again for your concern, and I kindly request that you now give our family the peace and quiet we deserve."

"That appears to be her entire statement for the moment Joe, and she is already moving inside the gates of Villa Azalea, and not taking questions. It seems the force, and in particular the top brass at Phoenix Park, have some explaining to do now."

"Thank you Michael, yes a dramatic climax to a dramatic story. What is the mood out there on Killiney Hill now?"

"Well we're all a bit weary of it, truth be told. Many of us wonder if there will be any resolution to this sordid tale, or are we to forever wonder how the authorities could be so inept—or if not, how the criminal mind could be so clever. We have to wonder that if a legend like Josh Morrison cannot be vindicated, how can any of us?"

"All important questions of course, Michael. Thank you for holding down the fort. And we look forward to hearing how this turns out. We'll keep an eye on the Morrisons, but in the meantime, we can't forget about Adopt a Cat Thursdays! With us after the break is CatsTrust Ireland, with some of the country's most adorable friends, all needing loving homes. Stay tuned."

68

"WHAT'S TAKING SO LONG?" DELANEY continued pacing, biting his thumbnail.

Chris shrugged. "Can't expect them to do this in minutes. Could take days."

They were all seated around the conference table in Store Street, staring quietly at the phone placed in the middle.

Dylan Morrison was believed to be somewhere in Kenmare, and the local branch there were working feverishly to find him. Chances were after getting off the train on Saturday evening, he'd used a taxi or public transport to reach the family holiday home.

The room was silent as the detectives waited for an update, any update at all from their Kerry counterparts.

Reilly wondered what Josh would think when this was all over. After he woke up having been brutally attacked and left for death by his own son.

Or actually not his son, it seemed. Maybe that was the whole issue.

Maybe Dylan Morrison had uncovered a horrible secret, and had lashed out because of it.

What's worse she realized, was that after this, three members of the Morrison family would likely be sent to prison. As much as this had been about Josh as a victim, it was also now about him being guilty of either manslaughter or accessory to murder.

Because what they'd found on Annabel was also hugely incriminating for Josh. Once all was over and done with, and he was conscious and improving, Josh Morrison would be tried for a crime that happened twenty years before.

Not that he didn't deserve it, but it would add much insult to a tremendous amount of injury. He would have a hell of a few months coming back around to the new reality of his life. And even after the legal mayhem passed, what of his life? His wife, kids, his past. His poor twelve year old daughter, suddenly left without a family. His celebrity and business. Everything that Josh Morrison counted on, would be gone. In a flash.

And, sitting in a coma, he still had no idea.

The masses prayed for his recovery, but Reilly for one dreaded it. To come back to the world after all this would be devastating.

So who was Dylan's real father? It had to be Cross, given the suggestions of an affair around the time of Dylan's birth. Maybe he'd threatened to expose the truth about the new baby's parentage on the night of the party, and Annabel had ensured that truth would never see the light of day?

The couple's complicated and nefarious past left a lot of sordid possibilities. All of them would be conjecture at this point.

If Dylan Morrison was found guilty, and Reilly believed he would be, then he was going to prison, no matter who his father was.

If Annabel Morrison was found guilty of anything, it would be protecting her son. Of trying to cover it up. Trying to pretend like it didn't happen.

Every person in that room desperately needed to go out and hit the nearest pub, but within a few hours - they hoped - they would have to conduct a very intense and cautiously constructed interview.

It wouldn't be easy and they were ready for several contingencies, but it would have to be cleared up once and for all whether Annabel had involvement in this or not.

If Dylan were to deny her involvement they'd have little to go on. But if it went the other way, they would need to proceed quickly and without incident.

Already the public was ready to tear down their doors for their treatment of the self-made princess, so any misstep on this part would likely result in the crucifixion of the entire department.

This time Helen Marsh was involved too. They needed the full support of the DPP.

Although Reilly hadn't heard as much, she was certain that earlier actions had created tensions between the detectives and the prosecutor's office.

Whatever tensions were there would need to be navigated thoroughly.

Much was riding on what would happen after the kid was brought in.

If the DPP wasn't completely convinced, there would be no telling if the testimony would work in court. They needed the strong and guiding hand of Helen to ensure the case would fly. Because after all, that's what this was all about.

If they weren't able to get a conviction, then all of their efforts would be for naught. Not only would Josh's attack not be vindicated, but neither would public opinion.

Much was riding on what would happen when that young man was brought into the room.

It was clear everyone was going to be doubly careful with the coming milestones. They couldn't risk another embarrassment. Another false lead.

This had to be buttoned up and bullet proof. There could be no mistakes. Nothing that would invalidate the evidence collected.

They had to be completely on book, on script and in formation. No renegades. No rogues. No hunches.

They needed things to fit into a nice and easy package, delivered to the courthouse with a big bow.

69

STILL FOR HOURS, THEY WAITED, going over everything, making sure all their ducks lined up in a perfect now.

And waited.

It seemed like days had passed by the time word made it to them that Dylan Morrison was downstairs being processed.

Once that was done, he was escorted straight to the interview room.

Reilly's heart was racing. At last, she was going to see the end of this case. The suspect was here. They would book him. This heinous chapter could end.

The group mutually agreed to start with Kennedy. The others would watch behind the two-way mirror, and begin to contribute as things escalated.

They wanted Chris for the real interview though, because his kindly, more easy-going demeanor would likely catch the boy off guard, and he'd be more inclined to open up.

Dylan Morrison was brought in by a uniform and sat without cuffs at the table. His hair was died black, he wore black rimmed glasses, a turtleneck and too-tight jeans.

His right hand was tightly wrapped in a make-do bandage. Blood stains had begun to appear on various parts, particularly around his thumb, and he had a notable callous on his right index finger.

Reilly saw that he fidgeted too much, tapping the heel of his size eleven Doc Martin boots rapidly, with no conscious realization he was doing it.

They let him sit, causing him to feel more and more discomfort.

Finally, after about fifteen minutes Kennedy came in. The dramatics were up to level ten. He clumsily held a huge pile of unorganized paperwork and files—Reilly knew them to be a prop—plus a clipboard, pen and two cups of coffee.

Struggling to get it all in, he stumbled then fumbled, dropping one of the coffees creating a huge and hot splash all over the floor.

"Feck it," he muttered. "Hold on." And he threw the files in a chaotic mess, sending them strewn across the table.

Dylan sat back and looked at the clumsy detective with surprise.

"I'd offer you a coffee, mate," he laughed. "But eh…"

He futilely tried to mop up the mess with a pocket handkerchief, cleared his throat and then sat, folding his hands and wearing a big grin.

"So. Josh Morrison not your dad, I hear?" he said, out of nowhere.

Dylan flinched and then stood up, "I want a solicitor."

"Right. Yes, you do have the right to that. I'll get you one. Stay here?"

Then he went out as abruptly as he came in. He walked into the back room and gave a quick bow for his performance, causing Reilly to smile.

"How long are you going to make him wait?"

"I think forty-five minutes, be enough? Good round frustrating amount of time."

"You know we're not getting anywhere without a solicitor anyway. Let the kid have one. What difference does it make? It'll go straight to a plea anyway."

"What is the plea?" Reilly asked.

Helen Marsh gave a brief sigh. "If there is…anyone else involved and he is able to disclose that information, we can alter his charge to attempted murder. Could reduce the sentence by a few years. If there is an accomplice, he or she would get the same charge."

"What if there is no accomplice?" Reilly asked.

"Either he claims innocent on attempted murder, and we charge manslaughter, or he pleads guilty for attempted and we charge that."

Dylan seemed very irritable. They watched him from behind the glass as he paced, looked around, walked back and forth—tried to see behind the two-way mirror. After a few more minutes of this, Kennedy returned, but didn't look so confident.

"What is it?" Chris asked.

"His solicitor is already here."

"His solicitor? He has a solicitor?"

Kennedy thumbed at the mirror and they all groaned when they saw Cormac Flanagan enter the room.

"For the love of…" Chris spat.

"And, well," said Kennedy turning red in his cheeks, "we didn't have a good discussion with him last we spoke, did we? Eh…just a few hours ago."

70

FLANAGAN LOOKED VERY HAPPY TO see Chris again.

"Oh, detective. Long time no see."

His weasel-eyes narrowed and that made Reilly happy. The guy had no idea what he was up against. She especially enjoyed watching his face when this time, she too appeared in the interview room.

"Ah great, Ms Steel. She's the one behind your mother's arrest," said Flanagan to Josh. "And now I suppose she is behind your arrest too. How much do you want to put the Morrison family through while you grasp at finding the actual criminal, Steel? It's almost as if you have a vendetta."

Reilly said nothing, just spun her phone around so that he and his client could both see the screen.

"Do you remember this Skype call, Dylan? You were on a train."

Dylan looked at her and then shrugged. She sped the video forward to a point and paused one particular frame.

"Detective Delaney called you at 12:30 pm Dublin time, which would have been 3:30 am Pacific Standard Time, the middle of the night. Why then, is there a reflection of blue skies and clouds in your glasses? Here. And here."

The table was silent, and as suspected, Dylan had no answer for that.

"What does that prove?" spat Flanagan. "So he wasn't in California at the time. Not as if he had an obligation to disclose his location."

"OK," said Reilly.

She opened another folder and then showed them the calloused fingerprints they'd taken from the worktop in front of the knife block, and at various other places in the Morrison residence.

"Why are your fingerprints at your mom and dad's place?"

"Is it a crime for my client to visit his parents?"

"It is to lie about his location when prints specifically prove his presence at the crime scene."

The table fell silent and then Flanagan shifted in his seat.

"Are you charging my client with attempted murder?"

Reilly pointed to his hand, "How'd you hurt yourself?"

Dylan looked to Flanagan who raised his eyebrows.

"I was doing some DIY at the house in Kerry, lost control of my saw."

"Dylan," said Chris. 'We can go through the motions. Examine your wounds and use forensics to connect them to the crime. They can very easily prove that you nicked yourself using, not a saw, but a knife. They will prove that the size eleven boot impression taken from the lane way behind your house, are the same as the boots you are wearing now. We can use phone masts to prove you were not just in the country, but at your house in Killiney, last Friday night. Just a few examples of the things that can prove you were there when your dad was attacked. Or we can just talk about your future. What it is you want to do about the spot you've found yourself in."

Again silence. Flanagan spoke at last, "What are you offering?"

Chris got right to the point.

"We know you did this, what we don't know is whether or not you were alone. Knowing that could make all the difference between a planned or spontaneous attempt to kill."

The young man was still avoiding eye contact, not displaying the qualities of an innocent person appalled at the directness of the accusation.

Flanagan spoke finally, "I need a few minutes to talk to my client."

They both stood and Reilly was following Chris out, when she stopped and turned. "We know you did it Dylan, but we don't know why. Frankly it's not my job to know why. But it may help your plea."

Flanagan glared at her.

"Josh isn't your father. That was it, wasn't it?"

Like a match, Dylan Morrison flared up, standing suddenly. "That bastard lied to me my entire life. My entire life!"

"Dylan!" Flanagan howled, trying to pull him back down.

Reilly left with Chris, while Flanagan desperately tried to work out something.

Back in the observation room, they all watched the solicitor try to talk quietly with Dylan, who wasn't having any of it. He was pacing, deeply disturbed.

"What about just asking him straight if Annabel was there?" asked Kennedy.

"He's too agitated," said Chris. "And Flanagan won't let him say one more thing. We just need to wait and see what he advises him to do."

Flanagan advised his client for a good half hour before he finally asked the uniform to see the detectives. He started in immediately, "My client needs assurances that the penalty for spontaneous would reduce the base charges."

Chris nodded. "Well that all depends on what your client is willing to share."

"He had an accomplice."

"If your client will disclose the accomplice, he will be charged for spontaneous attempted murder, reducing his baseline custody time to five to ten years."

"My mom," Dylan said quietly. "It was my mom. She was there. She came in drunk, stumbling around a little, and then started drinking even more. Snipping at Dad… at…Josh. Like she always did when she was drunk.

Except this time I was there. I was just home for a couple of days, and they were talking about the separation, and Mom was being nasty, trying to turn me against him. And that's when she said it. That's when she blurted it out, that I was hers and not dad's."

He stopped, the pressure of the confession choking him. Recovering, he continued.

"And dad…Josh…admitted it to me. Told me Mom was telling the truth - as if it was no big deal. So I just lost it. I saw red. The more I thought about it, the more pissed I became. I just came unhinged. Mom was weeping on the table and Dad…Josh just got up and started making fucking *tea*, as if was all no big deal! I don't even know why, but I was standing by the counter and I picked up the knife. And I went for him - the lying hypocritical bastard who'd always made me feel like I could never measure up, couldn't follow in his footsteps and be the big rugby star he and everyone else wanted me to be. I hated that shit - always hated playing sports. I was no good at it. And I especially hated that stupid fucking college, and those rugby arseholes who thought they were all so fucking fantastic…"

Ah, Reilly thought, remembering the family portrait and recalling how unhappy she'd thought the son had looked in that college jersey.

A lifetime of failing to live up to expectations both public and private, and disappointing the man who, in the end wasn't even his father, had sent the kid over the edge.

"Mom…she said she'd take care of it. She gave me some money and rushed me out the patio door. Told me to head down to Kerry and lay low for a while, until everything blew over. She'd talk to Josh afterwards, she told me. She'd take care of it."

The room was silent as his words settled in.

"Josh's phone messages were deleted, why was that?" Chris asked.

He shrugged, "Maybe to hide the fact I was in town? Josh had picked me up from the airport that evening, and we'd been discussing where we should meet outside arrivals."

Just then Kennedy came in with a uniform. "Mr. Morrison, come with us, please."

He duly cuffed Dylan Morrison and took him away.

Afterwards, Chris stayed quiet at the table, absently looking at Flanagan, who finally stood up after a time.

"I want to be with you when you pick her up," the solicitor said quietly.

"I can't let you get to her first," said Chris. "You know that."

"I know, but I want to be there."

71

FLANAGAN WAS A DEFENDER. HIGHLY paid and entirely in the confidence of his client. Clients, even.

Still, there was something a bit odd about all this, Reilly thought.

The man seemed completely upended and by his shell-shocked demeanor, it was clear that he felt out of his element, perhaps out of his pay grade.

He was convinced all along his clients were innocent, wasn't he? And when confronted with evidence nearly impossible to refute, he immediately had to go into mitigation mode.

What's worse, Chris had sat in that interview room just the day before with him and laid out their entire case.

He knew they were out to get the client. He especially knew how they were out to get the client. And he'd laughed at them.

Once the case was laid out, the son of bitch had started laughing.

None of that mattered now. The shoe had dropped. They'd been right all along and now Flanagan had to do the right thing.

He had to defend his client in the best way legally possible. He was going to make sure she didn't get the full book thrown at her. That her trial would go smoothly and the charges minimized. He would make sure that once sentenced, that Annabel could get out on good behavior. That custody was loosened. That she would have a life and career after the whole thing.

How could he make this process as painless as possible?

That was a job Reilly could never understand, and she witnessed it a lot. Once it was clear the state would win, no matter how the case was stacked, the solicitor immediately went into damage control. Trying to minimize the effects of the sentence on the client. She could never do that work. In her opinion these so-called precious clients deserved every bit of punishment the book suggested. That's why there *was* a book.

"Why do you want to be there for the arrest?" she asked him now, as they made their way up the driveway behind the detectives to the Morrison house.

"This may be difficult to understand Steel, but I consider the Morrisons friends. I've represented them for more than twenty years. This is an utter tragedy and I want to be there for Annabel's support."

"And to help build a defense case."

"The defense of my clients is always my top priority. But there is more to it than that. I was at their wedding.

I was there when the kids were born. I saw Dylan off to university. This is every bit a personal tragedy as it a professional duty. I want to see to it that she has the support she needs."

Reilly stayed quiet after that. She wondered if his personal relations were somehow clouding his judgement.

It was perfectly ethical, of course, for a solicitor to be present during an arrest, just very rarely done. Too many things could go wrong, she supposed.

She just wondered if he was being honest. If he was looking for some sort of mess-up that could be used against them.

In truth, the whole thing was rather unconventional. But then, most things about this case were rather unconventional.

The house was still mobbed by media and as the cars went through the gates, questions had been lobbed at them from all quarters.

"Did you find something else?"

"Are you making an arrest?"

"Didn't you already do this?"

"Detectives! Any comments? Updates?"

Chris and Kennedy went in first with another uniform.

"Mrs. Morrison? Detective Delaney here, please open the door."

There was no response. The media was overtly watching, rapt, from the gateway.

"Mrs. Morrison! We have a warrant."

Nothing.

He gestured to the uniform who kicked in the door. The cameras loved it. Flashes, shouting, questions, scuttling of reporters.

Quite the different scenario than at to hotel where they'd whisked her away for questioning without anyone's knowledge.

Chris went inside first, followed by the others. The lights were out. It was completely quiet inside. Reilly looked closely around. It seemed too still, yet there was some sort of tension around. Her heart rate was going crazy.

"She got the news and buggered off," said Kennedy. "That's just great."

"I'll check upstairs, Kennedy you and Rourke check the back. Reilly stay put."

She snorted at that and followed Chris up the stairs as he cautiously hit the landing.

"Mrs. Morrison? Are you home?"

Rourke shouted from downstairs, "All clear down here."

Then Kennedy called up. "I think she buggered off."

Chris and Reilly proceeded down the hall to the master bedroom and stopped suddenly. Chris turned around, visibly annoyed she had followed, and gestured for her to go back down.

She shook her head and he gave her a stern look. Reilly shook her head back. He sighed, rolled his eyes and then continued forward.

Then she heard it inside the bedroom. Muffled crying.

"Mrs. Morrison, is that you? Don't worry, we'll sort this all out."

Chris slowly went into the room, and terror clinched as Reilly suddenly thought of something.

Her heart stopped, and she lost her breath as she remembered what Lucy had found in the wardrobe last time they were here.

"Chris…"

72

ANNABEL WAS SITTING ON THE bed with her back against the headboard, pointing the shotgun at them.

Her face was streaked with tears and worry. Her clothes unkempt, and hair wild. She was sobbing uncontrollably as she pointed the weapon.

"Okay. Okay, Mrs. Morrison. You don't want to do this," said Chris. "Remember your daughter. You don't want Lottie to grow up knowing her mother shot a policeman. Now please, put the gun down."

Annabel shook her head, grief warping her beautiful face.

The woman was desperate. That calm, cool, calculated persona completely fell apart in the face of her collapsing life. She was a wild animal, incapable of doing anything but reacting. The most dangerous type of animal, cornered, desperate. Worried about her kids. Her whole world falling apart second by second. Everything she thought safe was now destroying her.

"You took my boy," she said between tears. "You have him. You took him."

"Mrs. Morrison, he is in good hands. Mr. Flanagan will work on the terms of custody. Please don't escalate this."

"…Flanagan…" she said, a roll of weeps forcing her to lower the gun, but then she straightened as Chris stepped forward.

"Don't move a step!" she warned.

"Mrs. Morrison, let's talk, okay? I know this has been horrible. Your husband was attacked. You tried to protect your son. No one wants to bring you more trouble, okay? We just want to get through this as peacefully and painlessly as possible."

"He deserved it," she whispered. "He let this all happen. He forced me to let it all happen."

"What do you mean?" Reilly asked, unable to stop herself.

"Josh is a coward," she spat. "He was always a coward."

"Please, Mrs. Morrison. Put the weapon down. If you shoot us your life will be over."

"I don't care about my life."

"What about your daughter, then? Think about Lottie."

Annabel started crying again, but held up the shotgun

"Ye all right up there?" Kennedy shouted guilelessly.

Annabel looked scared and sat up. "Tell them to go away!"

"Kennedy, everything is under control," Chris said calmly and loudly. "We are talking with Mrs. Morrison now. We're talking, aren't we?"

"Hey!" someone else shouted from below. "Hey! No! You can't go up there!"

"Who's that?" Annabel said and jumped to her feet, wildly casting the shotgun around.

Reilly turned and wanted to scream profanities at the sight of Flanagan running down the hall.

"Annabel! Annabel, don't do this!"

She trained her gun on the solicitor.

"You. This was all you. Every part of this was you."

"You don't want to do this Annabel. Please lower the gun and let the detectives take you in."

"You'd like that wouldn't you?" she said beneath a growl. "You set this all up. You told us how to stage it, how to make it look like an accident. You did all of it. You scared my coward husband into it. You made murderers out of us! You convinced us they would put us away forever. Now look at us! Look at what you did! My life is over! My boy… my sweet Dylan. Years being made to feel small by that sniveling spineless rat of a husband. This is all your fault!"

Reilly felt faint as the connections starting coming into place. No wonder the entire thing seemed watertight. No wonder everyone got away with everything.

This solicitor master-minded the whole thing. But why? Oh, she could suspect. And she guessed that it was coming out now. She should have seen it all along. He was too close to them; he had his paws into everything they did.

He was the master puppeteer, keeping them safe from prosecution all of these years. He was the one that kept their life in balanced control, always holding the murder above their heads. And when they were finally ready to call it quits, he was the one that insisted they tied "secrets" into their money. Not to protect them, but so that his involvement would never come to surface. As a couple he controlled them. As individuals, he was at risk.

Kennedy and Rourke were carefully approaching from behind, even as Flanagan held his hands up in the bedroom.

"I only did it for you, darling," he said just above a whisper, tears starting to form.

"I know," she said falling into tears again. "I know you did. I'm sorry. I'm so sorry."

"Don't," he whispered, coming closer to her.

Then she fired. A deafening blast split through the room, and Flanagan fell backward, stunned and stuttering as his chest erupted.

Reilly was too stunned to move, but Chris wasn't. He leapt forward to tackle her, but she was too quick. She turned the gun on herself and fired.

Reilly knelt over Flanagan, but the light had left his eyes. He was gone and the lack of a pulse confirmed it.

Seconds later, Annabel Morrison was gone too.

They stood quietly in the room, in disbelief. Shouts erupted from outside as the media undoubtedly heard the gunfire. Uniforms were rushing in. Someone else radioed the incident in.

Reilly wanted to cry, she wanted to scream. She wanted to throw something through the window. It wasn't supposed to end like this. Not like this. This wasn't justice. There could be no retribution. It would be yet another ghost she'd have to shoulder—that all of them would have to shoulder.

The memories would be replayed time and time again. They would wonder what they could have done differently, how they could have moved quicker. How they could have prevented this disaster.

The silence was broken by a text Chris received. He reluctantly checked his phone.

"Josh Morrison is conscious."

73

"ONE OF DUBLIN'S MOST PROMINENT families, he was the nation's star athlete, and a multi-million euro business tycoon. She, a successful entertainment personality rising the media ladder to become the star of Dublin's favorite morning TV show.

A son in Silicon Valley. A beautiful young daughter.

Was the Morrison family as picture-perfect as it seemed? Or was there something beneath the surface, a sordid and confused past, hiding a ticking time bomb?

"In this special Prime Time Report we will go deep into the history of Josh and Annabel Morrison, childhood sweethearts and Ireland's glossiest power couple. We will meet old school friends, teammates from Josh's rugby years, and some of their closest friends and business associates.

"You will see a picturesque life sitting precariously on a house of cards. You will learn the dark secrets that poisoned them all these years, and the events that would lead to their bloody collapse.

"Join us as we go behind the scenes, concluding with the investigation that sent the country into a tail spin. Join us as we Uncover The Morrisons, tonight's Prime Time Special Report."

74

REILLY SIPPED COFFEE, WATCHING CHRIS play with his biscuit. The cafe was noisy, allowing them to be anonymous. She liked the way his brows furrowed when he was thinking really hard about something.

And he would get fidgety. Such a cool, collected guy, yet anyone that knew him would get strong signals whenever he was uncomfortable.

"What's up?" she asked.

Chris shrugged and avoided eye contact, looking out the window at passersby.

"We've been a team a long time, Reilly. I should know when to listen to you."

"Oh, yes," she said containing a laugh. "And I should continue to overstep boundaries, and work behind your back. A very productive way to find the bad guy."

"Well that might be true," he said loosening up a bit and offering a smile. "But something was bugging your gut."

"I'm supposed to be looking at evidence, I'm not supposed to have a gut. *You're* supposed to have a gut."

"And I didn't," he said. "The fact that Annabel could realistically be responsible was so far removed from any possibility in my mind."

"Well it wasn't her, as it turned out. And petty jealousy shouldn't constitute a gut feeling."

He chuckled at that. "Jealous? You - jealous?"

"Petty jealous," she corrected. "Not enough to swing chandeliers over, but yes. A bit. Women like that, they always get everything they wanted. It was true in California and it's true here. So many people like that. Celebrities living in a different atmosphere to everyone else."

He smiled but said nothing.

Reilly changed the subject after the silence persisted too long. "Are you mad? I mean that I confided in Kennedy instead of you?"

"Yes, actually," he said with no hint of irony. "That really hurt. On many levels. I always thought you and I could talk about anything, but I *knew* Kennedy and I could. I mean, things are grand between us all the same, but that really stung, Reilly. You better not make a habit of it though," he added grinning, "Josie would flatten you."

She nodded, and now was the one avoiding eye contact, "I suppose the whole thing was a mess. And the Morrison thing too. And just for the record, Pete's not my type."

He nodded and blushed a little, "I don't know, Reilly. There's a lot of mixed signals lately, so I'm just going to come out straight with it; I'm sick of guessing. What's going on? I mean with us."

She took a breath, and then subsidized some time with a sip of coffee.

"There will always be an us I suppose," she said. "Let's not make it complicated."

"That's pretty vague."

"It's a weird time, Chris. I'm vague on purpose. Because when this is all over, and everything is on the right track and I feel like myself again…after all that, I know you'll still be here. And so will I. Let's just leave it at that for the moment, and see how things go."

Much later, Reilly went home, the weight of the world falling from her shoulders as she closed the door of her flat, and collapsed on the bed.

Her shoulders were relaxed, she felt calm and collected. Watching the ceiling for a while, her eyes then settled on the unclean and increasingly evaporated fish tank.

Glubs was inside dancing around with his angelic fins. Or was Glubs a female? She didn't know how to tell with fish. She'd always thought of him as male.

Hours later, she started wondering if the Morrison cat was going to be okay. Or if it needed a home, and if her landlady would allow it. And if she did steal the Morrison cat, would it try to eat Glubs.

Two hours later, she checked the time. It was 1:30 in the morning Florida time.

Digging out her phone from her pocket, she found and opened FaceTime and then thumbed a message to Todd.

You awake?

The "typing" message appeared.

Sadly.

Insomnia must be contagious.

:D

Do you want to talk?

Yep, he responded.

She dialed him. He was lying on his back in dim light, unshaven, squinting and without his shirt.

"Nice."

"You flirting with me?"

"Not exactly." She smiled. "How are you doing?"

"It's more important if you answer that question."

"Much better. We got the bad guy."

"How did it turn out?"

"Not very pretty, and I'd rather not talk about it. Needless to say, I was right all along."

"Of course you were."

"That's not true. I was partially right. But I was right about the most important aspect of it."

He laughed, a steady and deep chuckle. "So how's Blob doing?"

"I'm guessing okay. How am I supposed to know?"

"Well if you'd stop drinking all that Guinness, and smoking those damn cigarettes…"

"And give up the finer things in life?"

"I heard in Dublin they treat everything with Guinness. Pregnancies included."

She laughed. "Not so sure about that, but I wouldn't be surprised."

He turned serious after a moment, "Reilly?"

"Yeah?"

"I really do want to be a part of this kid's life you know."

"I know," she said softly.

"I'm going to find a way to do it."

"Great. Let me know how I can help with that."

"You could give me a place to stay," he said.

"What do you mean?"

"I'm coming out in a couple weeks, it'd be great if I didn't have to spring for a hotel."

"Well that's kinda…unexpected."

"I'll behave," he said.

"That I seriously doubt." Then, without giving it too much thought she nodded and said, "Okay, sure. Why not."

And much later, after she and Todd Forrest had chatted for an hour about the kind of things Reilly Steel had never in a million years thought they'd talk about, she lay back on her pillow, and drifted into glorious, dreamless sleep.

75

"I'M GLAD, TO BE HONEST. Well, maybe not glad… relieved. I know I deserve it. I deserve this. I need to serve my time. All those years of hiding from the truth, it ate me up like a cancer."

"Do you think the jury took pity on you?"

"I think they wanted to. They could have given me more time than they did. They could have given me a life sentence. After all the deception, I'm surprised they didn't."

"Still seven years is a long time."

"It is. I have a lot to think about. A lot to replay in my mind."

"And how are you doing now?"

"Much better, thanks to all the wonderful staff of St Vincent's hospital over the last year."

"No, I mean how are you doing? Your wife dead. Your longtime friend and confidant murdered in your home. Your stepson in prison. Your daughter taken into care."

"It's devastating. I mean, what do you want me to say…it all fell apart. Everything fell completely apart. All while I was in the hospital, out cold. Not a night goes by that I don't regret that lie though. And all those years of lying to Dylan. To the public. But now—well it was a high price, but I feel the debt will be paid."

"Big words, don't you think? Your son - Ian Cross's son - tried to kill you."

"Even while he was attacking me—and truthfully I remember very little—even when he was attacking me I knew I deserved each one of those wounds. I thought I would die. I think I hoped so."

"What's next?"

"Nothing's next. The Morrison legacy ends, that's what's next."

"What's going to happen to the business?"

"My very capable board of directors will figure it out."

"If your wife was alive, what would you say to her?"

"Don't make me answer that."

"You don't have to."

"Maybe…maybe I would say to her—that it isn't worth it, the fame, the money, the spotlight."

"Do you have regrets?"

"Of course. I regret everything."

"Do you have anything you want to say to Dylan?"

"I guess…I don't know. I just have to say that I know he deserved better. He did what he could with the hand he was dealt. I just…I never wanted him to be something he wasn't, truly. Dylan - son - you deserved better."

"Thank you so much for talking to us, Josh. Despite what's happened, I'm sure the entire country will join me in wishing you well in the future. You'll always be our hero."

ABOUT THE AUTHOR

Casey Hill is the pseudonym of husband and wife writing team, Kevin and Melissa Hill. They live in Dublin, Ireland.

TABOO, the first title in a series of forensic thrillers featuring Californian-born CSI Reilly Steel was an international bestseller upon release. It was followed by subsequent books, INFERNO (aka TORN) HIDDEN, THE WATCHED, TRACE and AFTERMATH. A prequel to the series CRIME SCENE, is also available.

Translation rights to the series have been sold in multiple languages including Russian, Turkish and Japanese.

For book updates, news and competitions, follow on twitter.com/caseyhillbooks or Facebook www.facebook.com/caseyhillbooks

Author website www.caseyhillbooks.com

Printed in Great Britain
by Amazon